SHAKUNI

SHAKUNI

Unravelling the Killer's Psyche

Harsha

NU VOICE PRESS

NU VOICE PRESS

First published by NU VOICE PRESS 2023
An imprint of Hubhawks Pvt. Ltd
www.nuvoicepress.com

This is a work of fiction and all characters and incidents described in this book are the product of the author's imagination. Any resemblance to actual persons, living or dead, is entirely coincidental.

ISBN: 978-81-963184-37

Typeset by Saanvi Graphics, Noida
Printed at Thomson Press
Published by Nu Voice Press

To the brother who went against god

PROLOGUE

"Beware that, when fighting monsters, you yourself do not become a monster...
For when you gaze long into the abyss, the abyss gazes also into you."
–Friedrich Nietzsche

"Give me the strength, Lord, to live with myself."

I loaded the gun.

It was pitch dark. Only a dim golden stream of light caressed her wrinkled face, making it distinguishable from the rest of her body drowning in the darkness. And in the glimmer, her eyes glowed like a starving carnivore in a black cave. Ready to pounce on its prey, rip apart its chest, drink its blood, and devour its innocent flesh. I couldn't take my eyes off hers, but I knew her rough fingers were peeling off the skin at the nail beds in the darkness beneath. She always did that. The flesh there was almost always swollen, red, and exposed. Like it stung every time she ran her hands through water or combed her grey, frizzy hair. And yet, she could never stop. She just had to keep peeling it off. Maybe that was the only desire we had in common: peeling off her skin.

No, I'm not deranged. I just wanted to peel her open and take a look at the soul that resided beneath. Was it the colour of her black sins, or was it the colour of the spotless white mask she fools the world with today, or fooled the world with five thousand years ago?

On 28th February, in that dark auditorium, I punished my first sinner.

Or should I say, on 28th February, the day of the play, I murdered my first sinner. I have begun to doubt my sanity. What have I become? What have they turned me into? Am I one of *them* now?

These questions have been troubling me for the past few weeks. They have been prodding my soul with their sharp ends, trying to draw out their answers. They force my eyes open throughout the night. *"Sleep is for the peaceful! For the innocent!"* They keep screaming. *"Not for you monsters. Stay awake. Dwell upon your miseries until they kill you one day!"*

"I wasn't always a…!" I scream in my defence. "I wasn't *born* a monster!" They look at me and smile. It's not a full smile. Its slightly uneven, sort of wicked. Evil. *"But you'll die as one…"* They wink, and the sun's rays kiss my cheek, *"Good morning…."*

But that's all they can do: keep me awake. I'm not afraid of them. I know they look terrifying. They have no eyes, but they can see me. They have no mouths but talk to me. They have no ears, but can hear me. They don't have a soul, but I know they can feel me. They're dark, like an abyss. I know their gaze would've petrified me once, driving me to kill myself. And yet, I'm not scared of them now and that is what haunts me. Have I become scarier than what I once feared? Have I become the monster I was once terrified of?

28th February 2010: The day keeps running in my mind. The day I chose revenge over mercy. Evil over good. The monster within over the almighty above. The narration was loud. My heart was racing. My eyes were glued to hers. Unflinching. I could feel streams of sweat trickling down my forehead, neck, and chest. My palms were wet and every expanse of my muscles twitched. My skin was bathed in bumps and my breathing was louder than a man on his deathbed. I kept gasping for air, harder and harder.

The play's narration kept falling on my ears: *The king who chose to be remembered as Gandhari's brother. Gandhari's brother. Gandhari's brother.*

My heart kept jerking my hand, making the gun in it shiver. "You don't want to do this. *Let it go, Shakuni!*" My mind kept trying to hold it steady: "She's your sinner. She deserves to die. *Yudhishtir deserves to die, Shakuni!*" The narration got even louder. *Gandhari's brother. Gandhari's brother. Gandhari's brother.* And in that very moment, my mind won. I was Gandhari's brother before Shakuni. I had always been and I shall always be.

I shot her dead. I killed Yudhishtir.

In the tug of war between my heart and my mind, I strangled my soul.

Hello…123 mic testing…123 mic testing…

I request everyone to silence their cell phone or turn it off now. Please take note that photography and video recording are prohibited during the play. In case of an emergency, there is an exit on each aisle at the rear of the auditorium and one at the front.

The moment everyone has been eagerly waiting for has finally arrived.

Brace yourself to go on a journey never explored before,
Get ready for the blockbuster of the decade,
Let the show…BEGIN!

CURTAIN-UP

I am Aryavarta,

The land of the triad; The Creator, The Preserver, and The Destroyer.
I have seen numerous ensnared in the circle of life, but only a few enslave it.
For I have seen them take birth but not die. They shall be alive till am I.
Hark, Oh, descendants! I am here to take you on a journey of one such man.
The charming crown prince of Gandhar, a master of the game of dice,
A devotee of Mahadev, a synonym of deceit, an illusionist, an evil trickster.
But more importantly, a brother. A brother who dared to go against God.
Be a witness to his intense journey, an untouched book covered in grime,
His journey from being a loving brother to the most loathed villain of all time.

Production No. 1
Elysian Theatre Company
Written and Directed by **Ryan Rana**

In a North-Western kingdom on Aryavarta's Earth,
Once upon a time, an intelligent little boy took birth.
His sinless-white skin, his amber eyes, his hair brown and curly,
A tinge of red on the nose and cheeks fair and pearly.
King Subala's youngest boy, the heir of the province.
He was Shakuni of Gandhar, their treasured crown prince.
Fabled for his generosity, his wit, his charm, his innocent glister,
Fabled for an inseparable bond, for the love for his little sister.
He raised her like a parent, protected her from grief, misery and distress,
Until one day, a ferocious lion invaded his province defenceless!
Gandhar saw Hastinapur's massive army coming its way,
An army large enough to erase Gandhar off the map in just half a day.
An army that enveloped the frail little kingdom like it was prey.
"The Prince of Hastinapur, I want Princess Gandhari to wed."
In a cold voice, the mighty Bheeshma commanded.
"Spare my daughter!" his princess's sorrows King Subala tried to prevent,
"After abducting the sisters of Kashi! Oh, Bheeshma, didn't you repent?"
Bheeshma growled, "Either the princess marries Hastinapur's blind Royce!
Or I shall wage war, Subala! And Gandhar's people will pay the price!"
"I am the valiant Shakuni's sister! I will protect my people, my motherland!
I will marry the Kuru prince!"
Between the tyrant and Gandhar, little Gandhari decided to stand.
The princess then took an oath, tied around her eyes a thick blindfold,
In return for the well-being of her kingdom, her life to Bheeshma she sold.
"I wish to never see your or your kingdom's face.
Darkness shall I rather embrace!

I, Gandhari, take a vow to live a life full of darkness till my last breath,
In your cage, Oh, Bheeshma, I shall await my freedom, my death!"
And his sister, her freedom, her peace, the poor brother couldn't save.
"I shall embrace her misery with her then!" a word to himself he gave.
"Princess Gandhari shall become the queen."
Bheeshma promised the lamenting father, the helpless king,
After snatching his daughter, his peace, his everything.
Before leaving, with tears, Shakuni looked at Arshi, his beloved wife,
At Uluka, their toddler unaware of the gloom that was to become his life.
"Crush this commander!" Arshi roared. "Make him pay for his sins!
Till death, stand by your sister's side! Don't let anyone touch her pride!"
"The throne shall always belong to you!" Shakuni's brothers cried.
"Bheeshma! The Lord will never forgive you!" People wept in woe.
And with wrath in his heart, the brother left for Hastinapur with his sister,
With wrath in his heart, the brother took a vow to kill, to die but protect her.
The brother took a vow to ensure his sister's sacrifice didn't go in vain,
A vow to end all her sufferings, end all her pain.
A vow that everyone who eyed her he shall slay,
A vow to make his Princess the Queen of Hastinapur;
Come what may.

1

"The Shakuni of our Mahabharata…" he said, letting out a deep sigh. The old man had been waiting for this parcel for a long time. He hastily tore open its packaging and gasped in euphoria, looking at the journal that had finally found its way to the author's house. His shrivelled fingers carefully examined the wrinkled victim of shelf-ware like it was some treasure. "Smells like an old room full of memories."

The journal must have seen over fifty years now—much more than the lifetime of a few humans he had come across. He grazed his hand over its peeling, hickory-brown leather cover and contently sniffed its worn-out, yellowish-white pages as he rifled through them.

Keshav Dham. The daughter-in-law. The secrets. The screams. The chaos. His mischievous eyes. Her crushed bones.

The words made his breathing more rapid as his jade-green eyes caught a glimpse of them.

"Sir, could you please sign here?" asked the courier girl who had handed him the parcel. But he was too absorbed. He was devoured, rather, by the cobalt ink that was beautifully engraved in cursive strokes on the pages bearing his past. An unforgettable one.

"Umm…" she cleared her throat, trying to get his attention.

No response.

"Sir?" she asked in a slightly higher pitch this time, drawing the plump, old man out of the reverie that he was dragged into.

"Oh, yes, I'm so sorry," he said, embarrassed, signing the sheet that she gave him.

"Sir, I'm extremely sorry to bother you, but could I please get a selfie with you? I've read all your books!" She crammed the paper back into her black cross bag. "And your films," she looked up, "I've watched each one of them like a hundred times!"

"Of course," he smiled. "You have no idea what this little parcel that you just delivered means to me."

"Thank you so much, Ryan sir!" she squealed. "You made my day! I'm going to frame this in my living room!" She almost jumped like a toddler after clicking a selfie with one of the most acclaimed directors and authors in the nation.

"Goodbye sir and thank you once again!"

"Who was it, Ryan?"

"Ira Di, it is finally here!" yelled Ryan as he darted inside to show the journal to his elder sister.

What is finally here? And who was it? Why are you running? What's that in your hand?

A jillion questions were shot at the unprepared old man as he entered his cosy reading room.

Like every alternate weekend, the five youngsters of the Rana family had gathered at Ryan's house to spend some quality time with their old grandparents, keeping alive the tradition that was cultivated since they were kids.

With fluttering eyes, the bespectacled, wrinkled man looked at the curious young lot who were prepared to shoot a dozen more questions at him. Avoiding their cross-examination and realizing his incredibly naïve mistake, Ryan cast a regretful look at his sister on the couch.

Ira defiantly glowered at her brother. "Ryan, you had to yell it out loud knowing that they're all here, didn't you?" she vigourously shook her head, making the white bob serenely resting on her thin and weak shoulders tremble.

Ryan sensed the fury that his sister had veiled under the polite question. "In my defence, Ira Di, you were the one who asked me who that was," he said as he tightened his red silk robe and sat in his reading chair, snuggling up to his dog, Simba, trying to avoid eye contact with Ira.

Ryan roguishly bit his tongue, looking at the young pairs of eyes teeming with curiosity. The attractive twenty-four-year-old Rohan, exuberant to debut in his grandfather's next movie, sat in a chair. Ananya, a young writer of the same age but a different metier, lay peacefully on the couch alongside the twenty-one-year-old sports fanatic, Eshan. Arya, a year younger than Eshan but the 'grandma' of the house, sat on the furry, soft brown carpet while Anuj, the youngest of the herd, a prodigy, sat on the beanbag solving a Rubik's cube.

Ira burst into pretentious laughter. "Yes, absolutely correct!" she said with a reverberating clap. "And what you yelled at the top of your lungs certainly was the answer to my question."

"Woah. Dadi, relax," said Arya, baffled at her grandmother's reaction.

"But what's that in your hand?" asked Rohan.

"And what is finally here?" asked Eshan.

"Great!" scoffed Ira. "Now tell them what that is."

Ryan looked at the three of them as they were desperately waiting for an answer. "Well, this is the journal which has the story…."

"Oh, my god!" Ira screeched in fury, cutting the man short. Blood gushed to her porcelain white cheeks. "Ryan, are you really doing this? I did not mean it!"

She hastily stood up, tossing the *pashmina* wrapped around her creased delicate neck on the couch, snatched the journal from her brother's hand, shot him a look of utter disapproval, and stormed off.

"Then stop saying things you don't mean," Ryan protested.

"Okay, now will someone please tell us what all this fuss is about?" asked Ananya, finally looking up from her phone.

"Nope. Not until your grumpy grandma permits me to, Anu."

"Dinner is served, Sir," informed a house help. "Ira ma'am has called everyone downstairs."

"Cool." Anuj stood up, still immersed in the Rubik's cube.

Ryan looked at the young boy, who had barely shown any interest in the journal. "Aren't you interested in knowing what the journal is about, young man?"

Anuj shook his head in denial without looking up and continued to solve his cube, oblivious to the ongoing commotion.

"Weirdo," Arya frowned.

"Come here," said Ryan, motioning for the house help to come closer. "Tell your Ira Ma'am that my audience has declared that they won't have dinner until they're told what exactly is in the journal." He winked at everyone.

2

Ira dashed into Ryan's reading room. It was spacious and two-storeyed with a wooden conical ceiling. It had polished wooden flooring of a slightly different shade of brown and wooden walls entirely used to shelve bazillion books, or probably more. Much, much more. It was like a warm and cosy brown timber box stuffed with books. And some more books. And some more.

Ira stood at the door, glaring at Ryan, irritated by his behaviour. The old woman was very well conversant with her brother's crafty tactics.

"Ryan, you're really going to have it from me now."

"Di, I'm seventy-one," Ryan dramatically gasped, with a palm on his chest.

"Well, act like that then!" Ira growled.

"What! *They* said all of that. Not me!" he argued, jolting his hands up in the air, questioning her 'spurious' assumption.

"I want you all down for dinner in less than a minute." She looked at the audience of five, disregarding her brother. Four of them looked at Ryan, gesturing for him to convince her, while the fifth, Anuj, sprang to his feet to leave.

"Anuj, sit down," Rohan hissed at his younger brother.

"They're eventually going to find out, Di, aren't they?" Ryan shrugged at his sister. "You do know I'm planning to write a book on it, right? And all of them read my books. I mean, I hope they do," he said, looking at the four faces with nothing but hope in his jade-green eyes.

"Yes, of course, we do," they chorused.

"How many has he written so far?" enquired Anuj.

Arya flung a cushion at Anuj. "Didn't you say you weren't interested?"

"You don't read my books?" the heartbroken old author asked his grandchildren.

"You narrate them to us yourself. Why would we read them, Nanu? Wouldn't that be like going all the way to the sea to see your reflection when you have a mirror in your room?" Eshan teased his old man, who stared at him with a face devoid of any expression.

"Remove the 'we', Eshan. Nanu, I swear I do," Rohan reassured him.

"That is great, Rohan. Why waste time listening to the narration then? I'm sure you'll love this one when it comes out," mocked Ira.

They begged their unyielding grandmother to let Ryan disclose the secret of the brown journal.

"You're not old enough," declared Ira. "Even your parents got to know about it just a few years ago."

Ryan burst out into hysterical laughter. "Di, wasn't I as old as Eshan when it happened?" he said. "I clearly recall it happened somewhere around 2010. I was just 21, you were 24, and Savya Da was 34."

"Fine!" Ira gave a gruff reply. "Let Rohan, Ananya, and Eshan stay back then. Arya and Anuj, down for dinner!"

"Please Dadi, don't do this," complained Arya and scooched over the couch, nestling up against her elder sister, Ananya.

"Dadi, she's twenty now. She's not a kid anymore, and as for Anuj, he turned eighteen last month," argued Ananya.

"Yes, eighteen and hungry," interjected Anuj. "Dadi, come on, let's go and eat."

"Let them hear it, Di. It's not that big of a deal," requested Ryan.

"It's not just about their ages, Ryan. Hadn't we decided the last time itself to never speak about all of it again?"

"But..."

"Ugh! You have always been a rebel, Ryan Rana." Ira sighed. "Alright then. Go ahead. Anuj, sit down. *It's story time.*"

Anuj apathetically dragged his feet back to the beanbag. "But I am genuinely not interested!"

Ryan took a knotty metal puzzle out of his pocket, a set of two springs inseparably intertwined with each other. He tossed it to Anuj and said, "Here, I got this for you."

The young boy accepted his consolation prize and slumped back in the slouched beanbag.

"Now, please proceed with the story, Ryan Da," requested Ananya.

"I know, right," said Arya. "I mean, what is all this about? And whose journal is that?"

Ryan smiled at the journal in his hands. "Inspector Nishika Mehta," he grinned at the memory of her beautiful face. "*My Nishi Di...*"

"This is a detailed description of the 2010 case by officer Nishika, who was investigating our case." Ryan raised the old journal up in the air. "She had a habit of writing journals about every case that she handled. *This one is ours.*"

A handwritten note tucked in the pages of the journal fell to the ground.

Dear Ryan,

I hope you get everything that you have been looking for in my little journal.

I thoroughly enjoy reading your books and watching your movies.

You must agree; I have been your first and your most loyal fan, haven't I?

Love to see how well Ira has been doing, too. Tell her I'm really proud of her. May god bless you both with the love and light you deserve.

Love,
Your Nishi Di,
-Nishika U. Mehta

P.S. Do not tell your annoying brother-in-law where I live. This grey-haired woman is a bit too aged to handle his hideous jokes now.

The few drops of tears that intractably escaped Ryan's eyes soiled a few words on the note as he read it. He passed it on to his sister.

With moistened eyes, Ira kissed the note and held it close to her heart. "I miss her…."

"How was she like, Dadi?" Arya hopped across the couch and snuggled up in her grandmother's lap.

"She was beautiful…." Ira whispered as her soft, wrinkled hands caressed Arya's hair, and her eyes smiled at the sight of the face her ageing mind was trying to put together. "She was very tall."

"Tall and slender and gracious and…" Ira sighed, "And just perfect. Thirty three…umm…no…Thirty—"

"Thirty-two," said Ryan. "She was thirty-two."

"Inspector Nishika…" he looked at Arya. "Her skin was the colour of beach sand," he smiled.

"And, oh, her voice!" he vigourously shook his head. "Strong and commanding. It knew exactly how to get things done."

"Yes. A voice that no one would imagine was hers," Ira chuckled, patting Arya's head a little harder in excitement, the face in her mind getting clearer. "A soft round face, big bright eyes…She had a baby face, you know."

"The silky dark raven hair—"

"Although, she rarely let them down," Ryan interrupted. "It was almost always in a neat and sleek top knot."

"Yeah," Ira smiled.

"I still remember the rough touch of her calloused palms," Ryan stared at the floor in a trance. "She was very hardworking. Very devoted."

"And so competitive," Ira laughed. "Always wanted to be the best."

"And she was," Ryan finally looked up.

"Were you guys close?" asked Rohan.

"Close?" said Ryan. "She was family."

"*Is.*" Ira smiled.

"But which brother-in-law of yours is she talking about in that note?" asked Eshan, yanking the old siblings from the slumber of memories. "And what do you mean by she was investigating *your* case?

"What happened in 2010?" asked Arya.

"And why—"

"Shhhh...." Ryan repudiated the examination, shredding the questions. "I will begin if you let me. And I will begin only on one condition."

"Now what, Ryan?" asked Ira.

"I want your active participation wherever needed, Ira Di. You know I'm going to need it."

Everyone stared at Ira with irresistible puppy faces.

"Fine. Whatever."

"Thanks, Di," he said. "Let's begin then, shall we?"

Ryan took a deep breath, sat on the edge of his seat, placed his elbows on his knees and leaned forward to do what he did best. He began telling a *story*.

"So, it all started after my first play," the old man sighed and looked at Ira.

"Did it really start *after* your play?" her eyes asked him.

Fifty years had passed, but neither of them had been able to silence the shrieks and gasps and wails that had filled the auditorium that day. The terror in the air, the gory visuals of *her* brain splattered on the back of her chair, of her bulging eye bathed in blood, about to pop out, and the faint scent of her blood, recklessly roamed their minds. Even today, *his* cries— "*Drishti? What happened? Oh my god! Blood! No No! No! Someone, please call the ambulance. My wife has been shot!*" His screams echoed in the dark depths of their souls, questioning their reality.

"28th February 2010," Ryan sighed. "I still remember that day. I remember every little detail of that dark day..."

"Nishika Di, you're going to love the show!" I said, squeezing her hand with excitement as I escorted her to her seat.

"I'm sure it's going to be lovely," she ruffled my hair.

"They'll finally know HIS story," I smiled.

Ryan opened the journal and started reading its first page.

CASE: SHAKUNI'S REVENGE

There were many factors that were important in an investigation—collecting evidence, interrogating the suspects, re-enacting the crime and a few more. But the most crucial part of a police investigation was finding out the *motive.* In simple words, it was the reason behind one's actions. But with the atrocious crimes that I had witnessed in the few years of my career, it wasn't just a reason.

It was a demon strong enough to push you off the edge of sanity.

A demon strong enough to drag you through the doors of brutality.

A demon strong enough to turn an innocent being into a beast who had no limits to his inhumanity.

Let me tell you a very interesting fact about this demon. It loved to eat. And guess what? It was always fucking hungry. Some of its favourite dishes might include blood, tears, and pain.

The cravings for which it hunted could be anything—the longing for a cold revenge on a scorchy sunny day or an irresistible, fuming hot rage, perfect in the heat of the moment. The sweet scent of unattainable love, the bitter but addictive taste of envy, or the spicy desire of lust. But sometimes, it hunted even without hunger, just for fun, you know.

'Motive' was a very funny six-lettered word when used in reference to a crime—was your reason strong enough to justify selling your soul to the devil in return for somebody else's misery?

Being an officer, this demon commendably helped me out in finding the criminal, but the problem arose when there was more than one.

Everyone involved in this series of murders seemed to be a convincing killer with a strong motive behind his or her actions. This was definitely one of the most crooked cases of my career.

The killer claimed to be Shakuni of Gandhar—the brother of Gandhari—a character of the *Mahabharata,* which took place in the *Dvapar Yug.*

Mahabharata, the war that marked the beginning of *Kaliyug.* It is said that the casualties of this devastating war were more than a billion. The unbelievable destruction left its land bereft of men. Weeping widows and children were the only inhabitants left.

You might have heard about a lot of people who claim to remember their past lives. Multiple researches have been conducted over decades by various philosophers, psychologists, researchers and hypnotherapists about the possibility of someone being able to recall their past life. But the mystery remains unsolved.

The killer, in this case, had a similar claim. He claimed to remember his past lives, in one of which he was the prince of Gandhar who was blamed for the destructive war.

I didn't know if it was really possible to have a memory of your past life, but all I knew was that the Shakuni of this Mahabharata also wanted his revenge. He wanted justice for his loved ones who had been wronged. He wanted the sinners to pay for their sins. But the most important question was—*How far would he go this time for his family?*

3

Nishika's Journal, 2010

Keshav Dham (Greater Kailash-I): A plush estate sited in the southern part of Delhi. An abode of the wealthy families of the city festooned with businessmen, justices retired from the bench, builders, and traders. In short, people who minted the kind of money that a bunch of their future generations could enjoy.

I moved into this bungalow society at twenty-two, about ten years ago, on 13th April 2000, with my aunt. She was an attractive, small-framed, and moneyed Chartered Accountant with a tiny face canopied by a classic 80s spiral perm brushing against her bony shoulders. The first time I heard about the Bathras was from the same aunt who came complaining to me about the weird family. Being the kind lady that she was, she had visited each of the families of the society with luscious French confectioneries that everyone had approved with a pleasant, hospitable smile except for the Bathras—one of the richest, highly esteemed, and shadiest families of Delhi.

An unsmiling, old and domineering father somewhere in his late sixties, Mr Dev Bathra. An upscale industrialist, he was the Chairman and Managing Director of the renowned Bathra Industries Ltd.

His spouse, Mrs Drishti Bathra, was a poised, beauteous lady always swathed in the classiest contemporary sarees I had ever seen. She greeted everyone with a charming smile, unlike her insolent husband. She was the only Bathra I genuinely respected and could even tolerate.

Mr and Mrs Bathra had four children. A stunning actress wearing her legs longer than usual, thriving in her late thirties—the woman, a bit too full of her own worth—Adah Bathra.

Her arrogant, truculent twin, Adar Bathra (a beefcake version of Adah with a few extra vertical inches and an added seventy pounds wearing a pompadour), was the eldest son who worked alongside his father in the Bathra Industries. The hypermasculine hunk was married to Urvi Bathra, a former teacher. Urvi was the kind of woman who'd shower you with compliments on your face and bitch about you the moment you turned your back to her, without even waiting for you to walk afar, making sure you heard it. Half her towering husband's height and ungraciously thin, her small face always had a sly smile. A smile you could easily tell was fake. A smile she made sure you knew was fake.

The third offspring was a charming outcast who had decided to swim against the currents of the river thronged by the businessmen of his family for generations and aimed to become a neurosurgeon— Savya Bathra.

The youngest son was a narcissistic spoilt brat who had never been denied anything in his life. A rangy young boy, bespeaking what his father must've looked like in his youth: an ugly soul in an attractive casing. Surprisingly, he was the only person around whom I had seen Mr Bathra smile. Undeniably the favourite offspring—Saarth Bathra.

"Their security guard didn't allow me in at first," said Shalini aunty. "When I told him the reason for my visit, he made a call from his cabin that was received by someone within the villa. The poor telephone couldn't endure the harsh, ear-splitting voice of Mr Bathra. Nishika, he asked the guard to shoo me off like I was some dog!"

I looked at my offended aunt and decided to pull the poor lady's leg. "So, you think it is okay to shoo off a dog, Shalini aunty?"

"Nishika, that's not what I meant, of course. You know, everyone in this society not only accepted my gift but also gave me a warm welcome. But these Bathras! Shooed off their neighbour without any sense of decency!"

"Sounds like my family," intervened a stranger standing at our door.

"I am Savya. Savya Bathra," he said, his eyes resting on Shalini aunty, "I live in the villa exactly opposite you—*the Bathra Villa*. I saw you leave my house looking a bit upset. So, I thought of checking up on you."

That was the first time I saw Savya. He was the kind of young man who was loved by mothers more than daughters. Having said so, I do not intend to convey that he was liked any less by the daughters. Two years older than me, probably 6'1, he was a warm-toned young man who had inherited the charms of his beautiful mother.

My aunt invited the boy inside with a sheepish grin, embarrassed that he had heard her rant. "Oh, I had come to gift you this little box of French confectioneries as your new neighbour, but it seems your father doesn't appreciate guests."

"Could I have some then?" he asked, stretching his mouth wide open like a toddler.

Shalini aunty unhesitatingly stuffed a macaron in Savya's mouth while adjusting the unkempt collar of his white shirt worn underneath a beige sweater vest. She lovingly gazed at the young man who had bonded with her in less than a minute.

"I have been living with that old man for twenty-four years now, and I know what you mean. Even I am not appreciated in that house, you see," he slurred with his mouth full. His words were everything but articulate.

"That's definitely a talented son right there. Speaking with such clarity, even with his mouth full. So full that all the tiny crumbs are escaping that big mouth of yours every time you open it," I taunted him, wiping the macaron off my cheek. Instead of showing any kind of embarrassment, he chuckled with my aunt at his goofiness and wiped the crumb off my forehead too. We both left my house together that day. Like every other morning, riveted to my disciplined routine, I was headed to the library to study for my entrance exam while he was off to God knows where.

He gracefully held out his hand to introduce himself. "Savya."

"Nishika," I said as I shook it.

The gallant gentleman opened the gate of my house, gesturing me to walk ahead. "So, Nishika, what do you do?"

"Well, I am studying for the SSC CGL exam. Wish to join the Police Force someday."

"Hey, that's great!" he said.

"I am here on a break, actually. I study in Australia. The Eastern State University," he detailed without being asked.

"Sounds good," I said.

"I study medicine," he continued. Again, without being asked. "Apart from the wholesome concept of saving lives—of course," he laughed, "It's the neurology part that really fascinates me. The neuroanatomy, the—"

"So, you want to become a neurosurgeon," I said, ending his upcoming thesis.

"Yeah," he answered, pursing his lips, giving me a look of condemnation for my dismissive behaviour.

"I'll see you later then," I said, in an attempt to end the small talk after throwing a quick glance at my watch, realising I was already quite late.

"I don't think so. I leave for college tomorrow, and I don't think my fortunate eyes will be seeing the face of my family for a long time."

Like all the other neighbours, I, too, had heard the loud quarrel that had taken place in the Bathra Villa the night prior. It was something about being a stain on the family's name and an unworthy son who was a disgrace to Mr Bathra. From what Savya told me, I assumed the argument had taken place between him and his father.

"Anyway, good luck with your exam then," he said, interrupting my thoughts and flashing a captivating smile.

"Thanks, goodbye," I said with a hint of a smile.

We both parted ways. As said, he left the next morning, and that was the last time I saw him in ten years.

* * *

The Bathra Villa was constructed with bricks made up of brawls and bickers. It seemed that arrogance, truculence, and disrespect were stirred in the air of their house. My studies were often disrupted by the regular blare of quarrels from the Bathra Villa. The family spared no effort in irritating me. Be it the ill-mannered punk, Saarth Bathra, who blasted atrocious verses under the name of music on the speakers of his flashy sports car every midnight on his arrival in the society, or be it the haughty actress who often fought with me when I didn't step back from complaining against her loud and shady late-night parties held in the Bathra Villa.

To my misfortune, the second storey of the Bathra Villa was clearly visible from my room, which added to the glory of their quarrels. Along with their exceedingly loud, unpleasant voices and cusses, I was even privy to unwanted violent visuals.

But time is an unbiased, fair gentleman. It passes regardless of your satisfaction or suffering, and it did. Ten years went by in a flash. I had completed my dream of joining the Police Force, and I considered myself tremendously fortunate for it.

But I had forgotten that when something is going too well, trouble is always around the corner.

Everyone thought that the case of the Bathra family that I had been assigned with began after a play, but only I know it began long before the play even took place. It commenced when *she* arrived in Keshav Dham. The newly wed daughter-in-law of the Bathras, *Ira Rana*.

Milky skin, high cheekbones, and a delicate heart face,
She stood before her new family, the Kurus, an invincible race.
But not her lustrous hair, her freckled cheeks, or her upturned nose,
Looking at the blindfold around her fabled blue eyes, everyone froze.
"For her would-be blind husband, it is a sign of love and respect!"
Shakuni fumed at Bheeshma's lie, at how her tragedy a secret he kept.
The brother observed them all, especially Kashi's abducted old sisters.
Their dismal eyes told a story, told the truth of
Hastinapur's hoax glory.
Shakuni looked at them, at their abductor, his heart filled with abhor,
He could see the suffering Gandhari was destined for.
In the flames of marriage, of her sacrifice, the sister was thrown,
Only her brother saw how lifeless, how numb the gleeful
girl had grown.
Soon the day of betrayal arrived; of his right, the blind prince
was deprived.
As the Ruler of the realm, Vidur pronounced Lady Ambalika's son,
Hastinapur crowned the younger prince, not the decided
elder blind one.
For Gandhari's sacrifice, her brother fought against the
decision unfair,
"If not the blind man, how can you make the diseased, dying
Pandu, the heir?"
The court split in two, between the wise Vidur and the outsider new.
When they asked the man most just the promise made to
Subala he crushed.
A vow of vengeance, then the betrayed brother breathed,
For in Bheeshma's loyalty to his words, he had once truly believed.

The defeat made the blind husband an inhumane beast,
After thrashing his poor wife, on her consent, he once tried to feast!
"I will kill you if you touch my sister again!" Shakuni attacked the blind man,
"Harm him and write Gandhar's end!" warned the entire Kuru clan.
"Let it go, Dada," at her brother's feet, the sister wept and wept,
"This is my life now," a miserable palm on her mouth she forever kept.
Even when brutally thrashed, even when mercilessly tormented,
Even when he swived concubines, even when he dragged her to his bed.
The brother heard her screams, her cries. Wept with her and wiped her eyes.
Helpless, he blamed himself for not being able to protect his sister,
Helpless, his tears and wails one day gave birth to an ***evil trickster****.*
Now the trickster waiting to strike one day got his chance,
When cursed, King Pandu carelessly abandoned his kingdom as penance.
"Oh, noble Bheeshma, obey your word! Make Gandhari the queen,
For more important than the man himself, his word has always been!"
Publicly he confronted the old man, successfully worked the trickster's plan.
But just when the power was about to turn his sister's fate around,
Partial for his beloved brother Pandu, in Vidur, a new enemy he found.
"Pitamah, what if Pandu returns? Wouldn't he feel betrayed by his own?"
Cunningly, Vidur made Dhritarashtra the acting king,
And poor Gandhari just a cushion to warm Queen Kunti's throne.

4

Nishika's Journal, 2010

A few months ago, I formally met Mr Dev Bathra for the first time after all the years that I had spent in Keshav Dham. He had come to my house along with his wife to invite us to his youngest son's wedding. Saarth was getting married to Miss Ira Rana, the daughter of a businessman from Mumbai. Mrs Drishti Bathra extended the invitation while he sat quietly like he had been reluctantly dragged along for formality, caressing the bushy grey-streaked chevron moustache he wore with pride.

I would have never predicted that the immature young man would agree to get tied to the strings of marriage at the age of twenty-four. Only a day ago, I had to ask him to move his steamy car, which was standing right in the middle of the street, blocking it. Thanks to my uniform and his compassionate (and evidently passionate) partner in crime, he refrained from arguing with me.

Apart from everything else, what left me sceptical was the date of the wedding. The marriage was going to be held on 10th January 2010—just a week from the date of the announcement.

"It was the bride's late mother's last wish," was the reason given to everyone by Mrs Bathra.

Shalini aunty attended the swanky wedding without me since I was working late that night and because I was least interested in watching the unnecessary display of opulence and pride.

"The bride, Ira, was gorgeous, Nishi. However, she did seem a bit off," Shalini aunty told me as she described to me her time at the wedding.

"Shalini aunty, have you been fortunate enough not to have encountered Saarth Bathra in all these years? Have you not met her husband?"

I often saw Ira sitting in the garden of the Bathra Villa, visibly lost and lifeless. A sight too miserable to ignore. She was like a body lamenting the departure of her long-gone soul. Her sylphlike stature was noticeably deteriorating since the first time I had seen her. The beautiful face had lost its charisma, and her soulless eyes were sunk into a dark and deep trench. Her sharp cheekbones and a narrow-angled jawline, once assets to her well-featured face, now manifested signs of malnourishment. In a month's time, she had started to look pallid and terribly shrunken.

Every other day, the residents of Keshav Dham spotted her husband fool around with distinct ladies in his car even after marriage— '*fooling around*' being the soberest term I can use here. It was more of shoving his tongue in—never mind, let's stick to fooling around.

On 13th February (almost a month after her marriage), as I left my house for duty at eight in the morning, I saw the young lady crying in front of an even younger boy, standing outside the gate of the Bathra Villa. That spot must not be visible from inside the house.

"Ryan, please stop creating a scene!" she said with her hands folded as though pleading. "Don't make my life tougher than what it already is. I beg you to stop fighting with everyone. *This is my life now*!"

"Di, I'm not going to tolerate it if that fucking bastard hits you once again. I swear to God, the next time he dares to touch you, I will fucking kill him!" he said, his voice paralleling the spiralling storm in his rageful eyes before he stomped off to his car and recklessly drove away.

"Is everything all right?" I asked the sobbing young lady. It was the first time I had talked to her.

"Yes, oh God, I'm so sorry," she said, wiping her tears as she ran inside the villa before I could ask her anything else.

"Did that boy just say someone hit her?"

I knew that Saarth Bathra was totally capable of doing something like that, and I wanted to help the girl. But first, I needed to find out if she was really being abused by her husband.

"Hey, are you new here?" I asked the boy the next morning when I saw him again on my way out. A striking, tall and lean youngster with jade green eyes complementing his fair skin, the boy was contemplating whether to respond to a stranger, his face bestrewn with suspicion.

"I'm Nishika, your neighbour, and apart from that great achievement, I'm also a Police Officer," I told him, realizing I wasn't in a uniform and my white shirt folded up the forearm, tucked in formal black pants wasn't really assuring safety.

I could see his face light up at the mention of my profession. "I'm Ryan…" he closed in near my face. "Nishika Di, I need to talk to you," Ryan whispered to me, adding an air of secrecy.

"I'm actually on my way to work right now, Ryan, but I can sure spare some time after duty, maybe."

"Great! I'll come to your house by 9 p.m. then."

"Ryan, weren't you supposed to be working on something? Isn't that why you have come here?" asked Mr Bathra in a sharp, interrogative tone, stroking his thick moustache from his balcony. He had an extortionately classy cigar crushed in his arrogant fingers and a jet-black silk robe relaxing on his somewhat overweight body. Maybe he didn't like the boy indulging in a conversation with me. Flustered, Ryan looked at his sister's father-in-law and left, muttering curses under his breath.

After an interminable day at work and with no memory of the plan Ryan had made fourteen long hours ago, I arrived home late at 11 p.m. to find the boy waiting on the stairs of my house. He ran to me as soon as he saw me. "Di, where were you? Even your house is locked."

I was a bit taken aback by the informality shown by him but still found it admirable. "My aunt is out of the country on a Europe tour, or she would've let you in. I'm extremely sorry. I forgot about this plan."

I invited him in. "How long have you been waiting for? Does your family know that you're here?"

"They're not my family. And no, they don't know. I told them I'd be out the entire night for some work," he replied, taking a stroll around my dramatically sombre, round-the-clock dull, yet soothing in a weird way, dark grey living room, touching and examining every little object in sight.

"And may I know where you're planning to spend an entire night in Delhi?"

He looked at me, clueless. "Let's see. I'll explore the city, I guess."

"At night, young man?"

"Yep, I don't really know anyone here, so that's the plan," he said, shrugging.

"Ryan, what kind of work grants you permission to stay out of your house for an *entire* night?"

"I've written and directed a play. It was an enormous success in my city, Mumbai, so I thought of organising it here in Delhi, too," he said proudly.

I looked astoundingly at the twenty-one-year-old boy who had a commendable achievement to his name at such a young age. "That's nice. What's it about?"

"It's about Shakuni from the Mahabharata."

Confused, I frowned at him. "The devious uncle who caused the war?"

I had never heard someone select that character from the epic as the lead of a play. An antagonist who was hated by everyone.

"Must be painful..." he whispered to himself before inviting a slight smile on his face.

"What?"

"For five thousand years, a brother has been solely carrying the blame for such a gruesome war. He didn't cause the war, Nishika Di," he sighed. "This is exactly why I chose this theme. He's one of the most misunderstood people in history. Everything that guy did was for his family...."

"There are always two sides to a coin." he continued after a pause. "Do you know there are people on this land who worship Shakuni even today?"

I swung my head sideways, twitching up my shoulders. "Really?"

"Yes!" he said. "The *Mayamkottu Malancharuvu Malanada Temple* in Pavithreswaram in the Kollam district of Kerala is a temple dedicated to Shakuni, appreciating the selfless man's love and sacrifices for his sister and his family. They admire his determination, will and courage to stand by a woman against a kingdom everyone dreadfully feared. Interestingly, there is another temple in the same district called *Poruvazhy Peruviruthy Malanda Temple,* built in remembrance of a magnanimous ruler of this land. The first ruler who disregarded the predominant, distasteful caste system—Suyodhan."

"Um, Suyodhan?" I asked, confused.

"Oh, right," he sarcastically laughed. "You might know him as Duryodhan."

"A temple dedicated to Duryodhan?" I was stunned.

"Yep," he smirked. "Folklores suggest that during the thirteenth year of exile, the Kaurava travelled throughout the land of Aryavarta in search of the Pandavas. One day, he reached this small village, parched and drained. Duryodhan requested a poor old woman for water, which she graciously offered to the crown prince. Her eyes soon fell upon the royal attire of the young visitor standing at the door of her dirty hut—literally falling apart at the seams—contently gulping down the impure water. With a trembling body, she fell at his feet, seeking an apology for her actions."

"Fell at his feet?" I interrupted Ryan, sitting next to him on the couch with two glasses of water for the both of us. "Why so?"

"In the era when an untouchable was scourged for even crossing an upper-caste's way, she had offered the crown prince of Hastinapur the insanitary water of her house," said Ryan, taking an exiguous sip from the extended glass as a formality.

"Duryodhan helped the old woman up, asking the reason behind her fear," he continued. "She informed him that she was an untouchable belonging to the Kurava caste. With hearty laughter, he wiped her tears and embraced the old woman, leaving everyone stunned. Grateful for her hospitability, he even granted her acres of land, jewels and money before leaving the village. The villagers, overwhelmed by the gesture of their benignant crown prince, built a temple in his memory that is looked after by a priest belonging to the Kurava community even today!"

I could see a noticeable change in Ryan's behaviour as he spoke about the unusual topic and characters of his play. "That's a unique point of view, Ryan," I smiled. "All the best for your play."

"Nishika Di, can I ask you a question?"

"Yeah, sure, go ahead," I said, expecting a casual question from the young boy.

"How far will you go to protect your family?"

The question caught me off-guard. It was nothing close to what I had expected. After a few moments of stuttering and hesitating, I said, "Unfortunately, Ryan, I don't think I have many people to protect. All I have is my aunt."

"Oh, I'm so sorry. May I ask how it happened?"

"I had a sister who passed away when she was quite young. She had been battling cancer, and I lost my parents in an unfortunate accident when I was sixteen. I live with my aunt, a childless widow. I am her world as she is mine."

"I'm so sorry," he said. "I'm sure they're all in a better place now."

I smiled at him. I was used to the sympathy.

"Ryan, is there a reason behind you asking me that question? Is everything alright?"

He looked at me for a few seconds, in which I'm sure a million thoughts crossed his mind. "Di, do you think taking revenge is a sin?"

"What?"

"You heard me," he said, smiling.

"Ryan, I–I don't know…I don't know if it's a sin, but with the crimes that I have seen, offenders, once upon a time victims, that I have met, it sure quenched the thirsts in their hearts they said…." I sighed. "Has something been bothering you, Ryan? You know you can share anything with me, right?"

Ryan looked at me, preserving the smile. "Will you help me out with my play, Di? I have no one to give me feedback on my work. I would've asked my sister, but she's busy with a lot of chores these days."

"That was not the answer to my question, but yes, sure, I'd be glad to help," I said. "And you can crash in my guest room tonight. It's not safe roaming around so late."

"Thanks, Di. You don't know how much this means to me."

Tousling the boy's hair, I returned his smile. "By the way, didn't you want to tell me something in the morning? What was that about?"

"Aren't we going to meet often now? I'll tell you everything."

"Okay, but—"

"Do you have anything to eat by chance?" he asked to divert me from the topic.

I took the cue and decided to let him take his own time to open up. We both had dinner together that night, unaware of the fact that it was going to become a ritual in the near future. In one meeting, anyone could define Ryan as a splendid boy with a lot of ambition and courage for his age. He slept in my guest room after having dinner and left early in the morning while I was still asleep. I kept thinking to myself the whole night, why would such a young boy ask me those serious questions? Questions that were so heavy to carry in one's mind, in one's heart. Was there any threat to him or his family? Was he planning to do something about it? Gazillion questions raced through my mind about these two fresh additions to the Bathra Villa—the miserable sister and her cryptic younger brother.

* * *

Present Day

Ryan glanced up from the journal to find everyone gaping at him, utterly speechless. The only sound that could be heard was the metal springs that clanged against each other as Anuj tried to detangle them.

"So, the brother-in-law of yours that Officer Nishika was talking about in that note is Savya Bathra? Our Savya Da?" Rohan looked at Ira, shocked. "He isn't your sibling?"

"No! Answer me first," Arya turned the frail and old Ira to herself. "Dadi, who is this Saarth Bathra? I hope you filed a complaint against that fucking son of a bitch," snarled the enraged girl.

"Language, Arya!"

"Dadi is right, Arya. But so are you," said Ryan. "He was definitely a fucking son of a bitch."

"Ryan!" howled Ira, giving him a look of criticism, her eyes wide open.

"But why was Dadi even married to such a man?" questioned Ananya. "What were her parents doing when their daughter was living such a despondent life?"

Ryan looked at Ira. "Now that, Ananya, your Dadi will answer."

5

Everyone turned their ears to Ira to hear the answers to their questions. Ira took a deep breath and began;

'Ryan and I were born and brought up here in Mumbai itself. We had a normal childhood but weren't really close to our parents. Both of them were busy individuals who hardly spent any of their time at home. I didn't see my father for months sometimes.

My father, Mr Adarsh Rana, was a reputed and, more importantly, a 'respected' diamond merchant. The owner of Ace exporters—a diamond manufacturing and exporting company from Mumbai. But in his own house, he was just a detached man who confined himself to his room whenever he was home. I don't recall having more than ten conversations with him in the twenty-four years that I lived in his house. My mother, Bhavika Rana, a successful corporate lawyer—the fiercest one I had ever seen, was equally uninterested in staying at home with her kids even for one day. Parents might not realize it, but it is almost impossible to hide their strained relationship from children. They understand everything; however hard you try to hide your problems. But in my case, they didn't even bother to hide it. We always knew nothing was normal between our parents. They barely talked to each other. When they did, I'd rather term it as an awfully aggressive quarrel with the use of extremely inappropriate language and verbal abuses—regardless of our presence. I had never seen them happy together, but neither did they care to get separated since they hardly saw each other's faces.

Ryan and I had made peace with the fact that we were unlucky not to have the loving parents that we always longed for, but at the same time, we weren't ungrateful for everything they provided us with. We found our happiness in other things and in each other. We shared an inseparable bond, even as kids. A bond that never lets us feel the void of not having experienced the love given to us by our parents. Our lives were much better before he barged in and destroyed them, causing irreparable damage. The tyrant industrialist from Delhi, infamous for his corrupt tactics, Mr Dev Bathra.

It was the first day of the year—the most dreadful day of the year. The worst day of my life. I remember standing outside dad's room, listening to their conversation. The conversation that shook me to my very core.

"It's either a yes, or I leak the tape… The decision is yours," he said with a crooked smirk. "Think about it, Rana, it is a

fucking good deal. The sale of diamond jewellery is expected to grow at an annual rate of 10% in the next six to seven years. Ten fucking per cent, Rana! With this joint venture, we can fucking rule the market."

"No." my father gritted his teeth. "You can leak the tape if you want to. I don't care about her reputation. I don't care what the world thinks of that whore," declared my father.

Mr Bathra smirked at my father as he kept the pen drive on the ostentatiously pricy black bar counter. "I know very well that you don't care what happens to your wife after I leak the tape, but I'm sure that even you will not be able to escape the thick, dirty smoke that will arise when I set on fire the hoax image of your picture-perfect family," he said, taking a sip of whiskey from his glass. "You're very well aware of the impact it will have on your business and reputation, Adarsh, aren't you?"

"Let's see," Mr Bathra took another sip with a devilish smirk. "A non-executive independent director of the Ace Exporters, also, the founder and chairperson of your group's philanthropic arm...."

"What will happen when the world comes to know about your worn-out relationship with your wife? About her extra-marital affair with my brother? Tell me, Adarsh, do you really don't care if I leak the filthy but undoubtedly enjoyable sex tape of your wife and my brother?"

I rushed to my mother's room to inform her about the inconceivable conversation that had unfortunately fallen on my ears, only to find her lying on the cold marble floor with a half-empty bottle of Vodka beside her.

"Mom! There's a man in Dad's room. He's…he's... he's speaking some ridiculous stuff! Please come with me!" I said, kneeling next to her, falling short of breath and words.

"Bhavika Patil, known to all as Bhavika Rana…" she said, staring at the ceiling, gently tugging at my arm, signalling me to sit down. "A poor but ambitious girl from Bombay with a million dreams dwelling in her eyes."

"Mom, please listen to me!" I cried.

"You know, Ira, I used to live in a BDD chawl in Worli," she continued, unheeding my request and crying, "It was a small, heavily congested 10x10 room with a little kitchen crammed with six people."

"Mom, why are you doing this? Please listen to me!" I yelled, my unfailing patience tested.

"I know…" she looked at me for the first time since my arrival. "Now listen, will you, darling?" she looked up at the ceiling again.

"My leech father wedded me off to a rich businessman's son who had come asking for my hand," she continued in a quaking voice, weak from battling the lump in her throat. "Apparently, a young man had seen me the night I was working as a waitress at one of his father's business parties. He had fallen madly in love with me, or rather, was simply infatuated with me. I had nothing against him, but I wanted to pursue my higher education. I had worked very hard, day and night, to get admission to a law school because my father,

a poor vegetable vendor, could not afford it. I tried explaining my situation and dreams to that mulish boy, but he said that he didn't have a problem with me pursuing my studies even after marriage."

My unsettled body finally rested on the floor. I sat down next to my mother. It was the first time she was sharing something with me. The first time I had a real conversation with her. The first time I met my mother—Bhavika Patil.

She held my hand. "It was never about him allowing me to pursue my dream. It was about what I wanted," she said, her tears hiding under her eyelids that she forced down. "I knew my success would weigh nothing in front of his huge name. However bright it shined, it would always hide behind the dark clouds carrying his glorious name. I wanted to become a successful lawyer on my own, and I sure did, but, 'It's all because of my influential husband', 'Anyone would become successful after marrying a man so rich', 'What problems did she even have to face? She's Adarsh Rana's wife!' they say. Even today, my career means nothing in front of my identity as Mr Adarsh Rana's wife."

An unnerving silence filled the room as she stopped to suck in pain, dying to break free. It was held in for too long. The ambitious woman tired of proving her worth to the world, the untameable self-made lawyer tired of fighting her husband's name, was not used to vulnerability. She was afraid of it.

"For the world, my story is classic, romantic and cliché—the rich boy falls in love with the poor girl and turns her life around," she finally spoke, the tears successfully swallowed. "No

one cares if the poor girl wanted to marry the rich boy! If she even wanted him to turn her life around! Why would they? Isn't it every girl's desire? Every girl's dream to one day marry a rich man madly in love with her beauty?"

She teared up again and looked at me, "I begged my father, but he was too awed by the proposal to even listen to me. After all, it was a proud thing for him. The time to hand over his 'heavy baggage of responsibilities' to another man had come. The time when he could roam around with his head held high amongst all our relatives. I tried to convince Adarsh to leave me alone, but my denial made me the forbidden fruit he became obsessed with. I even tried to run away. My father begged me not to stain our family's name. He begged me not to do such a thing, at least for the sake of my younger sisters, whose future lay ahead of them. 'Who will marry the younger sisters of a girl who ran away? People will make shameful assumptions about you and them!' he said. He then did something that shattered me into a thousand pieces. He clasped my younger sister's arm and dragged her before me, placing a knife in my hand, 'Kill her rather than make her suffer for her entire life!' he growled."

"Mom," I hugged her cold bones lying on the floor, numbed. "I'm here," I said, trying to soothe her.

Defeated by her fear, vulnerability slowly rolling down her face, she broke out into soft sobs. "I still remember the unfortunate day of my marriage. Everyone was enjoying the grand celebration of my sacrifice. Of my slaughter. My father then blessed the young man to rape his daughter every single night in the name of marriage. It was the grand celebration of a socially accepted rape by a man I was forced to marry."

It must've been the first time she had allowed herself to fall weak since her forced marriage to my father. I'm sure she had never shared her sorrows with anyone. For me, she had always been a quarrelsome mother who fought with my father for no reason. That was the first time I saw her as an individual. A miserable being. A wronged woman.

"I met Aman Bathra, Dev Bathra's cousin, last year regarding a case. It was the first time I felt something for a man. Unlike your father, he appreciated me. He filled the void in my heart. I thought I had finally gotten the love everyone wished for. The love that I had never experienced. The love that I thought I never would." she laughed, the stream flowing down the corner of her eyes now vigorous, endless, rejoicing its victory.

"I'm sorry, Ira, I couldn't be the mother that you and Ryan deserved."

The next day, Mr Bathra signed the deal with my father in our living room. Ryan and I dejectedly watched the two men shake hands.

"I would like to put a cherry on top of this cake, Mr Rana. I want your daughter, Ira, to marry my heir, my beloved son, Saarth," he said.

"Excuse me?" I bawled at him, enraged by his audacity. "What do you mean you 'want' me to?"

"My sister is not some cherry on this fucking cake made up of muck," argued Ryan as he charged at Mr Bathra.

My indignant father pushed Ryan away. "Go to your room right now, you two!"

"Dad, No!" I'm not marrying some random guy I don't even know. Especially not his *son!" I said, glaring at Mr Bathra, my blood boiling. "I know everything that you and your brother did to my mother."*

I ran to my room after being slapped by my father in front of the devil that fed on that feud. But Ryan stayed back. To fight for me.'

With moistened eyes, Ira looked at everyone and then at Ryan. "He was always there, you know," she smiled. "To fight for me."

"This is…this is just…" Ananya took a deep breath, trying to absorb what she had just heard. Her eyes were wet, her voice shivering.

"Anny, you okay?" asked Rohan.

"Yeah," she said quickly, wiping her tears, "Yeah, I am…."

"What happened next? How did he convince your father?" asked Eshan.

"He didn't need to convince him," Ryan replied in a trembling voice, narrating the story further.

'My father looked at Mr Bathra with a smirk, "And what's in it for me, Mr Bathra?"

I looked at my father, disgusted. "Dad, what do you even mean by that? Are you out of your mind?"

"My children would never dare to talk to me like that, Adarsh," said Mr Bathra, further infuriating my father.

My father asked me to go up to my room. He slapped me for putting up a fight for my sister. Kept doing it until I finally left them alone.

Mr Bathra sat down on the couch, grinning at the delightful sight of me getting kicked out. "Ah, kids these days do not fail to shock me every single day," he smiled. "Adarsh, now that we're partners in business, the most crucial thing we need is cooperation. We need to share a good rapport to avoid any conflicts and difference in opinion. If tied in this beautiful relation, I think it will make it easier for me to 'co-operate' with you."

"I like it," said my father and sat down next to Mr Bathra, discussing the details.

"Adarsh! How dare you! Do you want to destroy my daughter's life now? Wasn't destroying mine enough for you?" boomed my livid mother, who I had brought along after telling her the entire incident. "Ira will not live the miserable life that I did. And Mr Bathra, didn't you get what you fucking wanted? What would you take to leave my house now?"

Mr Bathra calmly got up from the couch and walked up to my mother. After getting too close to her, making her extremely uncomfortable, he whispered in her ear, "Mind your words, Bhavika. I still have your dirty little secret with me."

I pushed the creep away from my mother, "What secret? Mom, what is he saying!"

"Answer your son, Bhavika," he said. "Ryan, turns out our interests are quite similar. Even I have directed a small piece of art. I'd love to show you my work, son. The actress—especially—has done a marvellous job."

With tears in her eyes, she helplessly looked at my father, who sat as a silent spectator to the entire scene. Unbothered by the situation, he continued sipping his scotch, looking at his wife with a straight face. She walked back to her room without saying a word. I tried talking to her, shaking her up. But she sat staring into nowhere, ignoring my presence, my existence.

Two days later, Ira Di came to me and declared her decision to marry Saarth Bathra. I begged her to give it another thought. I stormed off to my father's room to fight with him for treating my sister's life just like another one of his business deals, but Ira Di ran behind me and clutched my hand. "Please don't ever question me, Ryan. Please don't do this. Be the one man in my life who respects my decisions," she cried.'

"Dadi, why did you agree to marry him!" the listeners asked altogether, dazed by what they were hearing.

6

The tears streaming down her eyes, Ira looked at the stupefied faces. The old woman braced herself and continued;

'I sat in my room crying for the rest of the day after Mr Bathra asked for my hand in marriage for his son. At night, I went to my mother's room to ask for her help, unaware of what had happened after I had locked myself.

Her body lay on the bed with her wrist slit wide open, as though cut multiple times to eliminate any scope of survival, to drive the soul out of the body. I sat down at her door, traumatized by the visual. The drops of blood from her cut-open wrist dribbled on the floor, creating a horrifically rhythmic sound. A sound that keeps ringing in my ears even today. That was her only escape from the hell that she had been living in for years.

The starving jackals—the ravenous news channels—pleased with the loaf of my mother's meat blazoned the news of her suicide—the breaking news of 'Adarsh Rana's wife's suicide.' But only I knew she had been brutally killed. Murdered. Slaughtered by the demon that now eyed my peace.

My father came to my room two days later and declared his decision. I revolted with all my might. Revolted against his selfish agenda that I knew would destroy my life. The astute businessman then decided to emotionally blackmail his daughter. He tried to convince me that Mr Bathra had been blackmailing him for this marriage in return for my mother's sex tape. He told me that all he wanted was to save mom's reputation. He begged me to think about my dead mother. But he didn't know that I had already heard his conversation with Mr Bathra. I knew he didn't care about my dead mother's reputation. That he had already signed the deal with Mr Bathra in return for that tape. I knew this was one of the strategies of the cunning and self-centred businessman. All he saw was his profit. And I didn't want that to happen at the cost of my life. At the cost of me.

"What is the fucking harm in marrying Mr Bathra's son? I've seen the boy. He is extremely good-looking, well-read, exactly of your age and most importantly, of equal social status. I don't want you to make the same mistake that I made. I married a poor girl who couldn't match up to my status or adjust to my lifestyle. Even after doing so much for that ungrateful woman, she cheated on me. But Mr Bathra's son

is a good guy. He would never hurt you. His family is modern and open-minded. They have no problem with you working after marriage. His father has a vast business which he will inherit someday, and Mr Bathra is even my business partner now. What is the damn problem?" he thundered, standing in my room, barking at me.

"The problem is that I don't want to marry him. I don't want to see the face of his father or anyone even closely related to him. I shall not marry the son of the father who killed my mom!"

Mr Rana then stooped to the lowest level. "Do you want me to tell the world what your mother did? About her fucking affair? Shouldn't the world get to know what I have faced because of her? Do you want people to talk filth about your dead mother? Do you want me to leak that sex tape, Ira?"

"Really? What about you then?" I screamed. "Will I not tell the world about the little brothel that you have been operating right here in your house under everyone's nose for years now? Haven't I seen your 'visitors', dad?"

He lost his calm. I could see his gritted fists and his tightly clenched jaw. "If you don't agree to this marriage, not just you, even your brother, will have to face the consequences," he said, a fierce finger raised at my face. "I will throw you both out of my house. Who's going to stop me? Your dead mother? Neither of you will get a single penny from me. I don't care what the world thinks of me. Live on the streets then, feed on this pride of yours."

He came near me and bent down to look into my watery eyes. "Do you want to destroy your little brother's future? All because of your stubbornness? Do you want all of this to happen, Ira? Because you know I can very well do it. I have fixed your marriage with Saarth in the coming week. You better get ready for it."

I knew my father inside out. He certainly would do everything that he warned me about. I couldn't let people speak filth about my dead mother. I couldn't let him besmirch her name. I couldn't let Ryan become a victim of my father's wrath. We both had nowhere to go if he were to throw us out of the house. No one to take care of us. I was completely helpless. I would rather see my life getting destroyed than my younger brother's. So, I decided to marry Saarth Bathra.

"I still remember the unfortunate day of my marriage. Everyone was enjoying the grand celebration of my sacrifice. Of my slaughter. My father then blessed the young man to rape his daughter every single night in the name of marriage. It was the grand celebration of a socially accepted rape by a man I was forced to marry."

My mother's words echoed in my ears. That was the moment I realised— pain is only felt by the one who has the wound. Others can only feel bad for you.

I was pushed into the same fire that had once feasted on my mother. The inferno that had feasted on numerous helpless women in the past. The diabolical flames that continue to feast on every other woman of this country, even today.'

With her shivering, wrinkled hands, Ira wiped her tears, "The time I spent in the Bathra Villa was the darkest time of my life. I had lost my very will to live. Breathing had become a task for me, just as difficult as waking up every day in that hell. I was the brand-new toy a father had gifted to his impudent son. None of the family members intervened when my husband harassed me, when he physically abused me if I didn't give in to his whims. All the Bathras seemed to be unaffected by the way he tormented his wife.

So many years have gone by, but that ugly scar doesn't fade away. Every night I can hear the racing thrums of my heart against my heaving chest. I can feel the trickling sweat on my forehead and the numbness in my limbs when I used to lock myself in the bathroom every night, far from his dirty touch. I cried tears of terror when he banged the bathroom door for hours, petrifying my soul. I cried tears of relief when he finally abandoned me. I remember it all, feel it all, live it all. Every. Single. Night.

Mr Dev Bathra had decided to marry his spoilt, dastardly son to me, hoping that marriage would knock some sense into the boy who lacked any kind of seriousness regarding his future—regarding the family business's future. He thought marriage would make the boy responsible.

Fortunately, a month after my marriage to Saarth, Ryan came to Delhi for his show along with our dog, Daisy. But what I thought was the only good news in my life turned out to be an even bigger disaster. Ryan couldn't watch my dreary state. He fought with every member of my family. He blew a gasket when he got to know that Saarth had been beating me, and none of the family members had ever intervened. I tried to calm him down but ended up inciting his anger for the Bathras."

Ryan gave out a sigh of discordance at his sister's words, "Yeah, right. You expected me to calm down and watch that fucking abuser hit you in front of your supposed new family and me. You wanted me not to fight with the lady of the house, a 'respected' woman known for her principles, who silently watched her son assault his wife? You wanted me not to put up a fight with the man who was the reason for your woebegone condition. The malign industrialist who won you in a deal. The man responsible for our mother's death!"

"Ryan, that's not what I meant," Ira tried to calm her brother down, who had rebirthed the spiralling storm in his rageful eyes, as deadly as it was decades ago.

"No, Ira Di. You meant it," he said. "You mean it now. You meant it, then. You wanted me to keep my calm when that stuck-up actress treated you like a servant of the house. Wasn't it she who accused you of sleeping with her co-star out of jealousy just because she saw him talk to you once? And then her arrogant brother, Adar, advised your husband to teach you a lesson for your behaviour. The best day of my life, even today will be the one when I broke that motherfucker's nose. And let's not forget his wife, the cause of all your fucking hardships! They all treated you like a punching bag brought into their house by Dev Bathra for them to release their frustration!"

Ryan looked at everyone and tried to gain back his sanity, "Anyway, let's get back to the journal, shall we?"

With trembling fingers, the old man flipped through its pages, not waiting for a response, to find the one where he had stopped.

"Ah, here it is."

With a rare smile, the little sister kept his hands on her womb,
On the blessing thriving in it that would slay their gloom.
Hooting in joy, he ran through the palace like an excited little boy.
The brother's bliss knew no bounds; his ecstatic skies knew no grounds.
In just a few months, Kunti too was mother-to-be,
To meet his Pandu, Vidur left for the forest in uncontainable glee.
The overjoyed Bheeshma, Shakuni watched in dismay,
Upon Gandhari's pregnancy, even a visit, the elders hadn't bothered to pay.
As though her unborn baby, the eldest grandchild to them, was of no worth,
As though before the two children, bias had taken birth.
Fifteen months passed, and more than thrice as large as any normal one,
Gandhari's abnormally growing womb horrified everyone.
Kunti, on the other hand, gave birth to Yudhishtir, her eldest boy,
Disregarding Gandhari's suffering, his birth Hastinapur celebrated with joy.
Maddened and drunk, "You are nothing but a curse of misfortune!"
To his room, the blind man mercilessly dragged his pregnant wife,
"Dada!" her gut-wrenching screams alarmed her brother, saving her life.
But the threshold was crossed of her hope, of her pain,
To deliver her child, she repeatedly struck her womb, her bane.
Not an infant, but she birthed something never seen, a lump of flesh!
Vyaas divided it into 101 foetuses and kept them in wombs of mesh.
Flowers were to bloom, a miracle for all, science for him, an artificial womb.
"Demonical will be the children born from an unnatural process!"

Vidur claimed they would bring utter misery, utter distress.
"Are you questioning the great Vyaas, your own father?"
Shakuni bayed,
Fuming, Vidur retreated, but the people he had cunningly swayed.
They protested to the King, "Slaughter the children! Put them on fire!"
To protect them all alone, the brother fought with the entire empire.
And just a few hours after the birth of Kunti's second son,
A movement was detected in the artificial womb, and at last, the brother won.
The sage pushed open the door, carrying in his hands a new folklore.
"First, Dada shall hold my boy," the sage handed Shakuni her bundle of joy.
Shakuni held him in his arms, and in an instant, their eyes met,
It was the beginning of a story the world would never forget.
"King Subala is no more!" a piece of news suddenly shattered their mirth,
Vidur thundered, "This child is the devil of doom on earth!
An ill-starred boy! Killed his own grandfather as soon as he took birth!
Before he grows up to be a curse, oh, King! His neck you should wring!"
"Not another word, Vidur!" the blind king finally stood up for his son,
But of little Suyodhan, people were terrified; the damage was already done.
Sushasan, Sama, ninety-seven brothers and a sister, Sushala, arrived soon,
The brother raised them like his own, like from his Mahadev a boon.
They reminded him of little Uluka, his son, they made him a father again,
An unfortunate, sorrowful father whose fatherhood Hastinapur had slain.

7

Nishika's Journal, 2010

I spent a lot of time with Ryan. He often brought a companion with him, Daisy—a year old, lily-white Labrador. Along with Ryan, I had developed a close bond with her too. He joined me for dinner almost every alternate day, and we discussed the storyline of his drama. Ryan had put an extensive amount of time and effort into his creation. He had researched in depth about the epic, especially the lead character—the prince who left his kingdom to live with his sister to protect her, how the man lived his entire life for his sister and her sons, and how he sacrificed his own life to ensure their well-being. I'm not going to lie, he did seem pretty entranced by the story of the brother.

He even told me everything that his sister had to face on a daily basis in the Bathra house—the abuse, the accusations and the misery. He told me how she had been dragged to the dark abyss by its Satan, Mr Dev Bathra. I tried to calm him down every time he got caught up in violent fights with the two brothers or with any other Bathra. I even tried to convince Ira to speak up against her in-laws. I assured her that if she was ready to file a complaint against them, being a police officer, I could easily take care of the rest. Her brother was ready to become a witness to her statement too, but she denied it. She feared the outcome. She knew what Dev Bathra and her father were capable of. Ira had accepted her misfortune and had decided to live with it. She had lost all hope and strength to fight. I felt sad for the wretched girl. I wished I could do something to put a smile on her face. What enraged me the most was the audacity of Mr Bathra, who walked with his head held high and chest pumped with pride after destroying the lives of innocent women. I couldn't imagine the pain Ira and her mother must've gone through. Ryan's anger against the family was justified to the hilt, but I was equally worried for him. I hoped he didn't do something that would land him in deep trouble someday. So, I advised him to focus more on his upcoming show, which was scheduled in just a few days.

Finally, 28th February 2010, the day of his play, arrived—A Sunday quite warmer than the cold week that had disappointed the Delhiites craving for the sun. A day that I will never forget. A day that no one seated in the auditorium would ever forget.

The Bathras were also going to attend the play to display a strong and lovely bond with their new bride's in-laws.

The director and writer of the play, who was decked up with a headset and surrounded by a huge huddle of performers carefully listening to his instructions, ran up to me and gave me a tight hug the moment he saw me enter the auditorium. He was beyond elated to see me. "Thank you for helping me out, Nishi Di. Come, I'll show you your seat."

"Nishika Di, you're going to love the show!" he said, squeezing my hand with excitement as he escorted me to my seat.

"I'm sure it's going to be lovely," I ruffled his hair.

"They'll finally know *HIS* story," he smiled.

The extravagant auditorium—*the Golden Box* (located in Greater Kailash-II)—was a massive hall entirely filled with people. It sure was a full house. I had been given a special seat on the balcony that was reserved only for the Bathras and a few more VIP families. My seat was in the last of the two rows. In front of me, in the first row of the balcony, sat Ryan, Ira, Saarth, Adah, Adar and his wife, Urvi. In the balcony opposite ours sat Mr Dev Bathra and his wife, Mrs Drishti Bathra. I wondered why they hadn't been given a seat next to their family. When I asked Ryan about it, he told me they weren't going to attend the show but somehow changed their decision at the last moment, and those were the only two seats available in the balcony where they could be accommodated.

The play began. I put aside all my thoughts and began enjoying the show. It was much more exhilarating and gripping than Ryan had described it to me. I was totally arrested by it until I heard a deafening scream echo through the auditorium.

"Drishti? What happened? Oh my god! Blood! No No! No! Someone, please call the ambulance. My wife has been shot!" screamed Mr Bathra.

I immediately called my team and the medical examiners to the spot. A backup force tried managing the triggered chaos in the auditorium, the wild audience who ran haywire after hearing about the murder, while we restricted the crime scene with barricade tapes.

Mrs Bathra's body lay in her chair, lolled to the right side. She had been shot exactly in the centre of her forehead, ensuring immediate death. The 9mm bullet was stuck in the wound from which the blood oozed upon her face. Her mouth was slightly open, as though her soul had left her body even before she could scream.

My eyes fell upon the other members of the Bathra family, who were made to stand far away from the body. Unaffected by the death of his wife, Mr Dev Bathra was calmly wiping her blood that had splattered on his right cheek. He stood next to Adah, who was lamenting in her brother Adar's arms. Adar wept silently while trying to console his sister. Urvi stood beside him, staring at Ira, who was comforting her petrified brother. Ryan looked like he had seen a ghost. Saarth stood at a distance from all of them, talking on his phone, unperturbed by the death of his mother.

Hunkered down, I examined the wound and the body for any other signs of injury. "How much is the distance between the two balconies, Sharma?"

The lanky man about to enter the wrong side of forty, clad in khaki, carefully peered at the two balconies, calculating something, "Approximately 50ft, Inspector."

"Thought so," I stood up. "This is a professional's work. It is impossible for an amateur to take this shot. She has been shot with perfection right in the middle of her forehead from a 50ft distance in a dark auditorium attracting no attention."

"You're right, ma'am. But the ones sitting exactly opposite to her were the members of her own family...."

I looked at the confounded Asst. Sub-Inspector, "Hmm... Search the entire auditorium. Look for the murder weapon."

Mrs Bathra's body was sent for post-mortem after being scrutinized by the medical examiners. On Mr Bathra's request, Commissioner Bahrelia—one of the VIPs personally invited by Mr Bathra—permitted the family to leave before we carried out further investigation of the crime scene.

"Sir, we cannot let them go," I insisted. "We need to check them for any kind of evidence before they leave."

The Commissioner was nonplussed by my suggestion. He pulled me to the side. "Inspector Nishika, what the hell is wrong with you? We're lucky he didn't hear you, young lady! Mr Bathra just lost his wife, and his children lost their mother. I cannot ask him to stay here if he wishes to leave. He is a powerful man with a vast reach. Do you want to invite trouble?" he said with a chiselled scowl. "Let them go. And that's an order."

After the Bathras left, we searched the entire auditorium for evidence and the murder weapon but, as expected, found nothing.

Taking into account the spot of the murder—which was under my jurisdiction—and the fact that I was well-acquainted with the family, I was officially assigned the case of the Bathras, my neighbours.

I went back home the night of the homicide, shaken by the incident. Considering the angle from which Mrs Bathra was shot, the only people who were seated in the perfect spots, winning the unfortunate title of suspects, were the Bathras and Ryan. I had a sleepless night for two reasons. A thought that kept arising in my mind, and the loud quarrels in the Bathra Villa. I wondered why they were quarrelling instead of mourning, but all I could do was wait till the next morning.

*"They call me **Duryodhan**, Ma," little Suyodhan endlessly cried,*
"They despise me, fear me, curse me! At even my sight, they hide!
*They say I'm their **doom**, Mama! Their **end**, a **monster**, a **demon!**"*
The damage Vidur's accusations had caused could just not be undone.
The name made Suyodhan feel evil, like a demonic brat,
Maddened, the little boy ran, begging everyone to not call him that.
Shakuni abhorred his image that had been created in every mind,
Abhorred how the innocent kid was by all maligned.
Adding to Suyodhan's misery, upon the beloved Pandu's sudden demise,
In Hastinapur arrived his cherished sons, the five stars of Vidur's eyes.
And for the five boys, their affection Vidur and Pitamah never hid,
*Suyodhan hated the love Kauravas never got, but Pandavas **always** did.*
Bheem often ruthlessly bullied the younger Kauravas for fun,
The hot-headed Suyodhan battered him then; an eternal enmity had begun.
To Gurukul, the boys were sent far from the palace, from childhood sins,
At mace fighting excelled Suyodhan and Bheem, at Medicine, Madri's twins,
At Politics, Yudhishtir; at Archery, Arjun, Drona's favourite prince.
And for this favourite, Drona once stopped heinously low,
Snatched from a young boy his dreams, not just his thumb and his bow.
Shakuni scolded Suyodhan for not standing up for the tribal young man,
"Never let a warrior suffer for being powerless due to his lowly clan!"
Years passed, to exhibit their mastery to the kingdom, the time had come.
Arjun entered the stadium, and with his archery, the prince awed every one,
"The greatest archer of Aryavarta!" Drona lauded Indra's son.
"I disagree!" a robust voice put an end to the celebration grand,
With a bow in his hand, a courageous charioteer's son dared to stand.

"Sutputra!" Jeered Bheem. "The reins are meant for you, you know!"
"Only equals challenge each other!" Drona growled. "Drop. That. Bow."
"He is equal!" Wearing his mother's fabled blue eyes arose a young man,
By the poor charioteer's son's side stood the said monster of his clan.
"I shall not let you sacrifice another Eklavya!" he gave Drona a fierce glare,
Publicly, the prince crowned Karna the King of Anga then and there,
*"**Till eternity**, Suyodhan," a true friend Karna had met in the world unfair.*
The awaited duel began but ended when suddenly fainted Arjun's old mother,
"Must be the sun," people murmured. "Or was it any reason other?"
To their home, their kingdom, when the Kuru princes at last returned,
Not the first conceived, but the firstborn was declared the crown prince.
Bheeshma sided with Vidur's say, Shakuni's he sternly spurned.
"Suyodhan isn't flawless!" Shakuni said, "But then, is Yudhishtir the right fit?
For Arjun, Eklavya getting sacrificed, how could that righteous man permit?
Couldn't he stop Bheem when mercilessly the younger Kauravas he bullied?
Couldn't he support Karna when the vain Bheem ridiculed him on the field?
Or, in the wicked caste system, does the righteous prince too believe?
With his bogus morals and ethics, how long will the people he deceive?"
Shakuni roared at Bheeshma, "Your promise lies unfulfilled ever since!
Ensure Gandhari becomes the Queen by making her son the crown prince!"
"If something happened to Yudhishtir," glared Bheeshma, "Only then will I."
The trickster within whispered to Shakuni, "Well, then he will have to die."

8

Nishika's Journal, 2010

The next morning of Mrs Bathra's murder, Mr Bathra and Adar came to the police station. They had brought a tape that someone had handed over to their security guard last night. Profusely sweating, the old man gave me the tape.

"Inspector, please listen to this."

'Every time you place upon my family your sinful eyes,
From his grave shall this brother arise.
Your end has been invited by every tear that my sister shed,
An end that shall entrench in your soul misery and dread.
For your nightmare is back, your death is near,
You callous Kurus! It is now your time to fear.
This brother shall slay you monsters hiding in human skin,
For the trickster is back, but this time he's here to win.

I know your dirty little secrets, I remember everything you did,
I know every sin that you successfully hid.
Every sin committed in this and in your past lives,
To write history, let's see this time who survives.
Who am I?
The brother of the sister you dragged to hell on Earth,
The uncle who lit the pyre of his ninety-nine nephews,
The man on whose soul, on whose name you left an ugly scar,
I am Shakuni of Gandhar!'

"What the hell is this!"

"We don't know, Inspector. The man who handed this over to the security guard ran away before the guard could catch hold of him. He had wrapped himself in a black shawl from head to toe. The guard couldn't see his face," said Adar, "And…This isn't the only one. There's one more..."

'An ardent follower of Dharma, the prince once again pretended to be,
An epitome of morals, of compassion, an endless sea.
Mrs Drishti Bathra, the woman with a heart of gold,
The cunning woman whose secrets shall now unfold.
A pure human filled with morality, with kindness,
Or maybe just sly enough to convince everyone of her righteousness.'

"Shakuni? As in the one from Mahabharata," I said, looking at the two Bathras. "And this righteous prince is?"

"Yudhishtir, who else?" answered one of the policemen. The entire police station reverberated with the raucous laughter of the men in khaki.

"This is surely some nutcase, ma'am," said one of the constables while the others discussed whether the false accusations made on Mrs Bathra in the tape were just an attempt to divert the case and distract us.

But what if there was a reason behind his accusations? What if they were true?

I had always respected Mrs Bathra and thought she differed from the other members of her family. She was known for her fair work as the Director of one of the city's most prestigious universities, the *Mittal Institute of Technology*, and for the charity work that she did.

"Throw away the tape, Mr Bathra. There's no need to worry," said Sub-Inspector Mishra—a generous brown man with a midlife balding, awaiting a promotion since forever—shaking his hand in rejection at the two anxious men.

"Well, I beg to differ," said a firm, polite and familiar voice, intruding on the boisterous laughter in the station.

Sniffing for its source, everyone threw their heads around to finally find Mr Dinesh Joshi, a distinguished quadragenarian criminal psychologist, entering the station. Mr Joshi looked at me with a well-bred smile, "I was here for the Anup Singh triple murder case, as requested, Inspector."

"Yes, of course. Good morning, sir," I said, offering him a seat before showing the way out to the Bathras.

Mr Joshi took a swig from the glass of chilled water, settling in the timber chair as he looked at Mishra. "I seem to have overheard the tape, Sub-Inspector. It may be too soon to throw it away. I think I know what this is."

I eagerly looked at him. "What do you mean? What do you think is it?"

"Delusion of Grandeur."

"What's that?" asked Mishra, scratching the round tiara-like bald spot on his head.

"It is a type of *Delusional Disorder*," said Mr Joshi, placing the glass on the walnut-coloured table. "As the name suggests, patients suffering from this rare but relatively severe mental illness are highly delusional. They live in an altered reality. They hold firm, *imaginary* beliefs, having no touch of realism. Beliefs that may sound erroneous and ridiculous to everyone around them. Beliefs that are so strong that the patient can just not be convinced otherwise, however hard you try. The delusions stay resolutely ingrained in their mind even if you provide convincing evidence about them being far from what we define as *real*. They start living a lie. Start living a life where they cannot distinguish between their imagination and reality."

"But...but how do we detect it in a person? What are its symptoms?" a paunchy Constable Naidu stepped in.

“It is difficult to detect this particular disorder in an individual,” answered Mr Joshi. “The exact number of people suffering from it remains unknown since most of them don’t realise that something is wrong with them, or they don’t believe they need any kind of treatment. Unlike the patients of any other disorder, the patients suffering from this particular disorder *behave quite normally otherwise.* Their behaviour isn’t abnormal or bizarre, and neither exhibits gross disorganization—”

I looked at Mr Joshi, confused, “I’m sorry to interrupt you, but what’s gross disorganization?”

“Patients with disorganized behaviours are unable to independently carry out simple, day-to-day activities. They might lose control over their emotions, responses and impulse, proving to be harmful to the people around them. Their behaviour is highly unpredictable and dangerous,” he explained. “But this is not the case with Delusional Disorder. An onlooker might not even notice anything wrong with the people suffering from it until the subjects decide to share their false beliefs.”

“What kind of delusions are we talking about?” I asked him, slightly resting on the table, curious to hear more.

“Delusions can be of many types such as being stalked, suffering from some disease, being related to a person you’re actually not, being watched or even beliefs like a particular person is conspiring against them.”

"For example," he said after a brief pause, analysing the disarrayed expression on every face. "There was a case of a forty-three-year-old woman from States who believed that she was pregnant when in reality, she was not. She was also convinced that her family members were conspiring against her and the unborn child and were planning to kill them. The woman refused to consume food prepared in her house or even drink water since she was certain that it had been poisoned by them. The diagnosed killed two members of that family as a result of her false beliefs and delusions. Upon studying her case in detail, it was later found out that the lady had been forced to abort her child by her parents when she was a teenager. The beliefs and delusions were a result of the trauma she had been through upon losing the unborn child she wanted to keep. Also, the two members that she killed had a history of physical abuse with the woman, which must've made her feel even more threatened," he explained.

Mr Joshi took another mouthful of water, moistening his throat, before continuing.

"In the case of Delusion of Grandeur, patients usually have over-inflated delusions related to themselves and their abilities. They might believe that they have supernatural abilities or extraordinary powers or that they are a totally different person. There have been extreme cases where patients were convinced that they have magical powers, are invincible or even immortal. Three years ago, in Germany, there was a case of a man, somewhere in his late thirties, harbouring a belief that he was immortal. He went as far as attempting suicide multiple times to prove it to the world. After listening to the tape, the conclusion that I would draw from it is that our patient here believes that he has the ability to *remember his past lives,* in one of which he was Shakuni. He believes that his loved ones are once again being wronged by those he hates and that history is repeating itself. Now either he is simply trying to distract everyone, or he actually believes in what he is saying, which might complicate the case even more."

"How can someone come up with such a belief out of nowhere?" I asked him incredulously, unconvinced by the entire theory.

"Inspector, sometimes trauma finds its origins way back," he said. "The lady who was delusional about being pregnant conceived her belief the day she heard the news of her pregnant friend's miscarriage. She began reliving the trauma she had experienced upon losing her own child. Her mind blew life in that cremated pregnancy, hence coming up with the belief that she was pregnant once again to get rid of the re-emerged misery. The entrenched feeling of failure for not being able to protect the child in her teens, somewhere buried deep within, arose from its grave. To deal with that intense emotion, the mind moulded a story, hence giving her one more chance to protect her child, which in reality, was *nonexistent*."

"Do you think there is a reason behind our killer's belief too?" questioned Mishra.

"Sometimes we tend to relate or empathize with the people around us, historical figures, or even fictional characters who have had life experiences similar to ours. Most of the time, these are traumatic experiences. Maybe after getting introduced to Shakuni, the killer started relating to him to a dangerous extent, thus reliving his own trauma. And to manage those emotions, his mind conjured up a belief, and he started identifying himself as Shakuni. He may also believe that his enemies have been reincarnated, and destiny has given him a chance to avenge the sufferings of his loved ones."

"Do you think it is possible for someone to remember his or her past life? Or is it impossible for something like that to happen?" I asked.

"People have been trying to answer this question for centuries, Inspector," said Mr Joshi shaking his head, fascinated. "Apart from common people, scholars with great calibres like Swami Vivekananda or the Greek philosopher and mathematician Pythagoras have claimed to remember their past lives and showcased a firm belief in the theory of reincarnation. The theory is that a certain facet of a human being is immortal, unlike the body that gets worn out with time. That this facet, known as the soul, transmigrates into another mortal after its prior home perishes. It is also believed in Hinduism that the ones who die with unfulfilled desires or wishes are unable to escape the circle of life or attain liberation and take rebirth to fulfil them."

"What about the other religions and cultures?" I asked. "Are there any evidence, mentions or beliefs regarding the phenomenon endured by them?"

"Of course, there are," The psychologist answered. "The concept of reincarnation is not just prevalent in Hinduism, but also Buddhism and amongst Greek philosophers like Socrates, Pythagoras, and Plato. In fact, neither is it of any less fascination to the Western world."

"Ian Stevenson," said Mr Joshi. "An American psychiatrist conducted under his supervision approximately 3000 cases of subjects who claimed to remember their past lives. His book *'Reincarnation and Biology'* includes several astonishing cases of children born with birthmarks unmistakably resembling the cause of their death in their former life as narrated by them. He suggested it is possible for memories, emotions like fears or phobias, or even physical features to travel from one life to the proceeding one. Stevenson cross-checked the various claims made by the subjects, like their former family members, cause of death, and their identity, with the family of the deceased the child identified to be. Shockingly, most of the claims made, and details narrated were a hundred per cent accurate and provided concrete proof for the proposed theory of rebirth, while a few weren't as precise. The convincing evidence provided by Stevenson is accepted by many but doubted by few who believe the claims to be cases of *Cryptomnesia*—the resurfacing of some memories that were either suppressed or hidden in the unconscious part of the mind that an individual misunderstands to be new ones."

"What about you?" I asked him. "Do you believe in reincarnation?"

"Inspec—"

"I do, ma'am!" Naidu interrupted Mr Joshi, unable to contain his enthusiasm. "Like lovers and soul mates, enemies too find their way back to you *to settle old accounts.*"

"Yes, ma'am!" Mishra exclaimed. "Even my mother believed in this. In fact, she often said that one often takes rebirth in his own family since they are the ones we have interacted with the most within our lifetime and have a lot of karmic debts with. She even says I am her grandfather reborn! What a fine man he was, a—"

"Mishra," I motioned him to stop and looked at Mr Joshi.

"I was saying, Inspector," he said. "I certainly would identify myself as a supporter of the theory, but in the case of this killer, I cannot arrive at any conclusion before talking to him myself."

"Hmm...So, does our killer carry himself as Shakuni did? Does he believe that he has a limp or something like that? Or maybe he suddenly starts behaving like Shakuni and then switches back to being himself?" asked Asst. Sub-Inspector Sharma, sitting down on the chair next to Mr Joshi.

"Not really," he replied. "The killer isn't confused about his real identity. He knows who he is in this life and will *always* act the same. He simply *believes* that he was Shakuni in one of his *past* lives. There isn't any reason for him to physically replicate Shakuni or showcase any sudden abnormal behaviour, which also makes it harder to identify him. And by the way, Shakuni had no deformity. He must've been a proportionately built man from Gandhar, present-day Kandahar in Afghanistan."

"Not physical, but we might need to focus on his cerebral and emotional traits. If the killer believes himself to be Shakuni reincarnated, his characteristics and thought process will be similar to Shakuni's. To identify these traits in the killer, we need to study Shakuni in detail. Thanks to the mythology enthusiast lodging in me, I was also one of the audience members of Ryan Rana's play," he said, allowing me a brief glance tailed by a gentle nod. "I'd say Shakuni was a victim who turned into a villain. An intelligent man, an artful schemer, *an illusionist deceiving us all.* So, I'd suggest we begin by looking for a *victim.*"

"What the hell is all of this!" I thought to myself, my hands on my head, befuddled by his theory.

The resultant expressions—more than transparent—that had taken over my face licensed Mr Joshi a peek in my mind.

"There's more, Officer," he said. "What might be a bigger problem is that if this disorder is not treated on time, the belief gets more ingrained and intense with each day of affirmation. The more he thinks about it, sees relative things, meets the people who are directly or indirectly involved in aiding his belief, the stronger it gets," he said, a sigh of concern ushering itself out.

The Criminal Psychologist looked at all the pairs of eyes that were glued to different things—the flooring, the desk, the ceiling, his face—having forgotten the instinct to blink, immersed in deep thoughts. "Well, I should leave now," he said, jerking me out of my thoughts. "I'll be back for the triple murder case some other time, Inspector."

"Yes, sure. And thank you so much for the generous insight, sir," I said, graciously escorting the man out of the station.

"What now, officer?" asked Sub-Inspector Mishra.

"The interrogation of the Bathras is scheduled for the day after tomorrow, isn't it?" I folded my hands. "Let's see what they got to say."

The mastermind came up with a plan, a scheme
unimaginable to any man.
Shakuni summoned the brilliant architect, Purochan, his trusted aid,
"In the forest of Varnavrat, build a palace," he told the master
of the trade.
"A palace for the Pandavas that they shall enter but not be able to leave,
A beautiful palace whose ugly truth no one would believe.
For what cannot be done by a dagger will be done by the house of lacquer."
But as Kunti and her sons were leaving, the truth discreetly Vidur exposed.
"Weapons aren't always made up of solid materials to commit
wicked crimes,
They're made up of matter impossible to gain control over sometimes.
When a forest is on fire, amongst all the animals brave, oh, brothers five!
Only the timid mice that hide in holes survive."
And in just a few days, as planned, Hastinapur was incessantly weeping,
Execrating the flames that fed on the defenceless when they
were sleeping.
The six were devoured by the ugly fire that had broken out accidentally,
But only one *stood with a smirk while the kingdom cursed it vehemently.*
The one closest to the Pandavas, the one who looked after them like his own,
On hearing the news of their death, not a sign of grief Vidur had shown.
"Find out what exactly happened that night!" Shakuni alarmed his spies,
"Maybe it was no accident." Vidur's persuasion made people surmise.
"It was Duryodhan and his uncle!" the rumours created a
terrifying uproar,
People started fearing and abhorring the prince and his uncle even more.
"The cunning brothers escaped! They are alive!" Shakuni spies informed,
"The old mother and her sons are safe, not one of them was harmed!
They deceived six beings whose remains could resemble that of theirs,
Exploited six poor lower castes for whom no one on this cruel land cares.

A Nishada woman and her five sons went to Yudhishtir begging for food,
What happened to them after that makes me a thousand times brood!
In the palace, their magnanimous crown prince offered the mother shelter,
And the same night, along with her innocent sons, he pitilessly killed her!
While his brothers dug a tunnel to escape, Bheem set ablaze the palace,
Showed the world his truth, how he is brutally callous."
"Those mice!" Shakuni cried, "For trusting them, the innocent paid the price!
And the people who have labelled me and my nephew evil and vile today,
Who loathe us and anyone related to us in the slightest possible way,
Tomorrow, these hypocrites will overlook this crime of their crown prince,
Only Mahadev knows Aryavarta shall enshroud his how many more sins!
How is he 'virtuous' after butchering those who went begging to him?
Righteous, they will call him even after knowing this sin hideous and grim!
The Bheem, who claims to be the strongest warrior on Aryavarta's land,
To burn six defenceless people in their sleep, how could he prepare his hand?
If us trying to kill them for our personal vendetta is a sin,
Isn't them killing six harmless people for their personal vendetta also a sin?"
Bheeshma made Suyodhan the new crown prince of the mighty empire,
But in the eyes of his people, he remained the cause of the hostile fire.
While the Pandavas escaped not only the flames but also the gruesome crime,
Thus remaining the heroes, hiding their sins and the truth till the end of time.

9

Nishika's Journal, 2010

An interrogation room was often dark, dull and misty. A ruse by the manipulators of the mind. The human brain is not very good at perceiving darkness. It panics, shudders and loses its calm, visualizing the monsters residing in the dark looking right at you. And time after time, without realizing there is nothing scarier than us humans, we let the fear fostered by darkness terrify our souls. We blurt out things our minds want to hide.

This large dim-lighted room was designed calculatingly. It had nothing but two chairs facing each other, distanced by a small wooden table. There was no chance of getting distracted. The only sight was the interrogator's face. The only sound was his unsmiling voice, his questions, his accusations. And until the moment you stepped out of that 12x14 area, you were under his control. The room and the man were capable enough to make you feel like the offender even if you hadn't committed the crime.

But not everyone fell for the schemer's tricks. Some were built differently. Even in the darkness, emptiness and the deadly silence that played with your mind, some had invincible shields protecting their vulnerability, which were stronger than the interrogator's desire to extract the truth. They kept lying. Real monsters that they were, fearless to an unsettling degree. The ones we should fear.

3rd March 2010, 72 hours after the death of Mrs Drishti Bathra, I interrogated all the members of her family to find out only one thing: all of them were hiding something—something dark enough to warrant the murder of the lady of the house.

#1 Adar Bathra

"Mr Adar, did your mother have any enemies?"

"No. She was a gem of a person. The most kind-hearted and compassionate human being I knew. Why would anyone have anything against her?" answered the bull-necked hunk with a knit in his bushy brows, his ashy three-piece suit unable to conceal the tension in his body.

"Why do you think the killer has questioned her ethics and righteous character?"

"The tape has been made to defame her," he asserted. "She was very stringent when it came to following her morals. She would never do anything wrong. Mom was known for helping others and even went out of her way to do so. *She was an angel.*"

"So, she always helped everyone but couldn't help her own daughter-in-law when Mr Saarth Bathra physically abused her?"

"How dare you! Do you even know who you are talking about? He would never harm any woman. Next time, keep in mind the family you are dealing with before making such preposterous allegations!" he warned me, snapping his fingers at my face.

"Hmm. So, nobody hit Mrs Ira Bathra? That's interesting. It is also drastically contrasting with what your sister told me. She said Ira 'deserved' the beating because she was sleeping with Miss Adah's co-star, Mr Vihaan Malhotra, wasn't she?"

Adar looked at me, bewildered. His anxiety was rippling through the room as he continuously bounced his leg and drummed the table in front of him without a rhythm. "That...that was just once. It was only because my brother loved his wife. He couldn't bear the fact that she was cheating on him. It was just...*heat of the moment.*"

"So, you did lie about him not hitting her then."

"Listen, officer! We are an honourable family! What that characterless girl did was something beyond our imagination. Contrary to her filthy and questionable upbringing, my siblings and I have grown up seeing the pure bond shared by our parents. Isn't my brother allowed to show his grief?" he bellowed in a fury.

#2 Adah Bathra

"Miss Adah, how were your relations with your mother?"

"What do you even mean by that question? Of course, they were great. We dearly loved each other," she said. Her words were followed by an in-sync toss of a shoulder and an eyebrow.

"Hmm... Do you suspect anyone? Especially after hearing the tape?"

"It is either that deranged brother who keeps fighting with everyone for no reason or his duplicitous sister who pretends to be what she's absolutely not: helpless and weak. The brother-sister duo is trouble," the brunette groaned, adjusting the shamrock green overcoat tautly wrapping her voluptuous body.

"What do you mean by the duplicitous sister who pretends to be what she's not?"

"Unlike everyone, I always knew Ira was not a timid girl. She was just pretending to be one. Everyone saw her real face when she aggressively attacked Urvi and viciously grabbed her by the neck over a petty argument."

"Ira? *attacked* Urvi? It doesn't sound like something she would do," I thought to myself, perplexed by what I had just heard.

"Miss Bathra, what was the argument about?"

"Urvi tweeted to pay her respects to my mother, and Ira got offended by it for some reason."

"Can I see the tweet?"

"Here."

Urvi Bathra

@urvibathra ...

I am extremely sorry to announce the demise of my beloved mother-in-law, Mrs Drishti Bathra. She was a selfless lady who lived her entire life for the well-being of others. But there is always a devil who cannot behold the sight of an angel doing good work on Earth for the people. She was brutally murdered during Ryan Rana's show, who is her daughter-in-law's brother. Ryan is the writer and director who shot to fame with his play which is about a savage villain. However, my faith in goodness is restored after seeing that the people who detested her when she was alive, like dear Ryan, are also grief-stricken by her death. This just proves that there really is no room for enmity in anyone's heart after the death of their enemy. So, why fill it in our hearts even when the person is alive?

May her soul rest in peace.

10:15 PM • Feb 28, 2010 • Twitter for iPhone

508k 216k 100k

"The tweet triggered Ira. She held Urvi by her neck and threatened to kill her," Adah added.

The tweet attracted a lot of unwanted negative attention. It indirectly accused Ryan. People had already made him the murderer. They had concluded that he was the one behind Mrs Bathra's death and protested against his upcoming shows, because of which they had to be cancelled. Due to this outrage, some people even stood outside Bathra Villa, where he was living, and burnt his posters, demanding justice for the godly lady.

"And exactly when did this argument take place?"

"The night of Mom's murder."

"So, that is what the commotion was about that night," I thought to myself.

#3 Urvi Bathra

"Why did Mrs Ira threaten to kill you, Mrs Urvi?"

"I merely paid my respects to my mother-in-law. I don't know why she attacked me like that."

"Don't you think your tweet has landed her brother in deep trouble?"

"It is the truth, officer. I just expressed my thoughts and emotions. Don't I have the freedom to express myself?" she asked me with her eternal sly smile.

#4 Ryan

"Did you hear the tape delivered to the Bathra villa last night?"

"No, Di, actually I was…."

"I'd prefer being addressed as an officer, Mr Ryan."

"Officer, I was not at home. The murder had a distressing impact on me. I needed some time alone, so I went on a drive, and it was almost dawn when I returned."

"The killer claimed to be Shakuni, the lead antagonist of your play."

"You saw the play, right, officer? Do you still think he was an *antagonist*?" he retorted, an edge of his lips slightly curved up.

"Mr Ryan, how are your relations with your sister's in-laws?

"They harassed her. They made her life hell. I don't have good relations with any of them, and neither do I plan on establishing any."

"What were you doing when Mrs Bathra was shot? Did you see anyone pull the trigger? Heard any noise?"

"No. Neither did I see anyone, nor did I hear any kind of noise. I was engrossed in the play, and the only thing I could hear was the loud narration."

"What do you have to say about Mrs Urvi's tweet, Mr Ryan?"

"It's a fact—I hated Mrs Bathra. The only thing wrong with the tweet is the claim that I'm 'grief stricken', which I'm clearly not. I still hate her."

"And as for my cancelled shows," Ryan gritted his teeth. "Let the world blame me for anything they want to. Let them make me the villain. I don't fucking care. But these Bathras won't stay the heroes for too long, officer, and that I'm sure of. Let them hide their sins and the fucking truth for now. The world will get to know everything one day. And I can wait till then."

#5 Ira

"Miss Adah said you attacked and threatened Urvi that you would kill her. May I know the reason, Mrs Ira?"

"I kept my calm when all of them accused my brother of being the killer, but I lost it when Urvi tweeted the message. Her note has made everyone believe the killer is my innocent little brother. She has destroyed his future! All his shows have been cancelled. He can't even step out of the house without protection. I know Ryan hates the family, but he could never kill anyone. And I will not tolerate anyone laying a hand on my little brother. I have suffered silently in that house since the day I first came here, but I will not let any of them ruin my brother's life. I love him more than anything, and I will not hear a word against him!" she screamed, standing up with a brutal force that blew off her chair. "I will always protect him, officer. *At. Any. Cost.*"

I was shocked by her behaviour. I had never seen her so incensed. I felt like…like she was somebody else at that moment…like even after all these days, I knew nothing about her. That there was a lot more to that 'weak', 'helpless' girl.

#6 Saarth Bathra

"Mr Saarth, who do you think killed your mother?"

"The only person I know who hated her was Ryan, but I don't think he killed her. He doesn't have the guts to. He's the dog who barks but doesn't bite," said Saarth, clicking his tongue.

"Did you see or hear anything on the night of the murder?"

"Nah. Not really. The play was too loud to hear anything else, and surprisingly, I was enjoying it. So, I wasn't looking here and there."

#7 Dev Bathra

"Mr Dev Bathra, did you have any enemies? You know, who would go for your wife to teach you a lesson?

"No. I don't have any enemies, and neither did Drishti."

"Are you sure about that, Mr Bathra?"

"I think I am. Do you think otherwise, Inspector?" he growled, crushing his teeth and withstanding my suspicious gaze with an untiring stare.

"Any take on the killer, Mr Bathra?"

"Now that's a question. I'd place my bets on Ryan Rana, Inspector. The boy *hates* us."

***

The autopsy stated that Mrs Bathra died because of extensive brain damage caused by the bullet and not because of any other reasons. After questioning the security guards of the auditorium, I learned how easy it must have been for the killer to carry the weapon inside. The two lousy fellows accepted that they didn't check anyone properly. Upon questioning the management of the acclaimed, high-end auditorium about their incompetent services, all they did was hang their heads low.

The other members of the audience that sat in the balcony gave answers that were similar to the ones the Bathras had given. None of them had heard the gunshot—presumed to be from a silenced weapon—due to the loud, ongoing play or had seen the killer.

My team and I searched the victim's house for evidence. That was the first time I went inside the Bathra Villa, the ancestral home of the Bathras. On the exterior, it was like any other opulent villa, but what lay inside could surely enchant anyone at first sight. Reflective of its wealthy dwellers, it had a flamboyant modern architecture, as though a page of a luxury magazine had come to life. The pristine glass walls let the lush, glossy black-themed interior glisten in the golden rays of the sun. Every object, right from the carpet to the vase that stood in the corner of the room, was handpicked from the finest of its lot, flattering the elegant and sumptuous interior. Mr Bathra had built himself a picturesque, exquisite mansion by destroying the lives of God knows how many people.

I personally checked all the rooms that belonged to the members of the family but didn't find anything notable. There was a licenced Beretta M9 in Mr Bathra's room, but he reasoned that the handgun was for safety purposes only and showed all the papers related to it. Ira had shifted all her belongings to Ryan's room for the time being and was sharing the room with him and Daisy. An almost empty box of Ambien, three empty strips of paracetamol and one of aspirin, and apart from the sleeping pills and painkillers,

Ira's drawers were overflowing with an unhealthy number of new and empty strips of Zoloft, Prozac, Celexa and a few more antidepressants that she couldn't provide a doctor's prescription for.

Ryan's cupboard was flooded with hundreds of books. Most of them carried information on the epic, Mahabharata, and the remaining few were crime novels and other mythology books. The only doubtful thing that could be easily smelled throughout the villa was the uneasiness and the hidden fear clearly visible on the faces of a few members of the family. The faces that were relieved when the police left empty-handed.

Mr Bathra, being extremely influential, had a lot of contacts in the department. He had been watching my every move. I had to find out what the Bathras were hiding from me. It was very important to dig out the secrets buried in their hearts and pasts. I had to reach the bottom of their dark sea without attracting the shark's attention.

Unable to endure the unwanted vigilance, I complained about it to ACP Verma, who was supervising the last case of his career. ACP Verma was one of the few officers whose loyalty towards their uniforms had always inspired me. A round married belly, burly shoulders trumpeting the three stars resting on them, a thick walrus moustache and the bushiest eyebrows I had ever seen on a man, the gazetted officer looked like an Indian version of Santa Clause without a beard. He was just as warm, just as jolly and just as gigantic. But unfortunately, the Indian version was unable to grant me what I had ardently asked for. ACP Verma offered me advice as compensation for not being able to take action against a man as influential as Mr Bathra. He urged me to proceed with the case by hiring a private investigator instead of approaching my regular undercover to prevent the information from getting leaked to Mr Bathra's well-concealed links in the department. Acting upon his suggestion, hoping to get some lead on the dying case, I found an agency in Nehru Place—*The Hidden Eye Security*.

I made up my mind to pay its office a visit regarding the case, unaware of what I was about to invite in my life, or rather, *who* I was about to invite in my life.

Unaware that I was. Of *him*. Of his mystical existence.

यदा यदा हि धर्मस्य ग्लानिर्भवति भारत ।
अभ्युत्थानमधर्मस्य तदात्मानं सृजाम्यहम् ॥
परित्राणाय साधूनां विनाशाय च दुष्कृताम् ।
धर्मसंस्थापनार्थाय सम्भवामि युगे युगे ॥

Whenever there is a decline in righteousness,
and an increase in unrighteousness,
O descendent of Bharat,
at that time, I descend myself on earth.

(The Bhagavad Gita; CHAPTER 4, VERSE 7-8)

Panchal invited Prince Suyodhan to her Swayamvar grand,
In Kampilya, arrived the crown prince to win Draupadi's hand.
But in case he failed, Suyodhan requested Karna to participate,
"But I am not a Kshatriya," Karna lowered his head, sighed at his fate.
"No such rules have been declared," Shakuni lifted up the warrior's chin,
"Even Brahmins are going to partake. The princess's hand, anyone can win!"
Shakuni looked around at the various powerful kings participating,
Shishupal of Chedi, Shalya of Madra, Jarasandha, Magadha's ferocious King.
But only one managed to fixate Shakuni's eye, the one an entrancing sight,
Dressed in the finest silk, yellow and bright, his skin as dark as night.
His sparkling almond eyes, eyes as cavernous as the vast unexplored skies.
His hair lustrous black, his lips crimson red, a peacock feather on his head.
A soothing smile on his face, he was much superior to the human race.
In his slender hand he held a flute, the being was divinity in its form absolute.
An avatar of Narayan for some, just a lowly gwala, a fraud for others.
Both, questioned and worshipped, but at his sight, a beat ***every*** *heart skipped.*
A hypnotizing effect Krishna had on Shakuni, on everyone around him,
The divine stories of his birth had always fascinated Shakuni to the brim.
"If you must, Mama, gape at the mace fighter next to him, the elder one,
The one I wish was my Guru," to Balram Suyodhan had pledged his devotion.
Drupad announced, "We look for the greatest archer on this land!
He who shall prove to be the best, win this conquest and my daughter's hand.
By looking at its reflection, aim at the fish's eye that spins above in the sky.
The bow welcomes every warrior on the stage, whatever be your lineage."
"Keep an eye out for Arjun," Shakuni alerted Suyodhan.
"The task put forward by the Drupad is with no one but Arjun on his mind,
The 'greatest archer' on this land he cleverly said he intends to find.
And the competitive Arjun shall never dismiss such an invitation, a test,

An invitation to prove to the world that he is unrivalled, the best!"
The swayamvar began, most couldn't even lift the heavy bow, what a shame!
Suyodhan raised it with ease, strung it successfully but missed the aim.
Karna then approached the stage and, seeking an approval, bowed to the King,
Drupad smiled at him but discreetly motioned to Draupadi something.
Karna strung the mighty bow, knelt, and aimed the arrow at the fish's eye,
"Stop! I shall not marry a sutputra!" through the stadium echoed a cry.
Kings outrageously laughed at Karna, who was aghast by the humiliation,
For no one had dared to criticize the King of Anga after his coronation.
"Draupadi!" Shakuni cried, "If you only wanted Kshatriyas to participate,
Couldn't you mention it or stop Karna when he sought Drupad's approval?
Till he strung the bow and aimed the holy arrow, why did you have to wait?
Why heartlessly humiliate an archer when he was about to hit the target?"
"This arrogant woman of noble birth," stormed out the fuming crown prince,
"Will pay for humiliating my friend because of his humble origins!"
Before leaving, Shakuni turned around to catch a final glimpse of ***him****,*
A glimpse of the enchanting being observing everything with a serene face,
A glimpse of his peaceful smile, his mischievous eyes, his charm, his grace,
Of the peacock feather swaying in the breeze, of his aura divine and blue,
Krishna smiled at him, and Shakuni smiled back, "Who really are you?"

10

Nishika's Journal, 2010

I was on my way to the private investigator's agency when I ran into Savya Bathra outside my house. It had been almost ten years, but he hadn't changed a bit. He had the same face, the same smile, and the same charm. Looked a little more attractive, maybe. The thirties had bewitched the messy-haired young man: neat, crew-cut hair, clean-shaven, and a lean, well-toned body. He was in a spotless white shirt which was slightly creased at the elbow pit where it sat rolled up. "Nishika! How are you?" Savya greeted me, trying to give me a side hug that I successfully dodged.

"We met once. That too, like ten years ago," I said, with a look of annoyance.

"Yeah, but we're friends, right?" he asked, his lips meeting to form a pout.

"Sir, I didn't even remember you existed until last week." (A lie, of course)

"Ouch, that hurt. I remember having a deep conversation with this beautiful girl before I left. Wasn't that you?"

"That lasted hardly for a minute!"

"That's what she said!"

I stared at him with an expressionless face, and my eyebrows raised above my hairline until his giggles finally came to an end.

"C'mon, you looked pretty serious. I was just trying to keep the atmosphere light," he said, winking.

"I look pretty serious? Aren't you here for your mother's memorial service? Don't you think your mood is a bit too jolly for the situation?"

He drew in a deep breath. "Unfortunately, or fortunately—only God knows—death isn't something new or unfamiliar to me, Nishika. It's something I witness every day. Something I cannot avoid, however hard I try. However hard I want to protect people from it…."

After a minute of silence, I asked him a simple question, "So, you started with your practice as a neurosurgeon?"

Savya nodded in response, "And you're an officer now!" he said, patting my back.

"Yes, one of the many reasons why you should maintain at least an arm's distance from me," I sneered, watching him roll his eyes and left for the agency, once again parting ways with Savya—not for too long this time.

"A private investigator will be assigned to you today itself after analysing your requirements. I will send you his number so that you can schedule a meeting with him whenever it is convenient for you. Please fill out this confidentiality form," the man sang monotonously, handing over an old crumpled piece of paper to me.

The office was nothing like the pictures that had been put up on the net. Instead of an extravagant and immaculate duplex office, it was a grotty little room with peeling plaster and just a middle-aged man working there. The doubts regarding the efficiency of the agency occurred to me as I was writing my name on the form. Apart from my first name, I ended up filling in the wrong information to avoid a meeting with their agent and left for the station, discontented.

* * *

"This is not expected from you, Nishika! The case has come to a dead-end. It has been six days since the death of Mrs Bathra, and you have no evidence against any of the family members and zero leads on the tape that was delivered to the Bathra Villa. You are not even able to predict the next move of the killer!" yelled DCP Chauhan as I stood in his office, staring at the wooden floor with my hands locked behind. "You have to foil the killer's next attack! My seniors are putting immense pressure on me to shut down this high-profile case as soon as possible due to the attention that it has attracted from the media. You are one of my best and most decorated officers, Nishika. Your credentials are irrefutable. Not everyone gets an out-of-turn promotion in just the first year of their service. And I respect that. But do not force me to hand over this case to someone else."

"Had we checked the members of the Bathra family the very night of the murder in the auditorium itself, I'm sure we would've gotten something at least," I muttered under my breath as I started my jeep.

"Help me, God!" I screamed, frustrated as fuck. I had a perfect track record of solving every case that came my way. I always loved being the best—the number one—and here I was, being warned to be replaced like I was incapable of solving this petty one. Bullshit!

After an entire day of conducting an inefficacious investigation of the murder that gave us no new leads, I reached Keshav Dham to find an unfamiliar old man sitting on the stairs of my house, waiting for me. He was extremely pleasant looking for his age, which I am sure was more than seventy-five. His forehead was glistening like a diamond, and so were his mischievous almond-shaped eyes. He was a swarthy man with features softer than petals but also as honed as a sabre. A bright yellow shirt, tidily tucked into his high waist black formal pants held up by a pair of suspenders, he was dressed with meticulous care. The well-groomed old man bore a warm, soothing smile on his face. Decorously taking off his brown vintage style ascot cap, flaunting his lustrous curly grey hair, he gracefully rose to his feet as soon as he saw me step out of my jeep.

"Officer Nishika?"

"Umm…Yes. Your good name, sir?"

"I am Krishna."

"Who?"

"Krishna…"

"Are you serious?" I scoffed. "Great! So now, after Yudhishtir and Shakuni, Lord Krishna has descended himself, nice. Why don't you truthfully tell me who the hell you are and who sent you here before I lose it all?"

"I really am Krishna! And I'm here because you asked for my help," he calmly replied.

"I? Asked for your help? Sir, I swear to God I have had an exasperating day. I am in no mood for jokes, and the only reason I'm still being nice to you is because of your age. I am going to simply walk up to my door and look back just once before entering my house. If I still see you here, pray to God for your safety."

"Ma'am, I'm not lying. I think there has been a misunderstanding. I'm Mr Krishna. Didn't you come to our office this morning? I'm the private investigator assigned to help you."

I slapped my forehead. "I'm so sorry, sir. I totally forgot. But wait a minute. I filled in the wrong information about myself. How did you find my correct address in this gigantic city with only my first name?"

"Isn't that my job, ma'am?"

I looked at the old man with a heavy heart, "I'm impressed, sir, but—"

"Give me a chance, at least. I am great at my job," he interrupted, as though he had somehow made his way through my mind, which was clogged with doubts regarding his efficiency considering the agency he was sent by.

But he was too kind and gentle to say no to. "In that case, Mr Krishna, meet me tomorrow morning at 10 am *sharp*. Let me give it a thought first," I told him.

"Sure. *Sharp 10.*" He put on his cap. "I won't disappoint, ma'am. I have ages of experience," he laughed.

"What?" I frowned.

"Nothing," he waved his palm, "Good night, Ma'am."

"Also, even if you decide not to hire me, I hope you get what you are looking for," he said with a warm smile before leaving.

After politely mirroring the gesture, I walked towards my door to unlock it.

"Nishika?"

"What now?" I mewled.

"Wow, even my voice seems to annoy you," gasped Savya.

"Oh, I'm so sorry." I sighed. "I thought it was someone else."

"Who?" he looked around.

"Nothing," I said. "Someone work-related. He just left."

"Really?" Savya raised a brow. "I mean, I didn't see anyone go out on my way in...."

"Huh? What do you mean?" I strode to the main gate and peeked outside. "Where'd he go?"

"How was he like?" Savya followed me.

"Umm...Grey hair...yellow shirt and...and—"

"Fuck it," I took a deep breath, shook my head and walked back to the door. "I'm really tired of this right now," I unlatched the door. "Are you coming in?"

Savya sat in my living room, surprisingly enjoying the cup of coffee made by me, which *no one* ever seemed to like. "Is someone troubling you, Nishika?"

"Apart from you? I don't think so...."

"Of course," he said, softly giggling.

"Actually, I'm here regarding my mother's case. I would like to help, with your permission."

"Uh—sure. I do have a question for you, in fact." I said, drawing my hair into a top knot.

"Shoot."

"Do you know anything about Delusional Disorder?" I asked him. "Mr Dinesh Joshi, a Criminal Psychologist I know, mentioned it after hearing the tape that was delivered to your house. He claimed the killer is *delusional* about being Shakuni reincarnated."

"I haven't heard the tape myself, but Adah did mention it to me," he said, "Well, I had taken psychology as an elective, and if Mr Joshi's diagnosis is reliable, we might have a problem here. It's quite a tricky disorder to deal with."

"And I'm sure Ryan's play has something to do with

all of this," he said, pulling out a CD from his jacket and keeping it on the table, "I watched the recording of the show very closely last night. Maybe this might give us an idea about our delusional killer and his targets—his offenders. Or maybe, the ones he loves."

"Even I have watched the recording numerous times since the case started," I said.

"So the ones Shakuni loved more than anything were Gandhari and—"

"Suyodhan," I promptly answered.

"Right," said Savya. "Balram's favourite."

"What? Balram's favourite?"

"Yeah," he looked at me. "At some point in his life, as he had always wished for, Duryodhan acquired advanced training as a mace fighter under Balram," he answered. "It is also said that Balram grew so fond of the Kaurava that he announced him as his favourite disciple. He was supremely impressed by Duryodhan's devotion to the mace, his arduous efforts to discard the caste system, and his unique decision to follow monogamy. Unlike many of the kings, Duryodhan was not a follower of polygamy and had only one wife, Princess Bhanumati, who he dearly loved and was immensely loyal to. He refused to marry any other princesses, even for political reasons that would prove to be beneficial for the kingdom. Balram even got Krishna and Jambavati's son, Prince Sambh, married to Princess Lakshmana, Duryodhan and Banumati's daughter."

"Wow, you sure know a lot about the epic," I said, impressed.

"Well, India's rich history has always been a subject of interest for me."

"History? So, you do believe that the Mahabharata happened?"

"Yeah, I do," he said, nodding.

"Coming to our Shakuni's enemies," Savya stroked his chin. "Nishika, do you have a suspect in mind? Someone who could've killed mom. Someone who might be suffering from the disorder…."

"I mean, your entire family, except Mr Bathra, sat in a position suitable for shooting your mom," I said.

Savya looked at the ceiling, his eyes narrowed, as he scratched his head as though in deep thought. "We're left with just one option then. We will have to research about each of the members of my family, including Ryan and Ira, in detail. What we are looking for is their past traumas, the secrets that they have been hiding and everything buried in their past."

"So, there's no other way to find out the delusional one?"

"Not really," said Savya. "You might spend an entire lifetime with a delusional person having a belief as absurd as say, he can talk to animals and never get to know of it if he doesn't share it with you. So, without everyone's exhaustive information, it might be extremely difficult and time-consuming to find our killer unless he himself comes forward and shares his belief. And unfortunately, we don't have much time. The killer is well aware of all his actions.

He knows exactly what he's doing and hence maybe taking extra precautions before executing each move. He might even be cautious enough to not share his beliefs and delusions with anyone to avoid attracting attention. This generally is the case with patients with this disorder. They avoid talking about their beliefs knowing they're unique and won't be accepted by the world."

"In that case, I know someone who can find this out. I'm meeting him tomorrow morning," I said affirmatively.

"That's great, so I'll see you tomorrow then?" he asked me.

"Yes, and hey, thanks," I said, smiling.

"Is that a smile I see? So, we're friends now?"

"Good night," I said, shooing him off.

Hope—the four-lettered word is the strongest and the kindest word in the entire world. It is the last string that holds you with all its might to keep you from falling off the cliff into the depth of darkness. But it can hold you just as long as you want to be held. The moment you cut that last string, you fall off in the hollows of gloom. But even in the dark, if you ask for its help, it'll appear in the form of a beautiful ray showing you a path. It'll be there for you every time you need it. Just a thought away. Isn't it beautiful? Something that is as kind as it is powerful? Just when I thought I had reached the dead-end, I was pulled up by not one but two powerful strings. I had met two bright rays of hope in the dark; *my long-lost neighbour and a mysterious private investigator.*

Prince Arjun had won Draupadi, proving to the world his worth,
Hastinapur rejoiced until what followed strangled its mirth.
On their mother's word, the brothers distributed the princess,
For bedding his sister-in-law, they spat on the righteous one in distress.
Not the throne of the heir, but Khandavprastha was given to him as his share.
Meanwhile, with his efficiency, Crown Prince Suyodhan impressed everyone,
Rejected the Varna system, upheld equality; he was no longer 'Duryodhan'.
A few years later, Nakul arrived in Hastinapur with an invitation,
In Indraprastha was Yudhishtir's Rajasuya yagnya, his consecration.
After the Yagnya, Yudhishtir felicitated the divine Vaasudev before all,
Everyone watched with content except one king present in the hall.
Shishupal ridiculed Krishna, insulted everyone who took his side,
Accused Bheeshma of impotency, mocked Yudhishtir's ethics, Bheem's pride.
But with the Sudarshan Chakra upon the completion of his sins hundred,
Krishna beheaded Shishupal, and the ceremony finally came to a blissful end.
Suyodhan then went to explore the palace, while Shakuni went to Vaasudev,
"I hope you are doing well, Mama," a warm smile the Lord gave.
"I am," Shakuni giggled, "Unlike your beloved 'Mama' Kamsa in the grave."
Krishna heartily laughed, suddenly through the palace, a loud splash echoed,
Shakuni took Vaasudev's leave, and in its direction, he hastily strode.
He growled at the Pandavas laughing while in a pond stood Suyodhan,
*"**Like father, like son!**" Draupadi's maid teased the drenched one.*
Suyodhan glowered at the laughing empress, rage streaming down his eyes,
The prince misunderstood that it was Draupadi's voice.
Suyodhan left burning in abhor, and with Karna, he decided to wage war.

But the trickster disapproved, "Not every war is fought on the battlefield,
The brothers will pay, but without sowing bloodshed, revenge we will yield.
Your insult we shall avenge, but with my mind as a chariot for your revenge!
A slave Yudhishtir is to the game of dice, to his gambling addiction,
And while awful he is at it, I can be defeated only by the Lord! No human!
But the Lord must've by now left for Dwarka! From a tyrant, he must save it!
I informed King Shalva how his unarmed friend Shishupal's throat was slit!"
And in Hastinapur began the game; a hideous scar on the land's name.
The trickster ingeniously lost in the initial rounds, creating an illusion,
After giving him false hope, the illusionist shattered Yudhishtir's delusion.
To save him from gambling himself then, his brothers put themselves at stake,
To win at any cost, his Dharma the gambler was ready to forsake.
The entire hall watched in disgust as he lost himself, too, as he lost his virtue.
"Panchali now, Mama!" In a fury his fists Suyodhan clenched,
"Suyodhan!" Shakuni screamed, aghast, "Your insult has been avenged!"
"But why spare her! For what she did to Karna, I just want to humble her!"
Suyodhan gave Yudhishtir a chance, suggested he put his wife at stake,
"Victorious I shall be this time; my chain of defeats Draupadi will break!"
The dice was rolled. He lost his wife. He committed the worst sin of his life.
A sudden ear-splitting thunder perturbed Shakuni, terrified him!
Maybe Suyodhan wouldn't just insult her, maybe he'd do something grim.
"What have I done, Mahadev!" Shakuni quaked, "What is it that you know!"
"For the sake of my family, Oh, Lord, how far was I allowed to go?"

11

Nishika's Journal, 2010

"I want you to get me each and every, significant or insignificant, detail of the Bathras, including Ira Rana and her brother, Ryan Rana," I instructed Mr Krishna, who had arrived at my house at the exact stroke of ten, as I had asked him to the previous night.

"On it, ma'am."

"And only I should be privy to this information, Mr Krishna...I hope you understand what I mean."

"Indeed, ma'am."

"Good," I picked up my coffee mug. "By the way, where did you disappear last night?" I frowned, taking a sip.

"I? Disappeared?" he overdramatically gasped.

"Yeah," I took another sip. "You just vanished in like thin air."

"Well, you caught me..." he dropped his neck and locked his hands behind him. "I lied to you."

"About what?"

"I'm not just a private investigator...."

"What do you mean?" I kept the mug aside, confused.

"I'm a...I'm a...."

"You're a what?"

"I'm a part-time magician."

"..."

He burst into laughter.

I pursed my lips, took a deep breath and picked up the mug again, "By when will you have all the data?" I cut his laughter short.

"Um...The eighth of March."

"The eighth?" I asked. "That's like tomorrow."

"Yes," he nodded. "I'll give you all the required information by tomorrow night, ma'am," he smiled. "Also, it will be easier for me to arrive unnoticed once the sun has set."

"Tomorrow night? You mean, what, around *thirty-six* hours? That's it?" I asked, flabbergasted by his confidence.

"That's nothing, ma'am. I hold an account of the entire world," he said with a little chuckle.

"Come again?"

"Nothing. I'll take your leave now. Lots of work to do," he said with a beam, heading for the door. But I stopped him as I had a strange thought. A suspicion.

An unexplainable gut-feeling, "There's one more person actually—Mr Savya Bathra."

"Sure, ma'am."

***

"So, did you find anything?" asked Savya, standing at my door with his hands buried deep inside the pockets of his (slightly faded) black sweats, around half past ten, soon after the lights in the Bathra Villa were dimmed.

"Not as of now, but I will surely get something vital by tomorrow night, I hope," I said, my fingers crossed, escorting him to the living room.

"I hope I'm not disturbing you," he said, settling on the edge of the couch, quickly glancing at the watch on his wrist. "Apart from the irrepressible urge to get a glimpse of your gorgeous face, it's a question that ushers me here today, actually."

I met his glance with an uneven smile. "Oh, it's alright. I hit the bed way past midnight. You see, there's one more loyal admirer in the queue that knocks on the door every day past ten—insomnia," I said.

"Just the two of us in the queue?" he shrugged with a smirk, watching me roll my eyes before abandoning him to bring coffee.

Savya hitched himself back against the faux-leather blue couch, getting comfortable.

"So, what was the question?" I asked, sitting next to him, balancing two steaming hot mugs of coffee, my late-night ritual, and offering him one.

"Thanks," he said, holding the boiling mug gently by its handle, brimming to the edge with coffee ready to jump out at the slightest turbulence. "And you complain about insomnia," he whispered with a scoff.

"What?"

"I had a small chat with Ira last night," he rephrased.

"Okay…and?"

"She told me about the time Ryan spent with you before his show to get your input. Could you please elaborate on his behaviour when he talked to you regarding the play? How was his body language while he talked about Shakuni? Did he seem excited? Or say, maybe enthralled by the character?"

I knew exactly what was going on in his mind. And as much as I wanted to believe in Ryan's innocence, I could lie neither to him nor to myself.

"Every time he talked about Shakuni or reasoned the brother's actions, he seemed completely engrossed in the topic. He was fascinated by the character," I answered.

"Maybe because he could relate to him. He has a similar kind of story, after all. His beloved sister was forced to marry an unworthy son of a powerful businessman. The sister is being tortured by her husband while the in-laws watch in silence. His presence has been unwanted in the house since the moment he arrived there," he mumbled. "If we consider Ryan to be the killer, he has already killed his first target, which was Yudhishtir…."

"Hmmm…Savya, is there anyone else who has suffered because of your family?"

"Unfortunately, there are many who have been a victim of their arrogance and brutality. It will be impossible to find out the number of people who have suffered because of them. That is also one of the main reasons why I choose to maintain a distance from my own family," he said, visibly dejected.

"Let's wait until tomorrow night, then, before we arrive at any conclusion," I suggested, keeping the flickering flame of Ryan's innocence from smothering.

"Maybe you're right," he sighed.

"Keep an eye on Ryan until then, will you?" I requested him.

"Of course," Savya assured me.

"I just hope the boy doesn't take any wrong step out of anger," I whispered to myself, worried.

"Nishika, do you think he is really the bad guy? The *villain*?"

"Ryan? No, I don't. I know that he's a great guy. I'm just concerned for him. He does hate all of them to a dangerous extent," I said.

"No, not Ryan. Shakuni. You know, like everyone else, do you also think he was really the bad guy?" he repeated his question, looking into my eyes, impatiently waiting for an answer.

"I don't know. And I don't care to be honest. All I know is that I have to solve this case before it is handed over to someone else."

"God, you're really competitive, aren't you? It's like deep-rooted in your soul…Don't care about anything else, just fixed on the bird's eye with the horse blinkers on, eh *Arjun*?" he said, laughing. "Don't worry. You will. I'm sure."

"What about you? Do you think he was the bad guy?" I asked him out of curiosity.

He dropped my gaze and stared at the floor.

"Savya?"

His neck bent low; he kept staring at the flooring in a deep trance.

"Umm…Savya?"

"I'd answer this question if I knew how far one is allowed to go for the sake of his family."

Her scream echoed in the hall, Sushasan dragged in the dynasty's downfall.

Petrified, Shakuni hissed, "Stop this right now, Suyodhan! This is a sin!"

"Her arrogance summoned this, Mama!" he growled, "Don't ruin our win!"

The wife of warriors, and a righteous gem, stood vulnerable right before them.

"Like she disrobed an archer!" Snarled Karna, "By snatching his bow!

Sushasan, disrobe her! Snatch her shame and how it feels she shall know!"

Roaring like a beast, Bheem charged at the prince to save his wife's pride,

But Yudhishtir stopped him, "We are bound by the game's rules," he cried.

As they watched her getting disrobed in dread, Krishna's name she recited.

*And the cloth didn't end, for **he** had come, her honour he had to defend.*

A wish the terrified blind king granted the wronged Princess,

She freed her husbands, they followed her out, their heads hung in distress.

"Mama!" Suyodhan said in fright, "One day, Yudhishtir will claim his right!"

"Enough, Duryodhan!" at Shakuni's words, Suyodhan stood in a daze,

His beloved Mama had used the name that had haunted him always.

But Shakuni thought of Gandhari, through hell his sister had already been,

If Yudhishtir did claim the throne, she would never become the Queen.

"Play a last round of the game! Everything lost, the winner can reclaim!

The loser gets an exile of thirteen years, and in the last one, he disappears.

For if he is caught, another twelve years of exile for himself he has bought.

God is on your side today," Shakuni said, "He shall end all your woes!"

Silencing his brothers' cries, Yudhishtir decided to play, only to lose.

Shakuni watched the Pandavas and Draupadi leave, frozen and glum,

"Oh, Mahadev," Tears of guilt flooded his eyes, "What have I become?"

"Dada!" Gandhari wept, "When they hurt her, how could you stay quiet?"

"I promise you, child, I'll convince Suyodhan!" Shakuni said in tears,

"He'll return everything when they come back after thirteen years!"

In the next twelve years, Suyodhan gathered the support of various kings,

Those against Yudhishtir for gambling his wife and brothers like petty things.

In the thirteenth year, the news of Keechak's death shook everyone,

The impossible deed of killing Matsya's commander, a mere cook had done.

Suyodhan attacked Matsya suspecting the cook to be Vrikodara Bheem,

But along with his charioteer, a eunuch, the prince of Matsya defeated him.

With the victory of Matsya, the exile period of the Pandavas ended,

Everyone knew the war was inevitable, the air was filled with terror and dread.

Shakuni sent Suyodhan to Dwarka, "At any cost, get Krishna on our side!"

"I shall not pick up weapons in the war, and partaking Baldau has denied.

So, you can pick my Narayani Sena or me," with a smile, the Lord said,

And while Arjun chose Krishna, "I choose the army!" Suyodhan declared.

In just a few days, Krishna arrived in Hastinapur as the messenger of peace,

"Give the Pandavas five villages, and the deadly war shall cease."

His uncle, his mother, and his conscience begged him to accept the proposal,

But the prince roared, "They won't get any land equal to the tip of a needle!"

"Listen to him at least, Suyodhan! He is Narayan himself!" Shakuni cried,

"Arrest Vaasudev!" Suyodhan commanded, "Mama! Gods, don't pick a side!"

"You have called for a grisly storm!" Boomed and vanished the divine form.

Before leaving, devastating news, discreetly to Karna, the Lord gave,

When informed, Shakuni mused, "What is it that you know, Vaasudev?"

12

Nishika's Journal, 2010

"Ask me what it is that I *don't* know," Mr Krishna said with a smile.

"Hm. So, you have all the information we need?"

"Yes, everything," he said confidently. "*I know it all.*"

The night that I had been waiting for had finally arrived. The clock crookedly smiled with its shorter hand a little above nine and the longer one a little below two. Prepared with his research about every person of the Bathra family and Ryan as I had asked for, Mr Krishna comfortably sat before me in my drawing room while I ground coffee beans on the centre table.

"Let me begin with late Mrs Drishti Bathra; she was 5'4 ft. tall with a bronze skin tone—"

"Mr Krishna, I know all of this. I'd appreciate it if—"

"Don't break my link. A bronze-skinned 5'4 ft. tall woman, born and brought up in Delhi, Drishti Ahuja, was in love with Mr Aum Desai before marrying Mr Bathra. He was a colleague who worked with her as a professor at the Mittal Institute of Technology. Their relationship didn't work out since the boy belonged to a different caste and was not accepted by her father. She was later married to Mr Dev Bathra (consensually). A year after her marriage, Mrs Drishti gave birth to identical twins, namely Adah and Adar. She gave birth to another son, Savya, five years later, and her youngest son, Saarth, was conceived ten years after Savya.

Mrs Drishti Bathra was made the director of the university where she was once a professor in, by her husband. The Mittal Institute of Technology is known to all as one of the most upright and fairly-operated universities, administered by respected faculty members like the late Mrs Bathra. It majorly functions on the funds by Mr Dev Bathra.

The charity work that Mrs Drishti did was authentic, but on the other hand, the disreputable woman was also distinctly ill-famed amongst the management of the university for demanding heavy donations from the rich for seats that their children didn't deserve and denying admission to the poor, whose children were unequivocally more deserving. She was also responsible for leaking examination papers to the children of her husband's business partners and her own twins. Even after all these years, long on sleaze and short on morality, these facts remain unknown to everyone outside the management since no one dared to speak them out loud, fearing her husband and her position.

Adding to the list of her perpetual malpractices, in 1993, Mrs Drishti had dismissed various acutely disturbing cases of ragging reported to her since her son, Adar and her daughter, Adah, both in their final years of engineering, were the main culprits. A student from her university repeatedly complained about being ragged and abused by a group of seniors led by her twins, but she ignored the grievous matter. Fed up by the intense torture, the student hanged himself on the ceiling fan in his hostel room. Mrs Bathra misled the people by bribing the teachers and a few fellow mates of that student and threatened those who were not won over by money. She declared that the boy was under a lot of academic pressure that he couldn't handle well. But after meeting with a few of his batch mates, I can confirm that the unfortunate act was committed due to ragging and ragging *only*.

Lastly, on the 28th of February 2010, Mrs Drishti Bathra was shot dead by someone who claims to be Shakuni from the Mahabharata."

"Mr Krishna, how did you get to know about the tape? It was kept extremely confidential by my team and the Bathra family, too," I asked him, stumped by the minutiae recited.

He smiled at me and continued, "Mr Dev Bathra was also born and brought up in Delhi. He is a rich magnate who inherited The Bathra Industries Ltd. from his father. Apart from the ancestral business, he is the founder and chairperson of *Angelwood Healthcare,* which is a grand hospital chain infamous for its exorbitant fees, and funds a renowned university and a few schools too. An unethical tycoon who can go to any lengths to expand his business, he snatched away an entire land from a poverty-stricken colony by promising the population relocation to a far better locality. He even guaranteed free admission of their children in his schools in return for the ownership of the land. After acquiring the property, he left the prior inhabitants homeless and stated that he had made no such promises. The crook has duped a lot of such penurious communities in similar ways.

As a self-proclaimed doting family man, Mr Bathra has subdued and concealed countless felonies committed by his family, especially his nefarious children. When Mr Bathra got to know about Bhavika Rana's affair with his cousin, he made a deal with the latter. He falsely promised to make Aman Bathra the head of the conglomerate's energy business in return for a sex tape. Mr Dev then blackmailed Mr Adarsh Rana to form a joint venture with the retail unit of his Bathra Industries, Bathra Brands Ltd. As per the deal, Bathra Brands Ltd. will hold a 51% equity stake in the venture. Mr Dev even fixed the marriage of his son Saarth Bathra to the same businessman's daughter, Ira Rana."

"Officer Nishika, who would you like to hear about next?"

"Anyone is fine, sir," I said. "Before we begin, coffee, Mr Krishna?"

"I'm more of a 'warm-milk person', you see," he chuckled.

"Sure," I said, pouring him some warm milk, parallelly, tossing the fresh coffee grounds in the filter, and brewing a good cup for myself.

The old man blissfully sipped the milk. "Ah, warm milk…the solution to every problem," he ecstatically sighed. "Thank you, Miss."

"Not a problem, sir," I said, steadily pouring water—perfectly boiled to 200—over the grounds.

"Let's continue with the daughter of the house—Miss Adah Bathra, a popular actress who is in a secret relationship with her co-star, Miss Devika Soni. Although unwilling, Adah had to conclude her relationship with the latter because of her orthodox mother, who was unsupportive of it. But Adah has recently been seeing Miss. Devika Soni again—a direct beneficiary of her mother's death, I guess. She had a disastrous relationship with Mrs Bathra, whose thoughts were utterly contrasting with that hers. Adah, since her childhood, was domineered by her repressive mother, who forced her decisions upon her.

An engineer who changed the course of her career, Adah decided to follow her childhood dream of becoming an actress after completing her education. Like always, her decision was opposed by Mrs Bathra, who had negative convictions about showbiz, but by convincing her father and gaining his support, she successfully made her way through the entertainment industry. She is also fabled for destroying the careers of umpteen newcomers who had no strong support to reach atop."

"Tell me about her twin, Adar, sir," I said, sipping the freshly brewed hot coffee while Mr Krishna was busy unfolding the Bathra chronicles.

"Mr Adar Bathra, the thickset felon, has his hands stained in a much darker hue of red than Adah in the 1993 ragging case. His shameful contribution in driving the poor boy to death was slightly greater than his sister's. Adar is said to have bullied and physically abused the boy on a regular basis.

After the death of the student, his parents tried their level best to take the case to court to punish his offenders, but the boy's mother went missing a few days after filing the complaint. The father and the boy's elder sister went dormant after the entire incident. I'm certain Mr Dev Bathra had something to do with the mother's disappearance. Apart from the ragging case, Adar's father has also suppressed several cases of drinking and driving, including a major one that caused the death of three people while two were left severely injured. A video of the big-headed man was making rounds on social media three years ago, in which Adar was seen beating up a poor security guard black and blue at the Delhi airport in a heated argument after the guard insisted on checking his identity card. The son of the guard pressed charges against Adar but was soon pressured to withdraw them by Mr Bathra. The old guard was unable to bear the assault and humiliation and died by suicide a few days after the incident.

Five years ago, on 9th September 2005, Mr Adar Bathra married the love of his life against the wishes of his family. The Bathras initially had a huge problem with the woman's financial status, which was a pinch before their mountain of wealth, but soon got along well with her."

"How were Adar's relations with his mother, Mr Krishna?" I asked him, succinctly jotting down salient points and making notes.

"They were good. He was her absolute favourite while she was worshipped by him."

"So, the only one Mrs Bathra was on bad terms with in her family was Adah?" I asked, tying my hair up.

"No," Mr Krishna shook his head. "There is one more who hated her for some unknown reason. A reason I am yet to discover...."

13

Nishika's Journal, 2010

"*There is one more who hated her for some unknown reason?*" I stopped writing and looked up from my journal, intrigued. "Who?"

"Saarth Bathra," said Mr Krishna.

"Hmm. Let's continue with him then," I proposed, turning the page, titling it—*Saarth Bathra*, ready to note down important points from Mr Krishna's research.

"The youngest son of the family," Mr Krishna began, "Dev Bathra's favourite child who has been brought up like a prince. A fervent boxer and a professional shooter—something to think about, maybe, the snob is fearlessly involved in illicit activities like arranging rave parties, consumption and dealing of drugs, and many more, but remains lawfully clean. Following the death of Mrs Bathra, Saarth is seen spending most of his time with his father these days.

He was married to Miss Ira a few weeks ago—10th January 2010—in quite a hasty manner. The fiendish spouse has physically assaulted Miss Ira on more than one occasion in front of his family, who never interrupted. But he could not get away with it for too long. Saarth was thrashed by his brother-in-law when he dared to lay his hands on Ryan's sister in front of him. The blows of his fist grew even more powerful when Ryan got to know that it was not the first time Saarth had assaulted his sister. He was also warned by Ryan to give up his wonton lifestyle, but he turned a deaf ear to his brother-in-law. Saarth doesn't share a good bond with his siblings, Adar, and Adah, either."

"How did Mr Bathra bear with his son getting thrashed by Ryan?" I asked inquisitively.

"He didn't. Mr Bathra would've literally killed the boy if *she* hadn't meddled in the affair."

"*She?*"

"Mrs Urvi Bathra, wife of Adar Bathra, a former educator who willingly gave up teaching after marriage. Urvi, a brilliant student and a college topper, is an alumnus of St. Jacob's College—a celebrated and one of the most expensive colleges in Delhi. After completing her M.Ed. here seventeen years ago, she shifted to a small, under-developed village where she provided basic education to the poor for free. She travelled all over the country for seven years rendering this imperative and gratuitous service to many underprivileged villages. On her return to the city, she worked as a teacher in one of Mr Dev Bathra's schools for five years before getting married to his son. Urvi's relationship with her in-laws is great. The daughter-in-law managed to impress everyone and bonded with all the Bathras in no time after the marriage, erasing their initial, unfavourable opinions. For a few years after getting married to Adar, Urvi was seen spending a lot of time with Saarth who she had the warmest rapport, but the two don't seem to be so close now.

The night of Mrs Bathra's death, Mrs Urvi Bathra took to twitter to express her sorrow and to pay her last respects to her mother-in-law. But clearly, more than an expression of grief, it was an implicit accusation, adducing how the woman was murdered during the show of a boy who hated her."

"I agree. The tweet undoubtedly was aimed at Ryan," I added. "Anyway, let's proceed with Ira. How was her childhood? What kind of a person was she before marrying Saarth? Tell me everything. Every little thing."

Mr Krishna softly nodded before gulping down the last sip of his milk. "Refreshed!" he exclaimed, an adorable childlike smile taking over his radiant face, forcing one on mine, too, looking at the contentment on his face. All because of a warm glass of milk.

"Miss Ira Rana," he continued, "Before marrying Saarth, she was a cheerful girl, passionate about art. An artist who used to spend all her days (and nights) painting. But sadly, she hasn't even looked at a brush since her marriage. Tracing back to her childhood, the little girl took upon her tiny shoulders the responsibility of raising her younger sibling after being neglected by their parents. She has been both a mother and a father to Ryan. From taking care of his studies and keeping a check on his habits and routine to ensuring important aspects like his dietary regime, she did it all. Miss Ira is extremely protective of her younger brother. In fact, it was for his sake that she agreed to marry Saarth Bathra. By sacrificing her own life and happiness, the sister secured her brother's life and future from her selfish and wicked father.

While summing up the misfortunes of her life, I can't exclude the heart-rending fact that the young lady has been a victim of domestic violence since the first day of her marriage. The accusation made against Ira by her sister-in-law, Adah, of having an affair with Mr Vihaan Malhotra was totally false and absurd, but she said nothing in her defence even after getting beaten up by her husband for it.

The young daughter-in-law, perceived as a lily-livered defenceless victim, startled everyone the night of Mrs Bathra's murder when she viciously attacked Urvi for landing her brother in trouble. None of the Bathras has dared to talk to or about Ryan in the villa since then.

Ira's mother, Mrs Bhavika Rana, died by suicide on the night of the first day of January, while her father continues to live in Mumbai."

"Who shall I continue with, Officer?" asked Mr Krishna.

"The only two remaining are Ryan and Savya, aren't they?" I asked, flipping my copious notes back and forth, counting the ones done.

"Yes, ma'am."

"Continue with Ryan then," I said, refuelling myself with the tepid coffee halfway down.

"Twenty-one-year-old Ryan Rana is famed for the top-selling play, *Gandhari's Brother*, which was written and directed by him. It is a mythological drama revolving around the character of Shakuni from Mahabharata. The critically acclaimed piece was a hit in Mumbai, due to which he moved to Delhi to organise one of his shows here. The boy is currently living in the Bathra Villa with the Bathras at his sister's request and because he cannot leave the city until the investigation is over and Mrs Drishti's case is solved.

Miss Ira's brother is hated by the entire Bathra family. He has been in legion feuds with four members of the family, namely, the late Mrs Bathra, Mr Dev Bathra, Urvi, and Adah. And worse, in extremely violent brawls with Adar and Saarth. On one such disastrous occasion, Miss Adah attacked Ryan with a knife when he broke Adar's nose for provoking Saarth to hit his wife for her illicit sexual relationship with Mr Vihaan Malhotra, which Ryan knew was a false accusation. Mr Ryan Rana has already been declared guilty of Mrs Drishti Bathra's murder by the verdict of the public in the wake of Mrs Urvi Bathra's tweet.

On a lighter note, the boy is very fond of dogs and has brought with him his little companion, Daisy, a white Labrador. Also, the only member of the Bathra family he hasn't fought with yet is the second son of Mr Bathra—Mr Savya."

"So, Ryan gets along with Savya…." I murmured to myself, making a note of what I thought was one of the three cardinal points of the night—the other two being Adah's animosity towards her mother for years on end and Saarth being a professional shooter.

"As a matter of fact," Mr Krishna added, "Mr Savya is the only Bathra who is on cordial terms with the Rana siblings and has a soft corner for them."

"Hm…" I said, cutting him a glance. "Let's call it a day with him then."

"Yes, ma'am," said Mr Krishna, firmly blinking his eyes. "The talk of the town—Mr Savya Bathra. A fine-looking man quite popular amongst the ladies for his good looks, he—"

"Of course," I reflexively scoffed. "Certainly the most handsome man I have ever seen," I whispered (or at least I thought I did).

"Excuse me?" Mr Krishna folded his hands, "*Most* handsome?"

"Have you seen anyone better?" I laughed.

"Well, if I may say it without immodesty," he nodded his head with his eyes closed, "You should've seen my younger self then."

After an exchange of a few inaudible actions, wherein his confident nod affirmed my right eyebrow raised in surprise, asking him—uh-huh? That good, sir?—Mr Krishna continued.

"Coming back to Savya—the *second* best, if you must award a title," he giggled. "The most personable Bathra you may find in the wicked villa. He pursued his entire education abroad at the Eastern State University, Australia and thus has been distant from his family since childhood. Even though Mr Dev Bathra firmly wanted him to join the family business, he decided to stick with his penchants and chose to become a neurosurgeon. The decision proved to build an unbridgeable ocean of tension and hostility between the father and the son. Savya's relations with the other members of the family are also not that great.

He was bullied by Mr Adar and Miss Adah as a child to the degree that severely distressed him; as a result, a traumatized six-year-old Savya tried to run away from his house. He had kept no contact with any members of the family since the moment he left the country and was not involved in any of their dirty deeds. He didn't even attend any of his brothers' weddings but was forced by Mr Bathra to attend his mother's memorial service, which brings him back here."

"Forced?" I asked him, taken aback. "He was unwilling to attend his own mother's memorial service?"

"To an extent, yes." He answered. "There's one more thing you might want to write down or consider, perhaps."

"Yes?"

"The second best—maybe—has *something* for you," he said, winking.

"Not related to the case, sir," I said, trying not to give a reaction before smiling (wider than my face).

14

Nishika's Journal, 2010

"You are a genius…." I gasped, beyond impressed.

"Mr Krishna, the information that you have gathered in less than two days is commendable!"

"No! More than commendable. Much much more," I said. "But how did you even…."

"Told ya, I'm really good at this," he said, neatly restacking his research papers, ready to load them back into his navy office bag.

"Sir, you—without a doubt—are."

With a beaming nod, he tossed the broad shoulder belt over his head, letting it lay aslant the chest with the bag resting low on the side, while he waved me goodbye.

"And you know what I am good at?" I asked him, "Being a host," I added, dubiously looking at the clock that vaguely looked like it was winking at me with its shorter arm at one and the longer one at two—or maybe it was just the late-night face pareidolia that had kicked in. Whatever. It was ten minutes past one.

"It's really late, sir. I suggest you stay back here. I'll prepare the guest room for you."

"It's okay, ma'am. I'll be alright. Thank you."

"I insist, sir. I am a police officer. The cases that I have been dealing with lately won't allow me to send you back all alone so late. It isn't safe at all. So, either you stay back or let me drop you home," I said in a firmer tone this time. He was a very old man, and I didn't feel it was correct on my part to let him travel at the ungodly hour. After all, it was my work that he had been caught up in.

"On one condition, then," he said.

"Anything, sir."

"Please call me by my name, ma'am. That's how everyone addresses me."

My face and voice clobbered by hesitation, I looked at him, "Mr Krishna, I'm sorry…I don't think I can. It would be uncouth of me to address you by your first name considering your age—I mean, the years that you have witnessed."

"Are you calling me *old*, ma'am?"

"No! That's not what I meant. It's just out of respect, sir."

"Well, I'm your grandfather's age; maybe you could

address me as Krishna Da then. I'm not really used to '*Mr Krishna*' or '*sir*'," he laughed.

"Ma'am? Is something wrong?" he asked me on catching sight of the one tiny stubborn tear bearing the weight of all my emotions that had broken free, shattering the walls I had built to hold it in.

"It's nothing…." I sighed, quickly wiping it away, trying to get myself back to being a tough woman, trying to raise my lowered guard.

"Caged emotions often act like criminals," he sighed. "It's important to let them free, child. What is it? You can tell me."

"I'm not caging them," I said. "I just don't...I don't like crying."

"Why?"

"Because I don't have anyone to wipe my tears."

"You always have yourself, child," he whispered.

"Wow…*You always have yourself*…." I repeated with a gasp. "Really, sir? Really?"

"Yes," he smiled. "Don't you think so?"

"You know what," I stood up. "What I think and what I don't think isn't what's important here. So, let's just wrap this up."

"But maybe I *can* convince you otherwise..."

"Oh, please stop." I snapped back.

"Sir," I took a deep breath, trying to regain my calm. "This doesn't really matter. What matters—"

"What matters is that you don't believe in the fact that you always have yourself." He said. "And we must change that."

"Mr Krishna," I pursed my lips. "You don't even know me that well to say anything about me. Maybe we should just stick to our business."

"Oh, I know you well. In fact, I know everyone well," he chuckled. "Maybe you should share whatever it is with me."

"Oh, really?" I folded my hands, frustrated.

"You want me to share what it is with you, sir?" I almost yelled. "Here!"

"I faced the ruthless beast called death at the age of five. Just five!" I screeched. "My two-year-old sister had cancer, sir. I have seen death feast over that innocent infant. I have seen that beast chew her flesh, reducing it to a skeleton, one breath at a time, one pound at a time. Slow enough to cause her pain worse than just killing her as though…as though it was enjoying the suffering. I have seen that tiny, frail, and dying body battling Leukemia for its life! That little body invaded by pipes and tubes keeping it alive. Not letting it go. Making it suffer the misery of life a human is bound to. I have seen my parents die every single day of their life for not having been able to save their baby. I have seen my father cremate his happiness along with it. I have seen my mother brutally throttle the last drop of hope flowing in her veins. The five-year-old who saw it all never left me, sir. She still lives within. You expect *her* to wipe my tears?" I said with a lump in my throat.

"No, I don't have myself, sir. I don't," I continued, "At sixteen. I lost both my parents in an accident. The eleven years of therapy had just begun mizzling its magic over my depressed mother. My father was finally getting okay with things. It was getting better. Everything was getting better. I had just learned to smile. I was learning what happiness feels like, and suddenly, in a breath, they were gone. Just gone…" the tears in my eyes whispered. "That sixteen-year-old isn't strong enough to wipe my tears, sir. She isn't."

"Nishika, it'll get okay…everything will get okay with time, *again,*" said Mr Krishna. "The sun doesn't set forever. It will come out again. Brighter than yesterday."

"With time," I scoffed. "Yeah, it will. Not because time *heals* you. But because with every passing day, the memories slowly begin to fade. Their beautiful faces, their cheerful voices, the memory of their touch, it all begins to fade. You never heal, sir. You just slowly forget how that day when you lost them felt. With time, the pain that was once new to you slowly becomes an everyday acquaintance. You don't get okay with the things around you, sir. You don't get okay with life. You get okay with the pain that deceitfully befriends you. You never heal, sir. "You never heal because the pain never leaves you. It becomes a part of you that your heart, tired of fighting it, simply embraces."

"What if you never let the pain take shelter within you?" he asked.

"I tried," I said. "I tried to focus on the *'good'* part. I tried to be grateful for the things I had rather than what I had lost. Both my parents—grey-suited investment bankers busy wiping their tears with money, hiding behind it—had left behind a huge sum of their hard-earned money, ensuring my well-being even after their death. My childless aunt took good care of me like I was her own daughter. It did help. All of it. But the good things just keep you from killing yourself when the worse is more. They can't cure anything. They can't fill in the hollowness. The void remains. Forever."

Mr Krishna sat beside me, patting my back. I always longed to have a family. I didn't have parents who would love and protect me, siblings who would trouble me or grandparents who would shower me with love and care. And here was a stranger asking me to address him as the grandfather I never had. The kind gesture made me extremely emotional. It filled me with tears. I don't know why, but the stranger didn't seem like one. He felt like family. His radiant, calming smile, his kindness, his sparkling eyes, there was something about him. Something that made me feel better after a long, long time.

For the first time, my tears betrayed me. He sat next to me and wiped them exactly like a loving old grandfather would. I had always suppressed my emotions. That was the first time I was crying in years. That was also the first time I had someone to wipe my tears.

He gently pats my back. "It's alright, child. You're going to be okay. I promise."

"Easy for you to say," I said. "You didn't lose your entire family in front of your eyes."

The man sighed, looking out at the beautiful full moon peeking inside the room through the wafer-thin spaces between the blinds of the large window beside.

"I did," he said, "I lost them all right in front of my eyes. My sons, my brothers, my blood, my generations. *My family.*"

I looked at him, unable to speak anything.

"And...I—I could not do anything at all to save them. I just watched them get devoured by death," he said, swallowing a deep exhalation.

"And why couldn't you do anything?"

"Because sometimes things aren't in our hands," he sighed. "I was...*helpless.* I was helpless before the misery of a mother."

I followed his stare to land my eyes upon the beautiful moon shining outside. Non-living, thus happy. Unlike all of us that watch it every day with the broken pieces forced together to keep pumping, to keep the eyes alive in the false hope of a better tomorrow. We watch it with our hearts weeping in someone's memory, in fear of the forthcomings, or just craving to get a glimpse of it, to see what peace looks like. The peace we are all missing.

"Helpless..." I smiled. "Don't blame yourself, sir."

"To be human is to be helpless before fate," I said. "To be human is to be powerless before the unknown ravages of the future the time is to show."

"I don't think so." He looked at me. "To be human is to be hopeful that your fate bears what is good for you."

"You call humans powerless?" he asked me. "I disagree. The almighty is aware of all the forthcomings. He knows it all. He has seen it all. But not humans; they know nothing. And do you know the amount of courage needed to live without knowing what tomorrow carries? Because it could be anything you might have to face. *Anything*. Yet the hopeful smiles don't give up. The valorous eyes wake up every morning to face what the day holds. The music of breath continues to maintain its rhythm. The heart drowning in fear, despair and darkness doesn't stop beating." He smiled. "To be human is to be powerful. To be human is to be courageous to stand in the face of an unknown future carrying a deadly tempest, challenging it to conquer that storm. To be human is to be brave enough to *believe* that you *will* be able to conquer that storm," he said.

"To be human is to be beyond powerful, I think."

"यतः कृष्णस्ततो धर्मो यतो धमस्ततो जय: II"

"Where there is Lord Krishna there is Dharma, and where there is Dharma there is victory."

Vyaas told the devastated blind king, on being asked who shall win
The Mahabharata.

Everyone awaited their last breath, their only liberation now was their death.
Old, frail, for the last time, Shakuni went to Gandhar, to his room estranged,
For hours stared at the mirror, watching the only thing that had changed.
"I have to go, Arshi," he embraced her, "Don't wait for me this time."
"I always will," his wife smiled, "Till my existence doesn't reduce to grime."
In Kurukshetra assembled the armies for a war the motherland couldn't bear,
But she endured it for every time her daughters wept in despair.
Shakuni saw Krishna, Arjun's charioteer, take him to the centre of the field,
Weeping, he dropped his bow, and before the Lord, the warrior kneeled.
Suddenly time stood still, and Arjun's chariot was back on the frontline,
"What even happened, Vaasudev?" A shiver ran down Shakuni's spine.
Krishna blew the Panchajanya, the war began, warriors fought fiercely,
But hurting the Pandavas, Bheeshma, Drona and Kripa avoided discreetly.
When on the ninth day, Bheem killed several of the younger Kauravas,
The grieving Suyodhan blamed Bheeshma's hesitant involvement for the loss,
Incensed by the accusation on the battlefield, Gangaputra then created chaos!
Krishna broke his vow when against Pitamah, Arjun couldn't raise his bow,
He picked up a wheel! To stop the furious Lord, Arjun fell at his feet in fright,
"Don't break your vow! With complete dedication, now will this Arjun fight!"
The night of the ninth day, Bheeshma told the Pandavas how to defeat him,
"Since Shikhandi was born a woman," he said, "I cannot fight him."
And the beginning of the tenth day marked his defeat, the end of his sorrows,
Using Shikhandi as a shield, Arjun laid the unarmed man on a bed of arrows.
Bheeshma could choose his death's time, a boon his father had given him,
Shakuni sat by the helpless man who would now see his clan's end grim.
Bheeshma hissed, "You poisoned Suyodhan's mind right from his birth!

You made him what he is today! The vilest monster on earth!"
Shakuni teared up, "When a child grows up being called the doom, a demon,
By his own people, his own family, Gangaputra, he eventually becomes one.
Minds were poisoned! But not by me, by Vidur for the love of Pandu's boys,
He made a harmless infant 'the devil of doom on earth' in everyone's eyes!"
Bheeshma roared, "Is he not? Against his own blood, who ever fought?"
"The love he and his brother always craved for he saw in your eyes for them!
He is fighting for that love! He isn't the one killing his elders for the realm!
Battling for power, the world sees the monster they made that boy at birth!
But I see a hated blind man's unfortunate child battling to prove his worth."
"Upon your father's demise," Bheeshma sighed, "They made you their King,
You should've escaped. Unlike us, you had a perfect life, you had everything."
"Rest well, Pitamah," with tears, Shakuni left alone Ganga's cursed offspring.
After an unarmed Bheeshma was defeated by Arjun in an immoral way,
Seven Kauravas killed Abhimanyu in a Chakravyuha on the thirteenth day.
On the fifteenth day, Krishna lied to Drona that his beloved son had died,
"अश्वत्थामा हतो नरो वा कञ्जरो वा!" To confirm, for the first time, Yudhishtir lied.
Drishtadyumna then beheaded the father beating his breast, lamenting aloud.
The next day, Bheem tore Dushasan's chest and drank his blood as vowed.
On the seventeenth day, Arjun smeared his hands in a defenceless's blood,
On Krishna's behest, killed Karna, freeing his chariot's wheel stuck in the mud.
"Is this dharma, Krishna!" Shakuni cried, "Arjun! What did you even get?"
Krishna preached something to the archer, who had collapsed in regret.
Shakuni glared, "How did the 'Lord' justify his sin to console his favourite?"

15

Nishika's Journal, 2010

Mr Krishna stayed back that night on my repeated requests. At around half past three, noticing the lights of the guest room that hadn't been dimmed yet, I knocked on the door with a jug of water and a glass in case he needed it.

While making for the door after keeping the tray on the desk beside his bed, the pace of my feet suddenly slowed down, catching a sight I couldn't ignore. Mr Krishna was reading a book. An old copy of the Mahabharata he had picked up from one of the shelves of that room.

"Does the epic interest you?" I asked him.

"It does. I always feel like I was a part of it, you know," he said, giggling.

"Are you not interested in it?" he asked me, keeping the book aside.

I sat down on the chair opposite the bed, "Sure I am. I have been reading a lot about it lately."

"Who was your favourite then?" he curiously asked me.

"Lord Krishna," I answered within a second.

"Ah. Never mind," he made a face on listening to my answer. "I don't like him that much."

"Why? I love him. I worship him. Most of the people who have read about him do. What's there to not like about him?" I frowned, slightly offended.

"There are a few questions that arise in my mind every time I read the Mahabharata. Maybe if you could answer them, I would start liking him."

"Go ahead. I'll try to resolve your doubts with whatever information I have," I said, bracing myself for the questions.

"If Krishna was on the side of Dharma, why did he kill all the warriors on the battlefield using treachery?"

"Was it Krishna's treachery, or was it their own *karma?* Maybe they didn't deserve a noble death. The reason for Bheeshma's death was ultimately the same abducted princess whose life he had destroyed. It is said Shikhandi was princess Amba reborn, who had pleased Lord Shiva in her previous life and was blessed with a boon that she would be the cause of Bheeshma's death in her next life. Dronacharya was killed when he was defenceless since he had slaughtered the dreams of a young defenceless tribal boy, Ekalavya, which was his worst sin as a teacher. Karna's tragic death was a result of the curses that he had unfortunately earned for himself. One—of forgetting every holy incantation when he needed them the most, which was given by his teacher, Lord Parshuram. The enraged teacher cursed his disciple when he got to know that Karna had lied to him about being a Brahmin. And the second curse—by a poor Brahmin whose defenceless cow Karna had once mistakenly killed. The Brahmin cursed the warrior that he would die a similar helpless death. So, everyone who died in the war died the death they deserved."

"Why did Krishna pick up weapons when he had taken an oath that he wouldn't? Was it so difficult for a Lord to keep his word?"

"He picked up weapons against Bheeshma to teach him that it is not wrong to break your vow if it is for the establishment of Dharma. That Dharma is more important than one's personal honour. Also, it was to motivate Arjun, who was reluctant to cause harm to Bheeshma. And technically, the wheel of a chariot isn't a weapon, is it?" I answered with an uneven smiled.

"If he was really a God, why didn't he stop the ugly war knowing its repercussions?"

"He tried, didn't he? He went to the Kauravas as a messenger of peace to convince them and prevent the brutal war. He even tried to persuade Karna to put an end to the war since he knew that all the brothers would accept Karna as the king of Hastinapur without fulmination. After trying to enlighten the misguided and advising them to embrace Dharma, he showed the world how one's end would be if one chose the side of Adharma. And that however small you are in front of Adharma, you shall always win if you are on the side of Dharma. The world needed to be taught this."

"Doing good," he laughed. "A last one remains, though."

"Prepared."

"Why did Krishna decide to fight from the Pandavas' side? They, too, had people who had committed some grievous sins at some point in their life."

"Was it him who chose sides? He gave Duryodhan and Arjun a fair chance to choose. It was Duryodhan who chose his Narayani Sena while Arjun chose the Lord," I shrugged.

Mr Krishna burst out laughing and clapped his hands, "The spontaneity with which you are answering my questions is impressive. It's like Krishna himself told you all of this."

"I wish..." I sighed.

"But do you like him now, at least?"

"I'll try," the old man laughed.

"But if you like him so much, why didn't you go to him for help?"

"What do you mean?" I asked, confused.

He showed me the book lying next to him on the bed—*Cases of the Reincarnation Type, Volume I: Ten Cases in India by Ian Stevenson.*

"Hey, where'd you get that?"

"It was in the living room," he looked at me. "In a heap of several others."

"Well, I am trying to get to know more about this whole reincarnation thing for the case," I said.

"Exactly! And you didn't even *include* the one by me… uh…by your Lord Krishna, I mean?

"I don't understand," I said. "The one by Lord Krishna?"

"Yes! The most important one," he raised his brows.

"*The most important one*?" I asked, perplexed. "I don't think so. I have all by Ian Stevenson, Walter Semkiw, Steven Rosen, William—"

"Here!" he pulled out a copy of the Bhagavad Gita from his bag. "What about the one from your favourite?"

"The Gita?" I frowned. "And reincarnation?"

"I mean," he shrugged. "The whole world says it has an answer to everything…" he extended his arm.

I took the Gita from his hand. "Which chapter talks about reincarnation? Page number?" I riffled through the pages.

"Now that you have to find out."

"You suggested this to me," I looked up at him,

raising the Gita. "And you cannot tell me the part or the page number?"

"Nope," he shook his head.

"But—"

"If you lose your weapon, I shall become your shield, not your sword. I'll always be there for you, but your war, you have to fight yourself."

"Do not question the origin of the bricks in the pillars that uphold Dharma,
Oh, King of Gandhar, for what matters is that Dharma triumphs atop.
For if their origin is to be considered," Krishna smiled at Shakuni's question,
"Who you believe is Narayan, too, was born in a place as sinful as a prison."
Throughout the battlefield spread the news of Karna's tragic end,
Soldiers wept at the traumatized Suyodhan, refusing to let go of his friend.
"Let him go, child," After consoling Arjun, Krishna comforted Suyodhan,
That was when Shakuni understood the Lord wasn't against anyone.
Shakuni watched Suyodhan go to the crematory, "They blame us for the war,
And I accept it, Vaasudev, for I have sinned driven by rage, grief, by abhor.
I will go down in history as the most loathed villain! And I deserve it!
But why will they go down as 'heroes'? Sins they too have dared to commit!
Shantanu's lust, Satyavati's greed, Drona's bias, his inhumanity is justified?
Amba, Ambika, Ambalika, Gandhari! Their entire life Bheeshma destroyed!
Vidur advised murdering an infant, convinced everyone it was a monster,
The brothers distributed Draupadi, and Kunti let that happen to her!
The brothers burnt alive a poor, defenceless woman and her five sons!
The emperor gambled away his brothers and his wife due to his addictions!
And Vaasudev, none of his brothers denied! Yet all of them are justified!"
"I forgive no sinner," Krishna smiled, "Some die, some live to pay the price.
History is written by the survivors, and only he who upholds Dharma survives.
Embrace it, Shakuni, and live to tell the world your side of the story."
"I won't betray Suyodhan; I helped him sin; I deserve an end grim and gory."
"You breathe for your family," Krishna smiled, "Anything I can do for you?"
"Kill me before Suyodhan. I won't be able to light the pyre of my nephew."

In the crematorium, Kunti revealed the truth of Karna's birth, his identity,
"I knew you were family," Suyodhan collapsed, "Dear Karna, till eternity."
That night Suyodhan sat on a hill staring at the blood-drenched soil before,
He put his head in his uncle's lap like always, "Mama, this blood, this gore!
Its sight is making me shudder, terrifying my soul! I am responsible for this!
May my end be horrifying! May I never see the realms of bliss!"
Consoling him, Shakuni sat unaware of the gloom awaiting him the next day,
Sahadev defeated Uluka and hissed, "For your father's sins, you will pay!"
"My son is innocent!" Shakuni cried, "By killing him, nothing will you gain!"
Sahadev laughed and pierced the sword in Uluka's heart over and over again.
"Sahadev! You shouldn't have dragged my innocent son into this dirty war!
Shakuni charged at him, "You should've kept him away from it!"
Sahadev blocked it, and with a fierce blow, the old man's throat he slit.
As the sun set, "Dada!" the weeping sister stormed into the battlefield in fear,
Shakuni tried to call her, but the dying man's gasps couldn't reach her ear.
"Your Dada has to go," before his teary eyes flashed his entire life,
His little girl's smile, his parents, his brothers, his nephews, his son, his wife.
Even in his last moments, he was worried for Suyodhan, for his little sister,
The world forgot he was a human, not just an evil trickster.
All because a man one day decided to leash and drag a lady to his kingdom,
And another decided to protect her, sacrificing his own life, soul, his freedom.
"In the circle of life, we shall meet again, donning new skins, a new name,
Tied in different bonds, but my love for you shall remain the same.
Infinite grim ends I shall embrace for my family," he smiled, closed his eyes,
"And to protect them, their peace, their smiles, infinite times I ***shall rise****."*

CURTAIN-DOWN

In the era where all killed for the throne,
He gave it up for his sister like it meant nothing.
I, Aryavarta, have seen some beautiful bonds,
The bond between this brother and his sister being one of them.
This was the journey of the King of Gandhar,
The King who chose to be remembered as Gandhari's brother.

The End (?)

16

Nishika's Journal, 2010

The truth-seeking shelter in the shadows of their gloomy past was dragged to the present. Dark secrets were unearthed. The coffins buried deep carrying the corpses of their crimes were dug up. All their secrets now lay exposed. On the ninth day of March—216 hours after Mrs Drishti Bathra's murder—I decided to interrogate the Bathra family once again after getting to know every little detail about each one of them from *Krishna Da.*

The interrogation room, unsatisfied with its last meal, hungry to devour the truth I was to draw out, welcomed in its bearers.

"Mr Saarth, how long have you been practising shooting?"

His puckered brows, trying to mask the fingers fidgeting with the edge of his checked button-down shirt below the table, "Since I was 13. Why?"

I smiled at the boy, trying his best to curtain his nervousness by fixing the few strands of his wavy hair that had landed upon his forehead (a clever con to wipe the sweat born at the hairline) and the over-the-top attempts of holding my stare.

I got up from my chair. Pacing behind him with my arms folded, I asked him, "The distance from your balcony to the one where Mrs Bathra sat was around 50ft. She was neatly shot in the middle of her forehead with precision, ensuring immediate death. It is quite a difficult target to achieve from a distance of 50ft in a dark room. How easy do you think it must have been for a non-professional to—"

"Stop right there! Why would I kill my own mother?" he grunted, making a forceful turn in his chair and looking at me.

"How was your relationship with her, Mr Saarth?"

"It wasn't so good, but that doesn't mean I'd kill my own mother."

"And why wasn't it good?"

"Every family has its own's feuds, Inspector," he said. "You would know if you had one," he scowled.

"Ah, we're getting personal now…seems like I have pushed a button, Mr Bathra, haven't I?" I smiled at the frustrated boy. "Ripped off a band-aid, maybe."

Saarth took a deep breath with his eyes closed, conquering the scowl with a nice foxy smile, channelling the Dev Bathra within. "No. It was a—um, a stupid reflex. I apologize, Inspector."

"Trained by the best, aren't you?" I scoffed.

"The best," he repeated, still holding the smile.

"Miss Adah, are you familiar with the name Devika Soni?"

"Yes, she has been my co-star in three films. Nothing else." Adah answered with an instant grimace.

"I never asked if there was something else, did I?"

"Uh...I...uhm...I was just. I—"

"It's okay, Miss Bathra," I nodded. "Only a human being enters and exits this room. The words meant to stay, stay."

"I don't know what the fuck you mean," Adah growled, tightening the muscles in her defined jaw.

"Language, Miss Adah," I warned her. "I can very well keep up with the dirt you bring in. And you don't want that, trust me."

"I told you we are *just* good friends, Inspector."

"No. You said you were *just* co-stars…." I reminded her with a smile.

"Um...yeah...that's…it's the same thing."

"Someone murdered your mother, Miss Bathra. And the only thing keeping us from catching the killer are the truths you all are hiding!"

"I am not hiding anything!"

"Hmm…So, that's it? Just a co-star to you?"

"Yes. Nothing other than that. *Nothing.*"

"Are you sure, Miss Adah? Maybe I should call her down to the police station to verify your statement."

"I will kill you if you dare to drag her in this case!" she fumed, thumping the table.

"Miss Adah, are you threatening to kill an officer on duty? This rage sure doesn't justify your statement of being just friends with her, does it?"

"Officer, have you forgotten who you are talking to?" she said, biting her teeth. "I can destroy your life in a snap!"

I could see the untamed fire in her eyes trying to intimidate me.

"You can try, ma'am," I said. "Now, if you're done throwing warnings and lies at my face, let's get done with this. A bit more smoothly this time, I suggest."

"I told you everything already," she barked at me.

"Bullshit!" I roared. "Stop lying, Miss Adah. Were you in a relationship with her, or were you not!"

Adah glared at the floor, avoiding the question.

"Oh wait…let me just modify it a bit," I said. "Have you been seeing her after the death of your mother, or have you not?"

Adah continued to glower at the floor. Her eyes were red, and her fists clenched. The muscles under her skin twitched.

"And this is not your first lie," I added. "What was it that you said when I asked you about your relationship with your mother the last time? '*We dearly loved each other,*' wasn't it?"

"I swear to God, I *will* fucking kill you," Adah hissed. "And. Walk. Out. Free."

"Oh, of course, you will. Like you planned on doing after killing your mother!" I yelled, getting up from my seat.

"Dearly loved each other? Miss Adah, you despised her! And so did she!" I continued, orbiting the set of chairs and table, unaware of the fury slowly taking over her, successful in not drawing any attention to itself. "You were sickened by her staunch repugnant beliefs. She was against your preferences. She was against every decision of your life that only you have the right to take! The homophobia against which you were trying to raise awareness amongst the society had its rigid roots deep in your own house. In your own mother! She dominated you your entire life. She shunned your every decision—be it changing your career or being with the woman you loved. You were fed up with the oppression. You want to live your life the way you want to, with whoever you want to. You were fed up with her interference and dominion over your life. So, you decided to put an end to it. You shot your mother during the play in the auditorium, Miss Bathra, didn't you!"

As I was unalarmed and unaware of the fostered rage within her, which reached its peak, she suddenly attacked me and pinned me to the ground, pressing my neck with all her strength, "I am going to fucking kill you!" Adah kept screaming as she brutishly choked me. The uproar hurried the four junior officers and ACP Verma, watching the interrogation through the unidirectional perspective glass inside the interrogation room. The four brawny men tried to pull her away, but the possessed woman was beyond any man's control. I slowly began to lose consciousness. A curtain of darkness lowered over my eyes. The sight of bulging veins strewn all over my face, as red as blood, forced a yelp of fear out of ACP Verma. My fluttering limbs had slowed down. I writhed in pain as my heavy eyelids began shutting. Before I lost complete consciousness or maybe even my last breath, Adah was pulled off me and dragged out of the room. Through a paper-thin, flickering slit, I could see a fuzzy image of the woman kicking her legs in the air, screaming something I was too numb to hear.

"Officer Nishika! Are you okay?" howled ACP Verma.

"Oh, my God. Is she breathing?" said Sub-Inspector Mishra as he hunkered down to check my pulse.

"What are you looking at? You idiot! Call the damn ambulance!" ACP Verma barked at Constable Naidu, who was too dumbfounded to move.

The agonising, jabbing sensation at the back of my head and neck slowly began to wane. I could indistinctly hear the agitated voices of the officers around. Drawing in deep breaths, I gathered the strength to open my eyes.

"Ahhh..." I groaned, trying to recover from the attack. ACP Verma and Sub-Inspector Mishra pulled me up, each tightly holding an arm, and gently placed me on the chair.

"Officer, are you okay?"

"Maybe," I whispered, still trying to catch my breath.

I squeezed my eyes shut, clasping my left wrist with the right hand, unable to deal with the searing pain. It was probably the first thing that had hit the ground when Adah pounced on me like I was her prey.

Miss Adah Bathra was taken into custody after assaulting and attempting to kill an Inspector on duty during the interrogation. I was in no state to conduct further interrogation. Cancelling the scheduled session, I rushed to the hospital with a swollen wrist, suspecting it to be broken.

***

"Not a fracture, luckily," Dr Gupta whispered to herself, carefully examining the X-Ray. "I'm sorry, but you're going to have to take some time off, Nishika. You need to give your hand rest so that it can recover quickly." She advised, keeping the sheet aside and grabbing a compression wrap.

"No doctor, I can't take an off. I'm working on a really important case. I can't lose it to someone else," I whimpered.

"I can't allow this, Nishika. I know how passionate and devoted you are towards your work, but I recommend you to give your hand complete rest for at least a few days," she declared. "And that's it. I'm not arguing about this anymore."

"But Doc—"

"I think she's right."

I instantaneously tossed my eyes at the not-so-new baritone standing at the door with pursed lips.

"I was down at the station. I heard what Adah did."

"Wow. Who's he?" Dr Gupta whispered. "God have mercy," the fifty-year-old teasingly murmured, winking at me.

I gently knocked on the diamond sleeping on the ring finger of her left hand, trying to awaken it from its slumber.

"For you, not me," she mouthed with an even smile, leaving us alone.

Savya strode towards me, greeting the parting lady with a courteous nod on his way in, and gently held my hand, examining it. "Is it paining, sweetheart?"

"A bit. It was..." I took a pause. "Sweetheart?" my freshly injured, slow-witted self frowned.

"So, your boyfriend can't even address you as sweetheart now?"

"What boyfriend? Savya—"

"Brain: check," he interrupted, tracing a tick mark in the air. "There's absolutely no need to flatter yourself," he said, an exaggerated (hoax) smile bridging his ears, scrunching his eyes. He dramatically shook his head, mocking me. "I was just checking you for a concussion."

I hastily looked around after staring at his face, which detained the melodramatic smile for a couple of good long minutes.

"Are you looking for something? Can I help?" he asked.

"My gun," I glared at him.

"Sorry," he said, suppressing his laughter. "And sorry again."

"What was the second one for?" I asked him, clutching his offered hand to get down from the high-raised bed I was sitting on.

"Actually, I'm also at fault for everything that happened. I should've told you earlier."

"Told me what?"

"Adah had extreme rage issues as a child. She had been consulting a psychiatrist for it too. She was even a part of an anger management group in her teens," he said. "I thought her therapy had been successful and that she was okay, but I guess she needs to restart her sessions."

"And you're telling me this right now?" I shrieked, spreading my eyes as wide as I could. "Savya, she almost killed me today. Wait a minute, how did my investigator miss out on such an important detail?"

"I don't think anyone would've been able to discover this information. My parents were apprehensive that the news of her mental health would have a negative impact on her career and future. So, they took extra care to keep the treatment arcane. No one other than my family knows about this."

"That explains why she attacked Ryan with a knife when he fought with Adar," I thought to myself, flabbergasted by the new-found information.

Savya's phone rang, disrupting my chain of thoughts.

"Yes, Ira? He did what? She did what? Oh, my God! I'll be there in ten minutes. Yes, I'm coming right away, don't worry," he said, throwing the phone back in his pocket apace.

I could sense the panic in his voice. "Hey, what happened?"

"Nishika...um—Adah," he fumbled, breathing heavier than ever.

"Adah, what?" I asked him.

"She...she..." he stuttered with impromptu wetness in his eyes.

"Savya, are you alright?"

"We have to go home right now..." he whispered, his eyes not letting go of mine.

17

Nishika's Journal, 2010

I gently placed my hand on Savya's arm. I could feel the muscles tensing, the skin bathed in goosebumps, and his body shivering. "Savya, what's wrong?"

"I can't..." he took deep breaths. "Nishika, we *have to* go home right fucking now!"

"Okay." I mouthed, rubbing his arm, trying to calm him down. "But before that, you need to tell me what has happened."

"Adah..." he said with a crack in his voice. "She ran her car over Daisy."

"No..." I said, ungrasping his arm in a trice. "Wasn't she...wasn't she in Police custody?"

"My father came to her rescue, like always," he said. "After being released from the Police Station, she drove straight to Keshav Dham, simmering with rage. She ran her car over Daisy, who was playing outside the villa with Ira."

"Is Ira alright?" I asked him.

"She is."

"Did they take Daisy to the vet?" I asked him, quivering.

"Daisy...Daisy died on the spot."

Hell for leather, Savya and I drove to Keshav Dham in his car to find Adar holding Ryan back by brute force. The apoplectic boy would've torn apart and through Adar's arms if we hadn't reached on time. Adah, on the other hand, was held back by Mr Bathra. A few surrounding neighbours, alarmed by the bedlam, tried to muscle in and help while others stood insensitively recording the clamour on their phones, snacking on the commotion.

"Popcorn, anyone?" Savya sarcastically asked the recording spectators dismissing them with a single question.

The others helped us both drag Ryan to my house on my appeal. Savya and I tried to calm the boy down whilst Mr Bathra and Adar lugged Adah back into the villa.

"Nishika Di, I'm going to kill her!" Ryan mourned, devastated. "She killed Daisy on purpose! She had threatened me that she would make me pay for the time I broke her brother's nose. She took the chance today. She took her fucking revenge!"

Savya pulled Ryan in his arms, patting his back, wiping his tears with the cuffs of his jacket, holding him in his grip with all his vigour until the boy calmed down. My eyes, bewilderedly looking for Ira, found her standing at the gate of my house, hesitant to enter. The disfigured body of the dog was sleeping in her trembling arms. She looked at me and back at Daisy. She looked at me again before she set her eyes on the red puddle formed by the streams of blood trickling down her body, gathering beneath her feet. I ran to her and to Daisy. Ira fastened me with a stare. There was no trace of emotion in her eyes. I gently took Daisy's body from her hands. I looked at the poor lifeless animal, her crushed bones, flesh ripped apart, and blood running down my arms that was rinsing the dry lawn red.

"Ira, are you okay?" I whispered, holding the body to my chest.

"*She shouldn't have dragged my innocent Daisy into this dirty war,*" she said, her eyes hooked on Daisy. "*She should've kept her away from it.*"

"Ira, it could've been an accident...."

"It wasn't." She said, looking at me. "I was sitting in the garden watching over Daisy. She spotted a butterfly outside the gate and ran towards it. I briskly stood up to follow her. Adah was outside the gate waiting in her car. She gave me a stern look and then looked at the poor animal in front of her car playing with the butterfly. I could sense the danger. Something was severely wrong with her look. It was...it was deranged. I ran towards Daisy as fast as I could, but before I reached her, she killed this innocent little animal right in front of my eyes."

Ira kept repeating the same line over and over again, "*She shouldn't have dragged an innocent in this dirty war. She should've kept Daisy away from it.*"

Savya came out with a weeping Ryan, still crushed in his arms. He tried to take in Ira, too, but with tears in her eyes, she stepped back, looking at the blood all over her body, afraid that she would soil his clothes. Regardless, Savya pulled her in and tried to console the two siblings weeping in his arms.

We buried the little animal in my front yard.

"Keep an eye on them, please. Make sure they're okay," I requested Savya.

"Don't worry, I'll take care of them," he assured me and left with the two.

The last ray of sun preventing darkness had given up, drowned itself to death on the horizon. Maybe it was disgusted by us humans. I looked around as the world slowly fell into a fathomless black trench. The light left us all that day and never returned, for the sun had set. Darkness had taken over the sky and the souls. I knew the sun would illuminate the black skies once again the next day and free them from the grip of this darker world. But what about the souls? Will it be able to rescue them from the world of night? Maybe not. Maybe that was the beginning of humankind's end. The beginning of an eternal night. For the sun did rise the day after, but that last ray never did.

I stood staring at the spot where Daisy was buried. Her playful barks echoed in my ears, the tail gyrating with joy at the slightest pleasures of life, never to move again. I couldn't believe she wouldn't smile again, come galloping at me with her soft, pink tongue, bouncing with every stride, snuggling up to my leg and rubbing her nose against it. She was gone like they were. Forever.

"What happened to your wrist, Nishika?" asked Mr Krishna, interrupting my thoughts, as he pushed open the gate and entered the front yard.

"I sprained it."

"How?" he asked, visibly worried for me.

"Someone was unable to get to me a vital piece of information that Adah had rage issues," I said, teasing the old man.

"She did?" he gasped. "I'm so sorry. I had no clue about it."

"I was joking, Krishna Da," I said, comforting him.

He smiled at the mention of his new title. Or perhaps at the removal of the old ones he disliked.

"It's getting dark out here, child," he said. "What are you doing outside?"

I let out a deep breath. "My neighbours…uhm…they… they had a dog. Daisy…She…she died...we buried her here," the gulp in my throat made me stutter.

"May her soul attain peace," he prayed with his hands folded and eyes closed. Before I could ask him the reason for his visit, he answered me as though he had read my mind. "I left my wallet here last night."

"Oh, I'll get it," I said. "But could you please help me out with something before that?"

Our three hale and hearty hands planted a beautiful mango sapling on the spot where Daisy had been buried. "She loved mangoes," I said, my habitually dry eyes slightly moistened, smiling at the sapling.

"I had always heard that dogs are 'police's best buddies.' I saw it myself today," he said, smiling at me.

"By the way, how did the…how did Daisy…Old age?"

"No," I said. "It was them."

"Who?"

"The honey guides."

Honey guides are birds that guide human beings to bee colonies. When the human breaks open the hive and take the honey, the wily bird feeds on the larvae and wax that lie inside the open and unprotected beehive. The bird that we think is helping us get the honey, in reality, is just using us to get its own prey. When I think of anger, I picture it like a swarm of honey guides. It guides us to its prey. We blindly follow the devious birds, controlled by them, thinking of us as the beneficiary, but the little demons just want to have their food without getting blood on their hands. The cunning predators hunt down their prey—humanity, using humans.

What I saw that day shattered my heart into a million pieces. A woman had killed an innocent animal to get her revenge against the people she abhorred, guided by her rage, guided by the honey guides.

* * *

"Nishu!" a voice whooped in excitement from the gate of the house, dragging me out of my trance. I cast my head behind to behold the much-awaited sight of the traveller who had finally found the way to her house, "Shalini, aunty! You're back!"

Possibly possessed by the spirit of a rootless wanderer, the small-boned urbane Chartered Accountant who looked like a penniless gypsy at the moment enthusiastically sprinted towards me to throw herself in my arms. The overwhelmed hugger, blinded by a rush of dopamine (or by the rush of something that would put me in a grave moral crisis sparking a duel between a niece and a police officer), ran to hug me, accidentally missed a step, and toppled over.

"Oh my God!" I ran to help her up.

"Ouf, my face," she garbled.

"Oh, I hope you're not," I whispered, *"Off your face."*

I gently compressed the gash on her forehead with a clean cloth to stop the bleeding as she sat on the couch, grinning at me (without blinking).

"We're going to have to go to the hospital, Aunty."

"Oh, it's nothing, dear. I'll be alright," she said with an even louder grin squeezing her eyes shut, dismissing my worries.

"What's that?" she shrilled, suddenly side-tracked. "Nishu, what happened to your hand?"

"It's a long story," I said, grabbing my keys. "I'll tell on the way to the hospital."

"Nishika, we really don't need to go to the hospital."

"Aunty—"

The persuading that I knew would last longer than whatever she was maybe on was shortly invaded by the ringing of my phone.

"Yes, Savya?"

"Nishika, could you please come to my house?" he said in a hesitant voice. "I know it's a little late, but Ira has been crying her eyes out since the moment we came back. I think it would be easier to console her if you were here too. I've already instructed the security guard to let you in."

"Of course," I said. "Just give me some time, please. There's been a small accident here."

"Accident? Are you alright? Is everything alright?"

"Shalini aunty is back from her tour," I said, vigorously signalling the tranced woman to pick her unwilling bum up as I unlatched the front door. "She tumbled while running up to me like a kid."

"It's really nothing!" her voice resonated from behind.

"Sure, I'll wait for you then. Take care of her," said Savya and hung up.

I left for the hospital dragging Shalini aunty along and returned to Keshav Dham in around half an hour. After tucking the lady in her comforter in another five to ten minutes, I hastened to the Bathra Villa to meet Savya.

We were in his room, discussing the abject events of the unfortunate evening, when our ears were ripped apart by a deafening scream that silenced more than one heartbeat each, stopping us dead in our tracks.

"Help! Someone, please help me!"

***

Present Day

"What happened?" the weather-beaten old man who had just entered Ryan's reading room cried, bowled over by the intense scream. His mouth stretched broader than his eyes, and his hands shot up in question as he looked at the grey-haired director sitting in his chair surrounded by an entranced audience of four—all startled by his abrupt interruption—and an uninterested boy engrossed in a puzzle.

"Ryan, why were you screaming for help?" he asked.

"Savya Da, I swear you have the worst timing. I was about to read out the most exciting part," said Ryan.

"Ryan, it's really not something to get excited about," said Ira.

"Will someone please explain to me what is happening here?" asked Savya, perplexed.

"Nanu is reading out Nishika Di's journal to us," replied Rohan.

"Who is reading who's what to you?" shrieked the stunned old man.

"And you're not just letting Ryan do this, but are also a part of it?" Savya asked Ira, surprised, after she explained to him the entire scenario.

"You know him..." sighed Ira. "He is as stubborn as he was fifty years ago. There's no winning against him."

"I agree," said Ryan, with a proud nod.

"It wasn't a compliment," Ira threw him a look. "Anyway, why are you so late?" she confronted the latecomer. "Where were you?"

"I was out for dinner," answered Savya, exploring the old journal that Ryan handed out to him.

"You already had dinner?" she groaned. "You knew the children and I were going to join you and Ryan for dinner today, didn't you?"

"Yeah, whatever," he said, immersed in examining the journal.

"Don't *whatever* me," said Ira, her hands on her waist.

Brushing aside the old woman, Savya looked at Ryan. "But Ryan, how did you find her out after all these years?"

"Let's just say I'm good at getting things done," Ryan scoffed with an inflated chest.

"Give me her address right now!" said Savya.

"I don't think I can..." he said, shaking his head with his lips tightly sealed. "She has already forbidden me from telling you that."

Sealing his lips even tighter, trying to suppress his laughter after seeing Savya's irritated face, Ryan mouthed, "Sorry…" further mocking the old surgeon.

"*Already forbidden me from telling you that,*" Savya parroted, scornfully mimicking Ryan.

His narrowed eyes nailed at Ryan, who was on the verge of losing to the rip-roaring laughter quashed in his chest, he fit himself on the bean bag, settling down next to Anuj, "Move."

"Yes, because this is the only vacant space in the two-storey room," Anuj coughed sarcasm, looking up from the puzzle at the old man beside him with a smile.

"Shh," Savya winked at him.

"Now, can we please get on with the story?" asked Ananya.

"Yep. Savya Da, please let him continue the story," requested Eshan.

"Sure. Ryan, go ahead," said Savya.

"You know what? Savya Da should tell the next part," Ryan suggested.

Ryan placed a pen between its pages and shut the journal where he had taken a halt before locking his eyes with Savya's.

Savya agreed with Ryan and continued the story.

18

Savya, 2010

Daisy's death had terrorized Ira. It was getting impossible for me to calm her down. I needed help. I needed Nishika. It had been nearly an hour or two since I had dragged Ryan and Ira to their room as fast as I could, steering clear of Adah to avoid another clash. Considering the rage boiling in each of their veins, a fight right now could be the last straw of someone's life.

"Kill me, Savya Da!" Ira wept. "I cannot live like this anymore! These people are monsters! Free me from this cage!"

"Don't say that. Shhh…" I said, patting her head as she leaned in my arms. "It'll be alright…."

"No. It won't," said Ryan. "Things don't get alright till you make them," he said, slowly back stepping.

"Ryan, where are you going?" I asked him, alarmed by the eyes pouring out molten fury, the clenched fists digging bloody crescent moons in his palms, and the chest puffing and blowing in wrath.

"Take care of my sister," Ryan whispered. "*And I'll take care of yours….*"

"Ryan!" I yelled and sprang to my feet to catch the boy who had stormed out of the door and realized Ira had fainted in my arms.

"Oh, good Lord," I said, emotionally drained and done for the fucking day. "Nishika, please come fast…."

"Savya?" Nishika hastily entered my room about an hour or half later. "The house help said you're in your room. Where's Ira?"

"Thank God you're here!" I said, finally putting an end to my eternal loop of pacing back and forth from my bed to the door.

"How is Ira? And where is she?"

I sat down on my bed, a deep sigh of respite breaking free from my mouth. "She's…I don't know. She fainted a while ago—"

"Fainted?" Nishika gasped.

"Yeah. But I guess she's better now. I put her to sleep in her room."

With fleeting relief on her face, she dropped the satchel on her shoulder down to the floor and sat down next to me, "And Ryan?"

"I don't know where he is," I said. "He left when I was with Ira."

"Did he seem alright?" she asked me.

"I wouldn't say so..." I answered, my elbows resting on my knees, palms bracing my frazzled face. "I hope he doesn't do something that he'll regret later."

Nishika placed her hand on my shoulder. "He'll be okay...."

I looked up at her. I could see the lines of worry contorting Nishika's face, who was equally concerned for the impetuous boy. "I hope so."

"Your hair," I gently fixed a few strands of her hair, escaping the bun messed up from all the relentless dashing around. "And how's your hand?" I asked her, removing it from my shoulder, taking it into mine, and tightening the loosened Velcro of the compression wrap.

"It's okay now," she sighed.

"You drove your aunt to the hospital by yourself, didn't you?" I asked her. "You're supposed to give it rest, Nishika. It is clearly not yet okay. The swelling seems to have increased, in fact."

"I didn't have an option. I couldn't let *her* drive," she said with a little laugh. "You should've met her. Although she says it's just the contentment of getting a glimpse of her niece after so long, the woman is—I'm pretty sure—high...."

"What!" I laughed, my mind finally on to something other than the dreary events of the day. The tensed, dim-lit room was lightened for a fleeting moment. A moment I desperately needed.

"Savya…" whispered Nishika after my faint laughs had silenced. "Could it really have been an accident?"

The question made me let go of her gaze once again. I put my head back in my palms, and with a heavy heart, decided to tell her the truth, "As far as I know, my sister is totally capable of doing something like this. I don't think she would've thought even once before killing Daisy."

"So Ira hadn't misunderstood the situation…Adah, really…" Nishika sighed. "Well, the girl was right…."

"About what?" I asked her, my head still lowered.

"She said that Adah shouldn't have dragged an innocent in this dirty war. That she should've kept Daisy away from it…." Nishika told me. "She really should have."

My dispirited eyes widened in shock at the discovery of something crucial. Something horrifying. I jerked my head up, "Oh, my god…Adah dragged an innocent in this dirty war…She… killed an innocent to get revenge against Ryan…*Dragged an innocent into this dirty war!*"

"Fuck!" I sprang to my feet. "Where is Ada—"

"Help! Someone, please help me!" Urvi screamed from one of the rooms of my house.

We hurtled in the direction of the scream as fast as our legs could carry us to find Urvi standing at Adah's door, rooted to the ground. Her quivering eyes were fixed on something terrifying inside the room. As the petrified woman's tears of fright guided our strides further, Nishika and I dashed inside. While the vigilant police officer—immediately on her guard—cautiously toed at the source of the dread in the air, my legs trembled to move ahead. With every step that she took forward, mine fell backwards. Swamped in sweat, with a heart beating a mile a minute and eyes screaming in horror, I stood paralyzed at the sight of Adah's body lying on the floor in a pool of thick blood slowly spreading out, marking its territory, colouring the dull porcelain tiles crimson. Dark blood seeped out of the fathomless hole in her chest. It was easy to make out that she had been *repeatedly* stabbed by a sharp object in her *heart* till her body was completely lifeless—or maybe even after it was lifeless for a long time.

"I saw him stab her! He jumped out the window and ran away!" Urvi screamed again, pointing at the ajar window in Adah's room, pulling me out of the sea of fear that was slowly breathing me in.

"Urvi, who?" asked Nishika, startled.

"Ryan!"

***

Two medical examiners squatting down on their haunches half a meter away from my sister's mutilated body were busy examining it. A forensic photographer was documenting the frantic footprints running from alongside the body to the window and out. Around seven officers, including

Inspector Nishika, tore apart every pillow and mattress and defaced everything that came their way in search of evidence. ACP Verma was in deep talks with my father in the hallway. I, unable to pull myself together, stood at my (dead) sister's door, too stunned to speak, watching them all. My eyes wandered about the room, observing every face, every action, and even the slightest of movements. My ears caught every word, every groan, and the faintest sigh thrown out in the air. I could hear one of the officers yawn, the flashes of the cameras. I could hear the female examiner whisper to the male one, '*which seems to have resulted in Cardiac tamponade*,' as he scribbled it on some papers while they passed by me. I could hear everything. But my mind was anchored. It was moored to Adah's lifeless face. Her hardened eyes were halfway closed, trying to watch us all. Maybe they were looking for the boy Urvi had seen stab her to death. The venom that she often spat from her mouth was replaced by dried-up streams of blood. The heart that I thought was black, the heart that I thought was a stone, looked so delicate, so normal...so human.

"Send the body for autopsy," Nishika commanded the two examiners on checking their report. "Mishra, fax Ryan's photo to the control room. Depart a team to look for him right now. Check every vehicle leaving the city."

Ryan's cell was being monitored. His photo was circulated in all the police divisions and broadcast on the news channels without let-up. Like bloodhounds, the police were on a hunt for the twenty-one-year-old who was accused of cold-bloodedly murdering *the golden girl of the nation, the resplendent actress Adah Bathra*.

"He was wearing an oversized peach t-shirt and charcoal cargo jeans," I told Nishika upon being asked.

"Nishika Di, Ryan is innocent!" Ira cried, interrupting us, clasping Nishika by her arm. "He would never do something like this. Urvi is lying! This is just another conspiracy of hers."

Nishika signalled me to take care of her and left to look for Ryan.

"Savya Da, he's not like this," Ira turned to me. "He would never do this. Please help us, Savya Da," she begged me.

I tried to calm her down, but I was clueless. I didn't know if Ryan had really killed Adah. I looked at Urvi, who stood next to my lamenting elder brother, staring at Ira. My father and Saarth stood in a corner, observing the investigation. I had always been detached from all the members of my family, but why weren't they grieving? My father had just lost his daughter, and my brother had lost his elder sister, but there wasn't even a hint of sorrow in their eyes.

"Is Urvi really lying? But why would she? If she is, why would Ryan flee like he had really murdered Adah? Had he?" I thought to myself, unable to process what had just happened. In the blink of an eye, I had lost my mother and my sister. The boy accused of killing them had escaped. His sister stood next to me weeping, trying to convince me of his innocence. An equally ruffled but doing something about it, unlike me, Inspector Nishika came back after around an hour to interrogate us all.

"Mr Dev Bathra, where were you when Urvi saw Ryan stab your daughter?"

"It was quite late. I was sleeping," my father answered, sitting on the black couch across from the officer. His hands were firmly placed on his knees, his voice as steady as always, his gaze unwavering.

"Did you hear any noises? Any screams?"

"My room is on the third floor, Inspector. Adah's room is on the first. How would I hear anything?" he answered curtly.

"May I know who else has his or her room on the first floor, Mr Bathra?"

"Just Adar and his wife apart from Adah."

"Mrs Urvi, please describe every event of the night in detail."

"Adah's body—"

"In detail, Mrs Urvi. Start from how you found yourself there."

Ten restless fingers tied in a knot, sat on her crossed legs fiddling with each other, "I had just had dinner with my husband and was on my way to our room to get his medicines. As I walked past Adah's unfastened door—slightly open, I heard some strange grunting noises coming from within. At first, I chose to ignore them. But on my way back, the persistent noise really unsettled me, and I felt like…like something was wrong. I slowly pushed the door open and saw Ryan repeatedly stabbing her dead body like a psychopath. And with every stab, he gruffed to himself the same line again and again: *You shouldn't have killed Daisy*!"

"Hmm…" said Nishika, her tilted head studying Urvi's body language as she spoke. "You *'saw Ryan repeatedly stabbing her dead body'*. Mrs Urvi, how are you so sure Adah was already dead when he was stabbing her?"

"I just…I thought…I…" Urvi stumbled over her words. "I don't know, I just…I thought she was. Maybe because she wasn't moving at all."

"So, you were on your way back with your husband's medicines…." Officer Nishika murmured, brushing her lip. "Which medicines? Elaborate, please."

"Uh…h—he has diabetes," she nervously answered. "Glucomet, and Janumet and…uh…this one…uhm…"

"Go on," Nishika patiently nodded.

"Um…Dionil. Yep, Dionil."

"Three medicines…" Nishika smiled. "Three medicines, and if I'm not mistaken, Mrs Urvi, I don't remember seeing even one in your hands when I saw you standing at Adah's door."

Urvi's unsettled eyes blinked twice as fast at the statement, "I…I must've dropped them or something, Inspector."

"Fair enough...although we didn't find any there," said Nishika. "Anyway, what happened next?"

Wiping the sweat collected on her upper lip, Urvi looked at Nishika. "I was transfixed by the blood-curdling visual. Suddenly, Ryan noticed my presence and looked up at me. The boy looked …like a monster! His eyes were blood red with fury, his chest heaving with every vigorous pant, his clothes splotched red. Every inch of them! Clenching the knife smeared in my sister-in-law's blood, he charged at me. I screamed as loudly as I could to seek help and get him caught, but the sound of the approaching footsteps alarmed him. He immediately jumped out of the window and ran away."

"So, no one other than you saw him?"

"Umm…No."

"He was stabbing her with a knife…hmm. Did he run away with the weapon, Mrs Bathra?"

"Umm…I…" Urvi moistened her chapped lips. "I don't remember, I...I didn't see what he did with it."

"Mr Saarth, where were you at the time of the murder?"

The loutish young man turned a blind eye to the officer even after she repeated the same question thrice, making her question her physical existence. The fourth time Nishika held him by his arm, forcefully turned him towards her and warned him. "Mr Saarth Bathra, do not force me to—"

"What the fuck are you going to do, officer? Arrest me? Shoot me?" he scoffed, carelessly chewing his gum. "You can do nothing."

"Listen to me, you bastard," Nishika raised a finger at the boy, losing her patience. "It is three in the morning, and I am not up for your fucking bullshit. Do not make me force you to talk...."

"This is not your interrogation room, officer," he sniggered. "This is *my* house. My territory. You cannot touch a strand of my hair here," Saarth whispered, gnashing his teeth and leaning forward, his nose almost touching Nishika's, intensifying the tension.

"Saarth." My father cut in, pulling his son apart.

Reading the lines on my father's face, Saarth looked back at the fuming officer. "I am mourning the death of my sister right now, and I want some time before I can answer any questions," he said with a sarcastic smile, nonchalantly chewing his gum.

"Get a grip on your son, Mr Bathra. I—"

"It's okay, Mr Bathra," ACP Verma interrupted Nishika, signalling her to calm down before the matter worsened.

"He will answer all your questions after a while, Inspector," my father told Nishika before hauling Saarth along with him to his room.

Her toned arms tightly folded, the muscles in her jaw stiffened, Nishika shook her head in contempt at ACP Verma, who helplessly sighed at her and requested her to continue the interrogation.

"Ira, where were you when the murder happened?"

"I was in my room sleeping when I heard an ear-piercing scream. I rushed down to see what had happened to find all of you standing outside Adah's room."

"Is there any place you think your brother might seek shelter in?"

"Not any I can think of, officer. He's new here," she answered with a quivery voice.

"We'll find him. Don't worry," said Nishika, lightly clasping Ira's shoulder.

"Ryan didn't kill Adah!" shrieked Ira, "He has suffered from Hemophobia since childhood. Even the slightest sight of blood makes him shudder. It terrifies him! It took me a great number of efforts to calm him down even on the night of Mrs Drishti's death. Even if he wanted to kill Adah, he wouldn't stab her," she wept.

* * *

Present Day

"Nanu, did you really...?" asked Eshan, shaken.

"No, of course, he didn't, Eshan," said Ananya. "You didn't, right?" she whispered to Ryan.

"Are we going to ignore the fact that that woman killed an innocent little dog like it was no big deal?" hollered Arya, disgusted and livid.

"Arya, calm down," said Rohan. "Nanu, you have Hemophobia?"

"You might get all your answers if you let me continue," said Ryan, as he re-opened the journal, cutting their string of questions.

19

Nishika's Journal, 2010

After interrogating the members of the family, I went to question the security guard if he had seen Ryan abscond.

"The boy had blood all over his hands. He looked mystified and extremely frightened. Mr Rana wasn't even able to open the bolted gate with his shivering hands. But before I came out of my cabin to get hold of him, he escaped."

"Did he have anything in his hands? A knife or some kind of weapon?"

The guard scratched his head, trying to remember everything about the boy. "His hands…umm…" he muffled to himself, squinting his eyes. "No. He didn't have anything in his hands."

"So, the murder weapon is somewhere in these premises even now…."

I instructed my team to look for it or any kind of evidence in the entire Bathra Villa. "Check every single room. Every little corner of this house. And if anyone stops you, inform me right away."

Supervising the subordinates with an eye, concurrently, I dialled up Mr Krishna, in dire need of his expertise and help.

"Hello!" he exclaimed, his soothing voice exuding abundant positivity any time of the day.

"I am extremely sorry to bother you so late—"

"Oh, it's all good," he said. "I don't really sleep."

"Uhm…okay..." I said, a little confused.

"Office hours: twenty-four hours a day, seven days a week—every moment at your service, child!"

His smiling words drew out of me a spontaneous chuckle of admiration, even in this grim situation. "Thank you, sir," I said. "I need your help."

"Is everything alright?" he asked from the other side.

"Ryan is absconding. He is accused of killing Miss Adah," I told him. "Could you help me find him out?"

"Yes, sure," he assured me. "I'll inform you the moment I get any news related to him."

A little relieved, I joined my team in searching for the villa, raising the number of hands tirelessly working on digging out the truth. The first room we inspected was that of the prime suspect, Ryan, and his roommate, Ira, on the second floor of the villa, subsequent to Adar and Urvi's room situated on the first. Next, we searched Mr Dev Bathra's room on the third floor, followed by Savya's on the fourth and Saarth's on the fifth (the last floor).

"Officer!" Sub-Inspector Mishra ran to me as I stood in Saarth's room. "Ryan has surrendered himself to the police!"

"What? When?" I asked, staggered but thankful.

"I just got a call from the station," he informed me, "Mr Rana surrendered five minutes ago. He has been taken into custody."

"I'll leave for the station then," I said.

"Can I accompany you, Inspector?" asked Mishra. "You shouldn't drive with that hand."

"Okay," I nodded at him. "I'll be down in a minute. Get the jeep ready to go," I told him, tossing my keys.

"Continue searching the house for evidence," I instructed Asst. Sub-Inspector Sharma. "And keep an eye on each one of them. Nobody leaves the villa till I return. I repeat, *nobody*."

The dreadful murder had swallowed an entire night. A dark infernal night that was ought to leave its mark on every heart that beat through it. The unconquered sun rejoicing at its triumph over the darkness, grinned at me as I walked out of the villa. The dawn brimful of brightness—

forevermore enchanting—tried to cast a saffron spell on my unflinching eyes marching ahead, hooked to the risen sun, but for once was unsuccessful. For even the mesmerizing sight of it couldn't put me at ease. I knew something was not right. Something wasn't adding up. I knew Ryan was innocent and not the cold-blooded murderer that everyone thought he was. But why did he abscond like a criminal then? What about the horrifying sight that Urvi said she had witnessed? There was a war going on in my mind. A war that only Ryan could put an end to.

"Good morning!" beamed the old man walking towards me, his soft skin carrying along an amber sheen.

"Good morning," I reciprocated with a smile, retarding my pace.

"Ryan is in the police station. He surrendered a few minutes ago," Mr Krishna informed me on my way to the ride juddering outside. "The boy looked very calm, composed and in his right senses."

"Yes, I got the news," I said. "I'm on my way to the station."

"Nishika," he said, taking a halt. "You look worried. Everything alright?"

"I'm fine," I said, my face curling up in a faint smile. "Just troubled by a few questions...."

"You have been tirelessly working on this case," he said. "You should get some rest, child. Did you eat at least?" the worried old man enquired.

"Only after putting an end to this draining and odious case will I rest Krishna Da," I sighed, my eyes hitched back to the sun still grinning at me.

"*Vijayi bhava!*"

"Pardon me?" I said, drowned in my beholder's beauty, not having heard what he said.

"I know you will," he smiled. "Well, take care."

I smiled back at him. I gently bowed and took his leave, picking up my journey to the jeep and to the truth I desperately awaited.

"Nishika!" he suddenly called out, watching me go.

I turned around and walked back to him, retracing the five steps. "Yes?"

"What's the time?"

A little bemused by the sight of a watch on his wrist, I said, "It's 7:15 am. Aren't you wearing a watch?"

"It doesn't work," he replied, looking at the archaic, jiggered gadget wrapping his wrist. "It stopped functioning years ago."

"Umm…why not get it fixed then?"

"Sometimes it is about accepting the broken the way they are rather than trying to fix them," he smiled. "For you can't always fix what is broken by someone else. To rearrange the pieces, you don't know how it was before it shattered."

"Who broke your watch?"

"Time."

"Is it that old?" I asked.

"Ages," he answered.

"And yet you're wearing it? Not going to throw it out?"

"I'm not going to throw out a poor thing just because it couldn't stand the ravages of time, because it grew old. I'm not a human's soul," he laughed.

"This little thing is the closest to my heart," he said, gently kissing the worn-out watch.

"Is there something special about this watch?" I asked him curiously.

"There is." He said, his eyes still caressing it. "It can't show me the ones yet to come but bears the moments spent with a person who is no more. This watch was gifted to me by my elder brother when it was first launched."

I smiled at the heartfelt sight of this man cherishing his watch, "You must've been really close to him."

"Of course I was," he said and looked up at me. "He was my very first hero—my *dau*. That's what I called him. He was the one who raised me when my parents were in the dungeo—" he paused. "Wow, nope…let's say out of town."

"Elder siblings are no less than parents. They love you, care for you and protect you," he continued. "They always look out for their younger siblings, *come what may*. They'll die for you. If needed, *even kill for you*."

"That's true," I said, looking at the broken watch.

"Nishika…"

"Yes, Krishna Da?"

"The heart is never void unless you are dead. There's always something that fills it. It could be anything. Love, sorrow or even revenge."

I didn't understand what he had said, but before I could ask him to explain it to me, the cryptic man waved me goodbye and left, leaving me alone with his words and with a task to decrypt them.

***

"Thank God!" trumpeted Mishra. "I didn't have to go back to my house the entire night because of this case," the Sub-Inspector let out full-throated laughter of relief. His jubilant celebration of words unconsciously accelerated the jeep, snipping a few meters to the destination.

"You don't like going back to your house, Mishra?" I asked him.

"There's a war going on in my house, ma'am," he whined. "My son wanted to be admitted to his elder sister's university—the Mittal Institute of Technology. But I firmly disagreed with his decision after getting to know the truth about the college. Now the whole family is against me," he loudly exhaled, swaying his head.

"Try and reason with him," I suggested.

"It's not that easy, Inspector," he said. "The boy and my wife keep trying to convince me that his elder sister would be there to look after him."

"Now you tell me, ma'am," after a long pause, he added to the conversation I thought had already puffed out its last breath. "Would you send your young boy to such a place?"

Mishra glanced at me every other moment, curious to hear my point of view. I was saved by a sudden phone call from the police station that further tested Mishra's patience.

"Yes, Naidu?" I said as I received the call.

"Officer…" said Constable Naidu, the low tone of his voice mothered by urgency and fathered by an unnerved fear. "Officer, someone left a tape outside the station."

"Another tape?" I asked, puzzled. "What is it about?"

"I'll play it once again, ma'am," he said and put the phone close to the cassette player.

'For his revenge against me,
Ruthlessly to death, he dragged another innocent,
A poor blameless was once again hauled in the cruel hunt.
The Pandava had to pay for it, and so he did.
Adah Bathra had to pay for it, and so she did.'

"Who is he talking about, officer?" Mishra eagerly flung at me another question, forgetting his initial one.

"Sahadev…"

"Who the hell is this killer!" the man yowled in frustration, slamming the steering wheel. "If the accused boy is already in police custody, who left this outside the station?"

"Maybe…maybe he paid someone to do it!" he promptly answered himself. "But why would he surrender then?"

"Ugh," he groaned. "Haven't seen a case more twisted than this in the seventeen years of my service!"

"What did you say?" I asked him, my brows meeting each other.

"Haven't…seen…a…case…more…twisted than this in the seventeen years of my service…" the addled man slowly repeated, emphasising each word.

That's when something dawned on me. Something that changed the entire course of the case and flipped my destination horizontally. "*Seventeen years…*" I murmured. "Seventeen years!" I yelled, triumphantly striking my knee.

"No. It wasn't Ryan," I said. "Mishra, take the jeep back to the Bathra villa right away."

"And as for your previous question," I looked at his face strewn with confusion, his hands in the process of backtracking the freshly made tracks of the jeep. "I wouldn't worry about your boy," I said. "Turns out Krishna Da was right. Elder siblings do look out for their younger siblings, *come what may...*"

The footsteps left behind on the unexplored road to the truth by the lost travellers, my much sought-after answers leading my way, like a powerful gush of wind having broken free from the prison of doubts and questions, I dashed straight into Adar and Urvi's room as soon as I reached the Bathra Villa.

"What now?" yelled its male occupant, angered by the sight of me standing in the doorway. With traces of tears shed for his sister in the corners of his eyes and a face red with fury and frustration, he glowered at me. "The room has already been checked by your officers!"

"Take him out," I calmly told Mishra, my eyes restlessly sprinting from one corner to another, from one object to another.

"Ma'am, I have searched the entire room myself," Sharma told me on Adar's not-so-peaceful departure.

"No," I said. "Let's take another look."

"But—"

"Recheck each and everything," I commanded him. "However frivolous it may seem to be."

We searched the entire room once again. From every drawer to the mattress that had already been torn apart, to the rumpled bedsheets, to the cupboards dishevelled during the investigation. All to find nothing. Disappointed by the shocking defeat of my speculation, I dragged my heels out of the room, my eyes still in disbelief and mind still unconvinced. My unwilling hands pulled the door to shut it—the door to Ryan's innocence—but just when it was to touch the frame, Mr Krishna's words echoed in my mind.

'The heart is never void... Something always fills the void.'

I rushed back in, pushed it open and looked at the raised circular wooden platform with the giant bed on it—located in the heart of the room. Circling it on all fours, I knocked on the platform till I found the spot where it was hollow.

"This section behind the bed is hollow…." I gasped. "Sharma, this small section is hollow! Did you check what's inside?"

"Uh...no…No, ma'am," he stuttered with guilt, "I didn't realize it was hollow."

I hastily looked around the spot, trying to figure out a way to open it and came across a small latch hiding on the broad rim of the raised platform, almost camouflaged in its surroundings. I unlocked the latch and slid open the little door to find my answers—the travellers believed were lost seventeen years ago—held hostage for twelve years in her heart and for five in the small enclosed space. On the discovery of the unexplainable material, Mrs Urvi Bathra was arrested for the murder of her sister-in-law, Adah Bathra and her mother-in-law, Mrs Drishti Bathra, by guilefully trapping somebody else.

20

Nishika's Journal, 2010

"Mr Ryan, what happened the night of Adah Bathra's murder?"

10th March 2010, 0900 hrs: The walls of the dusky interrogation room, at odds with the glimmer spread outside, stood eager. Impatient to grasp the words, Ryan's mouth was to heave out. Impatient to satisfy an atom of their sempiternal thirst for truth.

"I drove to the Police Station after leaving my sister with the only trustworthy man I have met in this city," said Ryan. "I wanted to file a complaint against Adah Bathra for her crime, but I never did. When I was around the corner of the station, I realized it was a futile move. Mr Bathra had managed to free his daughter—effortlessly—just a couple of hours ago after she had severely injured a police inspector on duty in her own police station. Why would she be held for murdering an animal? The poor lives no one gives a fuck about—"

"Profanity is frowned upon, Mr Ryan."

"I'm sorry," he immediately apologized.

"Please continue."

"So, I drove back to Keshav Dham and stomped directly to Adah's room with the intention of fighting with her. I wanted to ask her why she had killed an innocent animal if her grudge was against me. I wanted to confront her about why she was such a lowlife cun—"

"Sorry," he sighed. "The woman killed my dog. It's just…it's just fucking difficult to settle for a 'bad person'," he said, air-quoting the term.

"Go on, Mr Rana."

"Anyway, I stood at the ajar door of her room, psyching myself not to do anything regrettable. I went inside…."

Ryan froze, reliving the nightmare. The visuals of the gore and blood he had witnessed forced his eyelids shut as his skin prickled with terror. He was breathing through his mouth, inhaling as much amount of air as possible. His forehead was flooded with sweat.

"You okay, Ryan?"

After a few moments of heavy silence and passing through hell, he continued. "She…she…Adah lay on the floor—static, blood squirting out of her chest. I was scared stiff by the gory sight, but somehow gathered all the courage that I had and walked up to her body to check if she was alive. I slowly crouched down to check her pulse, but my shivering, enfeebled feet slipped, and I fell in the puddle of my misfortune," he said, looking at the dry stains of blood on his clothes, explaining the history of their origin.

"What happened next?"

"Just then, Urvi, who was standing at the door, cleared her throat, seizing my attention," Ryan continued. "Blotched in Adah's blood, I looked up at her evil smile glaring at me. I requested her to come and help me, but she continued to stand in the doorway—no sign of the wicked smile's departure—rather than helping. Then, out of nowhere, she asked me—*Ryan, what have you done?*—I tried to explain to her that I hadn't killed Adah. With that sly smile, she shook her head, clicking her tongue and said something that made me jump out of my skin— *Ryan, I just saw you stab her. Why did you kill her? Oh my God! Why are you coming towards me with that knife?* —It didn't take me a second to figure out what she was doing. I knew no one would believe me. I tried to reason with her, but she started screaming for help. I didn't know what to do. All I could think of was escaping the house."

"What made you surrender then?"

"Realization," he answered. "After running away for hours, I decided to surrender myself. I realized that my running away was only going to help Urvi push the needle of doubt towards me."

"And I knew you'd save me if I was innocent," he added with a smile.

* * *

"Mrs Urvi Bathra, will you please care to explain what all of this stuff hidden in your secret space is?" I roared, smacking the table. "These charts with everyone's daily routines, habits, allergies, history and whatnot. These pen drives and CDs. Photos of all the members of the Bathra family out of which Adah's and Mrs Bathra's have been crossed?"

Urvi nervously looked at the evidence, "I...Officer I—"

"You what?" I yelled. "And what were the two murder weapons doing in there? The knife smeared in Miss Adah Bathra's blood, and this!" I raised the evidence pouch containing the Glock 26 fitted with a silencer, "The bullet from which is proven to have caused the death of Mrs Drishti Bathra!"

"Officer, I don't know where the knife and the gun came from," she cried. "I didn't kill them!"

"Really?" I scoffed. "So, you do know where this other stuff came from?"

Wiping the sweat of fright strewn on her forehead with the back of her palm, she looked at everything placed in front of her on the table and then looked back at me. "I'll tell you everything, officer, but I didn't kill them...."

"All ears, Urvi. All ears," I said in a stern voice, sitting on my chair, fixing my eyes on the woman.

"I was born in a small remote village—*Saretttha*—in Rajasthan to a poor family. I'm sure you haven't even heard the name, Inspector," she said in an intimidated voice, pausing to look at the floor.

"Silence is the last thing I want to hear from you right now, Mrs Urvi Bathra," I curtly said.

Her eyes still lowered, she continued. "The only dream that my illiterate parents had was to educate their children and provide them with a better life full of opportunities. I have seen them strive day and night to earn money for my brother's and my education. In that small conservative village—unknown to you all, disregarded by you all, forgotten by you all!" she said, her voice louder and eyes raised, surly at me. "My parents had seen a boundless dream. A dream that seemed impossible to everyone at first. No one from our village or the neighbouring villages had been fortunate enough to get educated. We didn't even know what a school was, Inspector!" Urvi screamed.

"Here," I said, offering her a glass of water.

"I am alright," she said, turning her head, denying it.

"Amidst this pitch-dark cavern of under-development and illiteracy, I was determined to strengthen my vision," said the spark in her eyes. "I told my father about my dream of becoming a teacher. The young girl from Sarettha wanted to enlighten her village with the rays of education. My parents sent me to Delhi with whatever money they had earned. They even sold our ancestral land. They traded their entire life's savings for my little dream!"

I could see a few tears hoarded in Urvi's eyes, the woman a word away from falling apart. Forbidding her emotions from flowing out, she quickly wiped them away.

"Take it," I said, offering her the glass of water again.

"Thank you," she said, declining it again.

"So, you came to Delhi…." I said, keeping the glass down on the table, motioning her to continue.

"I studied very hard to get into one of the best colleges of Delhi—St. Jacob's College. I also worked on the side to help my parents pay its sky-high fees…." Urvi sighed. "Although saying 'worked' might be an understatement here, Inspector," she added, her words leaving herself in stitches.

Like a maniac, Urvi laughed for about five whole minutes, clapping her hands, shaking her head, and wiping the tears flowing down her cheeks. Tears that she thought she had been successful in convincing me were of *laughter*.

"Urvi…" I said, trying to calm her down.

"Worked my fucking ass off!" she screamed, an abrupt upheaval in her emotions. "I needed to get independent as soon as possible so that my parents wouldn't have to pay for my necessities. I wanted them to save their money for my younger brother's future—my brother *Vikrant.*"

"Vikrant Barmer: Suicide Case—1993," I said.

"No!" she bellowed, jumping to her feet and bashing the table. "It was not a bloody suicide!"

"Vikrant Barmer: Ragging Case—1993!" she roared.

"Vikrant Barmer: *Murder* Case—1993!"

21

Nishika's Journal, 2010

I calmly looked at Urvi and bent down to pick up the pen drive and two CDs that leapt to the ground when she banged the table.

"I'm sorry," she muttered, taking her seat.

"Continue."

"My brother got admission to Mrs Bathra's university *purely* on merit and began pursuing engineering there. We both wanted to make our parents proud. The two of us used to meet for an hour every weekend to spend a little time together that we had managed to fit into our hectic schedules. He used to tell me everything—how his week was, his studies, his friends, but he never told me about *them*. He hid from me the appalling torture that he was facing every single day of his life! His seniors,

Adah and Adar, used to rag him. They had chosen him as their target. It started with little jokes and jeers. It always does, you know. Starts with something you can easily take until it gradually grows to an extent where one day you suddenly realize they're killing you a little every day. What followed were light smacks on the head whenever they saw him, insults and distasteful comments on his economic background. A few days later, they locked him in the washroom for two days to starve. Then one night, they shredded all his books and burnt all his clothes. When that wasn't 'entertaining' enough for them, they made his roommates defecate and piss on his bed every single day. Making him lick their spits, their dirty foot soles, stripping him for what they called just 'harmless fun', parading the boy naked around his hostel every night! They left no stone unturned in making his life hell. Adar even physically assaulted Vikrant when he finally tried to stand up against the torture. My brother helplessly cried before the 'godly' director of the university more than a thousand times, but Drishti Bathra did nothing. Vikrant kept suffering in silence to avoid disrupting the already difficult lives of his family members. But he couldn't hold on to hope for long. 3rd August 1993—I got the news of his suicide. I received the biggest shock of my life. I knew the reason given by the director was not true. Vikrant would never die by suicide under academic pressure. My brother was an extraordinary student. I knew she was hiding something. On a quest for the real reason that cruelly hung him to the ceiling fan of his hostel and strangled him to death, I secretly met his batch mates and begged them to tell me the truth. Inspector, I can't even tell you all the horrible things my brother was made to go through!" she finally broke down.

I got up from my seat and stretched the glass of water to her mouth. Urvi took it this time, gulping it down without a break, finishing the water in less than ten seconds.

After a few minutes of grieving, she collected herself and continued. "I blamed myself for everything. I cursed myself for not being able to protect him. I told my parents every piece of information that I had gathered from his batch mates. They decided to fight for justice. My father borrowed money from the entire village to hire a good lawyer and filed a complaint against the siblings who had tormented Vikrant and the director who had deliberately spread the wrong word. He requested I stay away from the matter to protect myself and my identity. But after a few days of filing the complaint, my mother disappeared. And we knew who was behind it. We knew it very, very well, Inspector. Mr Dev Bathra can go to any extent to guard his children. It was an open threat to withdraw the complaint. We could sense the danger hovering above us. My father and I immediately fled the city and went back to our village."

"Hm..." I said. "And returned after seven years, right?"

"Yes. Seven years..." said Urvi. "We were on the run for seven fucking years. Running for our life, Inspector! We kept changing locations and phone numbers and hid our real identities. I knew Dev Bathra wouldn't give up looking for my father so easily. During those seven years, I planned my revenge against the Bathras. To my good fortune, I had already completed my education. So, I was able to develop a strong reason for my disappearance from the city by roaming around the country and educating the poor for free as a form of social service. And to the Bathras' misfortune, they weren't aware of my existence."

"How did you get in touch with Adar Bathra?" I asked her. "How did you become the 'love of his life'?

"That dumb bastard," Urvi laughed. "I came back to Delhi in 2000 and began working in one of his father's schools that I knew was managed by him. It took me three and a half years to catch that fish, one and a half years of drama and done—I married that bull in 2005. That bastard fell so badly. He just wanted to marry me as soon as possible. Dumbass didn't even give Dev Bathra a chance to do a detailed background check on me."

"Wow..." I mouthed. "Was it *easy* to live with your brother's killers, Urvi?"

"Easy?" she chuckled. "Not even close, Inspector. I was successful in marrying Adar and entering the Bathra Villa but not their lives. Those rich assholes strongly disapproved of me. Their attitude towards me changed only after a few months of ass-kissing. What was tougher than winning them over was the amount of self-control needed to not press that bastard's neck every night I saw him sleep peacefully right next to me. It was an effort to not scrape off his skin every time his filthy hands touched me. Oh! The chains my mind had to tie my hands with to stop them from poisoning Drishti Bathra's food! The efforts needed to resist the impulse of pushing Adah down every time I sat drinking with her on the terrace. You can't imagine how badly I wanted to shoot Dev Bathra with his own gun!"

"Five years, Urvi. You stopped yourself for five years!" I said, dramatically clapping my hands. "Well done, woman."

"Revenge is one hard-to-please devil, officer," she smirked. "Not everyone can delight him. He isn't for the weak to worship. He demands utter devotion. He demands your darkness, the darkest layer of your skin. He demands time, every breath of yours. He demands the evilest shade of your soul. All of which can only be offered to him by those scarred to death. And for ones who manage to please him...he will place the world at their feet!"

"You know why they say Revenge is best served *cold*, Nishika?" she said, shifting to my first name—getting more personal.

"Longer the wait, greater the hunger, tastier the food," she laughed.

"I had to wait really long for a single opportunity," Urvi sighed and continued. "Until then, I studied everyone's schedules, habits, and every little detail of theirs. Finally, five years later came the beautiful day when Ira Rana married Saarth and entered the Bathra Villa. She was a frail, cowardly girl. A weak human being trapped by beasts. And there is no place for the weak in this world. I decided to take my revenge using her. I instigated everyone against her. My plan got a major boost when Ryan came to Delhi. The foolish boy always picked up fights with everyone who mistreated his sister. I knew exactly how I was going to get my revenge. According to my plan, I continued to instigate everyone against the two. I wanted the siblings to lose their calm and do something that I could use against them. During one of Adah's parties, I fed the doughnut of doubt to my dear sister-in-law. I pointed out to her how her co-star Vihaan Malhotra was besotted by Ira's beauty. I knew Adah was too proud of her looks. She couldn't bear the attention Ira got. A week later, she accused Ira of having an affair with her co-star. Poor Ira had nothing to do with that guy, yet she was beaten up by her husband. I even instigated Adar to provoke Saarth. Ira's puerile little brother fought with everyone for his sister," she laughed.

"Really, Urvi?" I yelled. "Instead of standing up for a victim who was being abused in front of your eyes, you decided to further exploit her!"

"So, I should've stood up for someone who couldn't even stand up for herself, Inspector?"

"The girl was suffering in silence for her younger brother. Ira knew she had no escape from the Bathra Villa till her father was alive. She was protecting Ryan and his future from her father's madness. Wasn't your brother suffering in silence for a very similar reason? For the well-being of his family?" I asked her, my face dripping with disgust at the sight of her. "I don't understand how you could do this to her even after knowing that your younger brother had once been the victim of such evil behaviour!"

"Every war has its casualties, officer," she said. "I don't care about her or her brother. I don't care about anyone. All I wanted was justice for my dead brother. The justice that could only be brought by killing his killers!" she screamed.

"And you were planning to achieve it by destroying somebody else's brother's life?" I hollered. "By putting the blood of your victims on somebody else's innocent hands?"

"Cut me some slack here, Inspector," she grimaced. "I am also a victim!"

"A *murderer,*" I corrected her. "You gave up teaching after marriage so that you could focus on your revenge. You cleverly spent a lot of time with Saarth, during which he introduced you to shooting. Without anyone's knowledge, you learned the sport, practised it for years and finally executed your plan in the auditorium by killing Mrs Bathra! You always knew the prime suspect would be Ryan—you ensured it would be him. Then, you empowered your plan by cunningly making him the murderer in everyone's eyes through your tweet. To leave no scope for his innocence to fight for him, you made the tape as Shakuni, the lead character of Ryan's play and hit two birds with one stone—Trapping him further and trying to bring out Mrs Bathra's truth. After attracting all the accusing eyes towards Ryan, you executed the next step of your plan. You killed Adah and put the entire blame on that innocent boy. But before you could get your revenge against Adar and Mr Bathra and lay the finger of blame on Ira, your little secret was disclosed."

Invalidating her loud wails and hollers and protests of not having killed the two ladies, the incriminating evidence that Mrs Urvi Bathra was found with charged her with the murder of Mrs Drishti Bathra and her daughter, Adah Bathra, committed to getting revenge for her dead brother.

22

Nishika's Journal, 2010

Ryan was not yet released. There were a few procedures due to which he had to spend the night of 10th March at the police station. I, however, was relieved after proving his innocence. That night, I wheeled back to Keshav Dham with satisfaction, respite and my fatigued yawns. My eyes, red from being forced open for about sixty hours, were revolting. My drained limbs cribbed before every movement, wailing for a good sleep, and the injured wrist—still swollen—begged for rest.

"Good night, Inspector," said Mishra, dropping me off at the gate of my house. "Take care of your hand, ma'am."

"Good night, Mishra," I said. "And thank you for the ride."

I walked (*read: dragged my body*) to the man sitting on the stairs of my house, awaiting my arrival.

"Congratulations on deciphering the case, officer," he clapped.

"Thank you," I puffed, throwing my groaning bottom on the stairs, settling for the hard cement over the soft bed inside.

"How's Ryan?" he asked me.

"He's okay," I yawned, resting the palms of my hand on the step behind, supporting my back, which refused what I had settled for. "He will be released tomorrow."

"What are you doing here anyway," I asked Savya with another yawn.

"There's a lock on your door," he pointed out. "So, I sat here."

"No," I said. "What are you doing *here*?" I repeated.

"Ah, no good reason…" he shrugged. "Where's your aunt, by the way? I wanted to say hi. Or more like 'high'…."

"Of course," I chuckled. "She left for Morocco this afternoon."

"Didn't she return from a Europe tour yesterday?" he asked, surprised. "She really loves to travel, doesn't she?"

"Maybe," I said, looking up at the unlit night sky, searching for the moon. "Or maybe…" I sighed, "We are all fighting our inner demons with different weapons."

"Weapons best suited in our grips," I said, looking at him.

"May we all win," he smiled.

"Hey," he said, nudging my shoulder. "Speaking of weapons, how did you know it was Urvi? That was brilliant! I would've never guessed."

"Actually, I'm not the only one who deserves the credit," I said. "It was my private investigator— 'Elder siblings will die for you. If needed, *even kill for you*,'—and that—'the heart is never void unless you are dead. There's always something that fills it. It could be anything. Love, sorrow or *even revenge*.' Yeah, it was all him."

"What?" he asked, jumbled by the bits and pieces that I had put together in front of him without a proper sequence.

"According to my private investigator's report, the student who had died by suicide in 1993 had an elder sister who went underground with her father after the boy's mother went missing. Urvi's story struck me at the exact moment. She had left the city after completing her M.Ed. here in Delhi seventeen years ago...."

"Seventeen years ago—1993!" exclaimed Savya. "The sister who went underground."

"Exactly," I said. "Upon her return, she directly joined one of your father's schools, conveniently fell in love with your brother, and in just one and a half years, the two were so deep in love that Adar went against the wishes of his family, his mother who he 'worshipped' and married

Urvi. I could smell the smoke of a scheme that she had been cooking."

"Hmm...also, I was eavesdropping on the interrogation that you conducted in my house yesterday at midnight. Her nervousness and answers were definitely suspicious."

"Oh, I see," I nodded. "Join the force already, will you?" I said with a sarcastic pat on his back.

"Whatever," he rolled his eyes. "But that was a great four, Nishika," he said, patting my back in return.

"A great four?"

"You know, two and two put together?" he chortled.

"..."

"That was the loudest silence I have ever heard..." he said, rubbing the back of his head.

I stared at him with a straight face questioning my choice of settling for the cement stairs and tormenting my ass, thinking of the far better possibility of me being asleep in my bed by now before his contagious laughter managed to crack me up at one of the most execrable jokes I had ever heard.

"Nishika, can I tell you something?"

"Yeah, sure," I said, still laughing.

"Your guard doesn't have to be so high up always. You should smile more often. You look even more beautiful...."

"Do I?" I smiled, meeting his gaze, bathing in the silver light of the moon finally out from the dark leaden clouds. "I'll try if you—"

An ear-piercing scream echoed in the entire society of Keshav Dham, ripping apart my words. A scream loud enough to awaken the dead. A scream that led us to the Bathra Villa before us. The only four people apart from Savya left in the devil's house that night were Ira, Saarth, Adar, and Mr Dev Bathra—and we knew who it was.

The two of us surged into Ira's room to see what had happened. She sat in the corner of her bed. Her head was dug inside the trembling legs folded close to her body, hands clutching them tightly to the chest, not leaving the thinnest space for air, and nails daggered in her arms, inviting blood. Ira was bathed in sweat. Her body trembled with fright.

I sat next to her, rubbing her back, "Are you okay?"

"Ira?" asked Savya, gently shaking her. "Ira, what happened?"

Ira shook her tucked-in head, refusing to look up. The trembling doubled, breaths quadrupled, and huffs of terror grew louder and stronger.

"Ira…" I whispered near her head, hoping it reached her ears. "Ira, it's okay. We're here."

Savya sat next to her shuddery frame. "Ira, look at me," he said, patting her back, trying to free her from herself. "I am here, Ira…what's wrong?"

"What in God's name is going on here!" Mr Bathra stood at the doorway tailed by Saarth.

"What the fuck was that!" yelled Adar, almost pushing Saarth aside, tramping his foot, and dashing into the room.

"Watch your bloody feet!" Saarth hissed.

"Why is she screaming like a lunatic?" Adar marched towards Savya, ignoring Saarth, who was moaning in pain at the door.

"Haven't you already made our lives hell, you sack of bad luck!" Mr Bathra growled at the girl. "You scream like that one more time, and I will throw you out—"

Savya gave a sharp look to Mr Bathra, his fuming eyes conveying the intent very well.

"Ask her to shut up then," Mr Bathra growled in response.

Ira looked up at Savya and me, trying to speak, but her locked jaw only allowed wordless gasps and deep exhalations. She suddenly thrust her arm forward. Her wavering index finger pointed at the open window—its door driven by the powerful strokes of wind, slamming it repeatedly against the frame.

"What's there? What happened?" I ran to the window.

"Ira, you're scaring me now," said Savya, turning her face towards him, slightly holding it by her chin. "Say something."

I looked outside the window, my eyes running as wide and far as they could. "Ira, there's no one here."

"He was here," she spoke in a hushed voice.

"Who?" Savya asked her.

"H…h... he…" she whispered in a palpating voice.

"Ira, who was here?" I asked her, sitting next to her again.

"The…the…killer…"

"Who Ira?"

"Shakuni!"

* * *

Present Day

"What!" squealed Arya.

"No way!" Both Eshan and Rohan yelled in unison.

"Dadi, really?" asked Ananya, shocked.

Ryan and Savya looked at everyone and then at Ira, waiting for her to say something. But the old woman kept staring at the ground blankly without responding.

Savya looked at Ryan and said, "Close the journal. Let me continue."

23

Savya, 2010

I was stumped by Ira's answer. I looked at Nishika, who was already looking at me, equally shocked.

"What nonsense is this?" Saarth asked scornfully.

"How can this be true?" my father said with a thick grimace. "Isn't the killer caught already?" he muttered, throwing a distasteful scowl at Adar.

"Maybe she's lost it," sighed Saarth. "Look what you got me, Dad."

"Leave." I glared at the boor.

"I don't even want to stay here," he wrestled back and stormed out of the room accompanied by my father. But Adar stayed back.

"Nishika Di, I'm not lying," cried Ira. "He was here!"

"Ira, tell me exactly what you saw," said Nishika.

"I was very happy about Ryan being proved innocent. I knew I wouldn't need the pills to sleep today—"

"Pills?" I interrupted her. "What pills?"

"Uhm…Restyl or Ambien works well for me," she sighed.

"*Works well for you*?" I frowned. "Ira, how long have you been on them?"

"I don't know…" she shook her head. "Ever since I came here, probably. Or just…I don't know," she dropped her shuddering face in her palms.

"*Ever since you came here*?" I mouthed, stunned. "You have been taking these every single day? Ira, these pills are addictive…there's a risk of overdose and—"

"It's just…" she whispered. "Nothing really helps me these days."

"No, you—"

Nishika sighed at me, motioning me to stop. "Go on," she tapped Ira's shoulder.

"I was saying….," Ira continued, "…as expected, in no time, I sunk into a profound sleep before waking up for no reason a few minutes ago. I had a very strange feeling. A feeling like…like I was being watched. Like someone was staring at me. Startled to the core, I hurled my head around to find myself alone in the room. Suddenly, the light blows of the wind making a scary whistling sound and gushing outside whipped my back. That was when I remembered that I had locked the window before sleeping."

"Are you sure you had?" Nishika asked her, walking towards the window, suspiciously peeking outside once again.

"Yes!" said Ira. "I am extremely sure."

"Hm. What happened after that? Why did you scream?"

"I sat on the bed, too numb with fear to turn around and close it. The tremor that aroused from the feeling of being watched was still making my heart throb out of my chest. It got worse when I could hear someone breathing. I was trying to locate the sound when his soft exhalations hit my neck and sent a shiver down my spine...."

Ira looked at Nishika with tears of shock once again flooding her eyes. "I slowly turned around and saw someone sitting on the bottom edge of the window looking right at me. My body froze. I couldn't utter a word. I could feel a sharp scream arising in my chest, strangled by fear. He kept staring at me. The scream kept trying to free itself. The only thing visible to me in the darkroom was his honey-brown eyes glistening in the moonlight. Then, he came closer. He gently stroked my hair with love, tucked them behind my ear, patted my head like a parent and kept adoring me. The moment it cut the ropes of fear into a million pieces, my scream rushed outside with all its strength pushing him off the window seal, forcing him to run away."

Nishika and I comforted Ira and went to my room. She sat on the bedroom bench, elbow standing on her thigh, her heavy-eyed face sitting in her palm, holding her exhausted chin up. I sat on my chair oblique to the bedroom bench, hooked to the clock, which was ticking eternally.

Tick. Tock. Tick. Tock. Tick. Tock. Before it slapped our ears with a loud chime at the stroke of eleven.

"Shit! The fuck was that!" she said with her red eyes stretched open by the sound. "I swear to god, for a moment, I thought I'd die of shock."

"You should get some sleep," I said with pity.

"My mind is on the run, Savya," she rubbed her eyes with the base of her palms. "It wouldn't let my body sleep."

"Same," I breathed, further slipping into the chair. "Nishika, did you see anyone outside the window?"

"No," she answered. "There was no one."

"It might be a hallucination then," I speculated, swiftly sitting up straight, intrigued by a thought. "In Ira's case, there could be just three to four identifiable reasons for such a hallucination. Either it is caused due to the psychological distress because of the trauma that she has suffered in the last few days, or maybe the prolonged use of Ambien, or something worse...."

"What?" she asked, her heavy lids shedding off all weight.

"Patients suffering from Delusional Disorder may experience hallucinations that are directly related to their delusions."

"Hallucinations?" asked Nishika, perturbed, "What kind of hallucinations?"

"Could be anything, but the most common ones are visual and auditory. For instance, if a person affected by the disorder believes that he is being stalked at all times, he might see a shady figure everywhere he goes or hear peculiar sounds coming from one of the rooms, even if he is alone in his house. The—"

"Savya sir, someone threw this envelope over the gate and ran away," said the house help standing at my door, interrupting us.

I took the envelope from him and opened it. "It's a tape...."

"Play it," Nishika stood up in alarm.

'The insensitive man remembered as honourable and wise,
Regardless of making a harmless child a monster in everyone's eyes.
Urvi's vile deeds aren't new to me,
Unfortunately, her heartlessness once again I had to see.
She cunningly escaped the last time,
But not again, she had to be punished for her crime.'

"*Vidur...*" I thought to myself, removing the tape from the player. "Ryan and Urvi are both in police custody. Do you think this was one of that bitch's plans to make her look innocent?" I asked Nishika.

"That witch is really sly, isn't she?" I added.

"Umm, Savya," Nishika called me. I twisted my upper body behind me to look at her looking at the unforeseen visitor standing at my door.

"May I?" he asked me.

"Uh..." I hesitated. "Sure."

"Officer, I need to tell you something," said Adar, directly walking up to Nishika. "I want to hand over all the evidence regarding the crimes and scams committed by my father. I will come to the police station tomorrow afternoon with them. In return for being a witness, all I ask for is protection. My life is in danger."

"Danger?" Nishika frowned. "Are you feeling threatened by someone?"

"Yes. By Mr Dev Bathra and his son, Saarth Bathra," said Adar and left the room before we could ask him anything else.

***

Present Day

"Why did he need protection from his own father and brother?" Arya intervened.

"Did he really give all the evidence to her?" asked Rohan.

"Only if he could've..." said Savya looking at Ira.

"Let's get back to the journal now," suggested Ananya.

Ryan nodded. He reopened the journal and picked up the story from where Savya had ended it.

24

Nishika's Journal, 2010

Savya's theory about the disorder and the related hallucinations kept me awake another night till three in the morning. But this time, I wasn't alone. A distant companion, unaware of my eyes, took impatient strolls on the second floor of the Bathra Villa till half past two. Her feet frantic with anxiety, Ira paced about the massive corridor for hours before settling in on a white marble couch gracing the black-tiled passageway walled by decorative veils and fell asleep there.

"I hope this is not what Savya and the Criminal Psychologist think it is," I thought, looking at the troubled girl shrinking every passing day, sleeping on the couch. "It can't be.... How can it be...? I am sure it is not," I tried to convince myself.

The next morning—Thursday, 11th March 2010—I called Mr Krishna and asked him if he knew the reason behind Adar's fear or if it was possible for him to find it out.

"Nishika, remember I had told you Saarth Bathra loathed his mother for a reason I am yet to discover?" he asked me.

"Yes," I said. "What about it?"

"The answer to your question lies in the reason behind the hatred the young man bore in his heart for his late mother," he said.

What Mr Krishna told me that day dropped my jaw to the floor. I sat down on the couch with my head in my hands. The doubts that had been planted in my mind after listening to Savya's speculation last night continued to nurture. The case wasn't over—more people were yet to die. It made me question my efficiency as the protector of the law. It had taken a severe toll on my mental health. The suppressed powerlessness of not being able to have saved my sister or parents rose from depths I didn't even know existed. I couldn't witness any more deaths of people I was unable to save. The hungry beast just wasn't leaving me alone!

"I can't do this anymore," I whispered, intense despair whetting my voice.

"Stand up, Nishika," Mr Krishna said decisively.

"I can't see any more people die, Krishna Da. I am unable to save them," I said with tears in my eyes, my head held tight by my hands, spurning its efforts of rising and looking at the old man. "I think I should hand this case over to someone else."

"Nishika, you cannot give up after coming so far," Krishna Da said in a calm yet firm voice. "You have worked diligently and determinedly on this case. You cannot give up after coming to the very end of it. It is shameful and craven to run away from the battlefield when you know war is inevitable."

"Krishna Da, I am terrified at the thought of not being able to save people when it is my duty to protect them! I wish I could've been able to save them all. Their blood is on my hands. They appear in my dreams, asking for justice. The justice that I am unable to deliver," I cried, finally losing to the anguish. "I am not worthy of this uniform, these stars, this noble profession! I don't deserve any of this."

"जातस्य हि ध्रुवो मृत्युर्ध्रुवं जन्म मृतस्य च |
तस्मादपरिहार्येऽर्थे न त्वं शोचितुमर्हसि ||"

"Death is certain for one who has been born, and rebirth is inevitable for one who has died. Therefore, you should not lament over the inevitable."

"Death is predestined, Nishika," he chanted the verse, sitting next to me. "Neither you nor can anyone else stop the phenomenon, however hard you try. You are merely doing your duty—your *Dharma*. Stop blaming yourself for their death and do what is right. Finish what has been started instead of running away like a coward!"

I looked up at him with tears in my eyes. "I can't...."

"I know you can do this, child," he said and helped me up. "I shall stand by your side till the very end of it. *Let justice prevail!*"

I wiped my quandary and fastened my shoes. I made up my mind to leave for the police station to meet Adar and collect the evidence from him.

"Krishna Da, should I drop you somewhere?" I asked him. "I'm on my way to the station."

"Let me drop you today," he insisted. "Let me be your *charioteer.*"

"Do you know how to drive?"

"I've been doing that for ages now," he said, chuckling to himself. "I have helped a lot of people reach their destinations, you know. I might've even helped you in some way or the other long ago. Maybe. Who knows...?"

"What?" I asked, confused by his words, following him out of the house. "Why do I never understand anything you say in the first go?" I sighed.

"Believe me," he whispered, turning around. "No one does...."

"But when did you help me long ago?" I asked him, locking the door.

"Nothing. C'mon, hurry, we're getting late," he grinned.

As decided, the old man dropped me off at the police station. "Nishika!" he waved as I walked out of the car, shutting its door.

"Yes, Krishna Da?"

"You're worth it all, child," he smiled. "Never forget that."

"Thank you," I whispered. "Thank you for everything...."

* * *

"Mishra, is Mr Adar here?" on my way to the cabin, I asked the happy-go-lucky man enjoying a hot cup of tea, oblivious to the world around.

"Not yet, ma'am," he answered, offering me a cup.

"Thank you," I mouthed, politely declining it as I headed inside.

The Sub-Inspector followed me to my cabin, his two middle-aged hands finding it difficult to balance the jouncing mountain of a dozen—supremely thick—important case files seeking support against his growing waistline. "Should I keep it on the table, ma'am?" he asked with his cheeks red and puffed, forearms shaking, and freshly moist face hidden behind the hill of files.

"Yes," I sat in my chair, throwing an eye at the clock. "It's almost two in the afternoon...Adar should've been here by now."

"Why don't you give his brother a call? What was his name?" he said in a crumpled breathy voice, finally cementing the pillar on the table. "Ah, Savya Bathra. Right, Inspector?"

I nodded as I made the call. "Yep, Savya Bathra."

"Yes, Nishika?"

"Savya, has Adar left Keshav Dham?" I asked him.

"Yeah. He left about an hour ago," he answered. "He didn't reach yet?"

"What? An hour ago?" I stood up.

"But the police station is just a few minutes from your society, Inspector," Mishra interceded with his hands on his lower back, the huffs in his voice everlasting.

"Savya, could you please give me Adar's or his driver's number."

"He asked the driver to stay back and decided to drive to the station himself," Savya replied. "Wait, I'll give you his number."

The number that Savya gave me had been switched off. For around thirty minutes, I called him persistently until my desk received a call. "Greater Kailash Police Station," I recited with no intonation. The receiver pressed between my ear and shoulder as my finger mechanically continued to dial Adar.

"I am calling to report an accident," said a hoarse, fat male voice.

"Where are you calling from, sir?" I asked him in an apathetic tone. My mind was being hogged by Adar while involuntarily picturing the voice to be of a heavyset man battling late forties, going thin on top.

"About 500m from your Police Station, opposite Capital Bank ATM," said the steadfast, calm voice.

"Okay. An officer will be there in no time," I tersely assured him, keen to place the receiver down.

"Don't cut the call, Inspector," he stopped me as though he had sensed the urgency. "You might want to know the name of the deceased...."

The leash tying my eyes to the screen of my phone untied, I placed the phone on the table and held the receiver in my hand. "Your name?"

"It's his name you might be more interested in," the voice replied.

I motioned Mishra to be ready for the jeep. "If so," I said, putting the phone in my pocket, my toes ready to leave any moment. "Tell me his."

"Mr Adar Bathra."

"Who the fuck—" the line disconnected before I could say anything else.

Three tons of a goods truck had run over Adar and his car, mercilessly crushing both bodies almost instantly. Heading a team of five, I immediately reached the spot to find the driver of the truck patiently sitting on the footpath, waiting for the police. Our rough unheeded requests that were transformed into frustrated pulls and push in a moment cleared the area mobbed by groans and gasps of pity, horror, and disgust. We fenced the spot of the accident, painted red by the shredded bag of blood with barricade tapes, and sent the handful of remains that could be identified as the flesh of a human amongst the other matter for post-mortem. The 6'4 ft. tall, once broadly built body was crushed beyond recognition.

Mishra dragged the man tranquilly seated on the footpath amidst the babel by his arm to me. "The driver, Inspector."

"Was it you who called?" I asked him, noticing his appearance—almost exactly like I had pictured him.

"Yes, Inspector. It was me." His voice confirmed the answer.

"Hm." I signalled Mishra to let go of his arm. "How did this happen?"

"I did it," he smiled.

"What do you mean?" Mishra yelled, grabbing him by his collar. "Naidu, get the Breathalyzer."

"No, I'm not drunk," he turned his head towards Mishra. "I killed him in all my senses," he looked back at me.

"Why?"

"Because I was paid to do so," he casually tossed his shoulders up.

I looked at him, flummoxed. "So, you killed him because you were paid to do so and now you want to surrender?"

"Yes." he calmly answered.

"Paid by who?" I yelled, frustrated by his calmness.

"Mr Dev Bathra."

Everyone was baffled by his answer.

"Why would Mr Dev Bathra pay someone to kill his own son?" asked Mishra, vigorously shaking the man, gripping the back of his pudgy neck.

With his eyes fixed on me, the driver said, "Mr Bathra also told me to convey a message to you."

"What message?"

The karma for the inhumanity you choose you cannot outrun,
I couldn't show him mercy, for he never showed it to anyone.
Call him Adar, call him Bheem, what he remains is a beast,
For revenge, he drank a human's blood like for him it was a feast.
This barbaric, prideful man death had to debar,
For he is not human enough to reside amongst the ones who are.

Mishra unclasped the man and trotted to my ear. "*Bheem...*" he whispered. "Four down, Inspector. Four down..."

* * *

"Mr Dev Bathra, you are under arrest." My booming voice scourged the walls of the Bathra Villa in perfect coordination with the foot set in.

"Arrested?" roared Saarth. "For what?"

Savya scurried to me. "Nishika, what is the matter?" he asked, confused. "Where is Adar?"

"Nishi Di!" Ira ran to me. "Is this about Ryan? Is he alright?"

"Ryan is alright," I told her, avoiding Savya's question.

"But where is Adar?" Savya repeated his question, shaking my arm.

"Savya, Adar..." I stuttered, avoiding eye contact. "He is—"

"Arrested? On what basis, officer?" Mr Bathra screamed at me, saving me from the most difficult part of the day. The worst nightmare of being a police officer. A part of the profession that I was never comfortable with. The part where I had to inform the members of a family about the death of their kin, or worse—his murder.

"What have I even done?" yelled Mr Bathra, charging at me.

"Arrest him," I ordered my officers.

"Mishra," I called the man closer than where he was standing in the team of five. "Inform the other members of the family about Mr Adar Bathra's demise."

The entire society had gathered around the Bathra Villa to watch the once-powerful businessman being helplessly dragged to the police station. The remaining two out of three members of the family seemed to be unaffected by the news, as expected.

The gleam of joy in her eyes lit up the walls of her dark cage. With a faint, uneven smile, Ira watched the police officers handcuff her father-in-law, lug him out of his house and throw him in the police van. Savya went to his room without saying a word—neither in support of his father's arrest nor against it. Saarth, however, was extremely livid. Being the only remaining faithful son, he tried to violently release his father from the police officer's grip, but all his efforts were in vain. I personally escorted Mr Bathra to the police station, which was going to be his new home. The only home he truly deserved.

"Why would I kill my own son?" he growled at me.

"Mr Bathra, did you know Adar was on his way to the police station when he was killed," I said.

He dodged my question and kept looking outside the window.

"So, you don't," I smiled. "Mr Bathra, your son was going to hand over to me all the evidence against you. He wanted to expose you."

Mr Bathra punched the metallic window net in a fury with a cuffed hand. "I knew he would do something like that. I always knew he would betray me exactly like his mother did. He was no better than me, officer. He was much worse!"

"Now that's debatable," I scoffed.

"At least I am not the one exposing the people I should be grateful to," he muttered.

"Wait a minute," I frowned. "So, Mr Bathra, you knew the truth?"

* * *

Present Day

"Which truth?" asked Ananya.

"Oh.My.God!" gulped Arya.

"No way!" screeched Ananya, squeezing the cushion in her lap. "Mr Bathra killed his own son?"

"He was the Shakuni?" yelled Eshan, smacking his forehead.

Ryan looked up from the journal at Savya. "Savya Da, I think it should be you taking over from here."

"Yeah," said Savya. "I think it's my turn again."

Ryan shut the journal and turned to Savya like everyone else. The narrator cleared his throat and continued the story.

25

Savya, 2010

I wanted to know the reason behind Adar's death. I wanted to ask my father why he killed his own son. There were so many questions in my mind that demanded answers. At breakneck speed, I drove to the police station along with Saarth—who was also on his way to dad, but with a determination to free him rather than question his actions. But sometimes, it's your path holding the destination that seems afar. It's the path that *is* your desired destination. On the way to the station, I got to know something that made my soul tremble in shock.

"Why was he going to the police station?" asked Saarth. "Didn't Dad's entire life go in rescuing him from there?"

I didn't know how appropriate it was to tell my younger brother about Adar's motive behind going to the police station, so I decided to ignore his question and keep driving.

"I know you know it, Savya," he whispered with his spindly neck twisted towards me. "You need to tell me everything so that it gets easier for the lawyer to help us release Dad. He's already at the police station, and I need to give him the details of the entire episode as soon as we get there."

"Are you sure dad didn't kill Adar, Saarth?" I asked.

"What makes you think I would know, brother?" he smirked.

"You have become an organ of his since mom's death, haven't you?" I briefly glanced at him. "You are always with him, like a shadow."

"Hmm…" Saarth pursed his lips. "Well, he didn't kill Adar but should have done so long ago, in my opinion."

"Saarth, why would you even say something so atrociously unsympathetic about your own dead elder brother!" I shrieked in revulsion. "He hasn't even been cremated yet. Can you stop disrespecting everyone for once, at least? Have some humanity, some shame!"

"Oh, you know nothing, brother," he grimaced. "The dark seeds of secrets sown beneath our family tree are beyond imaginable. Anyway, how would you even know? You ran away like a coward long ago, didn't you?" he scorned.

"I didn't run away, Saarth," I said, looking at him as he

shook his head with disdain from the corner of my eyes. "I chose not to live in the hellhole Dad had created."

"Which sane person would want to be a part of the family that nurtured nothing but demons," I murmured.

"Oh really?" he laughed. "Demons? My dear angel?"

"Yes," I said. "I know everything that you all have been doing. I also know how your asses were all saved by Dad. You better not point any fingers at me, Saarth. I know about all your wrongdoings, too. Just because I wasn't here doesn't mean I don't know what all dirt and sins you all have been decorating Dad's hell with."

"You are the one that hits his wife, and I am a coward?" I added after a slight pause, incensed.

"Don't bring that bloody bitch into this." Saarth scowled at me. "I fucking hate her. She deserves every bit of it!"

"Asshole," I muttered.

"Since the very first day of marriage, she dared to run away from me," he continued. "She dared to deny *Saarth Bathra* of what he wanted! And then she had the audacity to sleep with the co-star of my own sister! You really wanted me to maintain my calm, Savya?"

"Really, Saarth?" I bayed. "Shouldn't you have respected her decision if she wasn't comfortable with you?"

"Did you even verify the baseless tip our wicked sister gave you?" I added with a blow on the steering.

"Excuse me?" he said with a shallow, surprised pant. "What do you mean—*respected her decision*? We are married. She is my damn wife! Why would she say no to me?"

"What do you think marriage is, Saarth?" I yelled, losing all my calm. "A fucking licence to a human being's consent? Something that gives one the authority over another human? Being your *damn wife* does not bind her to say yes to every demand of yours against her own wishes, you fucking moron!"

"And was that the only time you hit her?" I snarled at him. "Because you thought she cheated on you? I know you have been torturing her since day one!"

"Mind your words, Savya. Don't you dare," Saarth raised his finger at me. "Nobody tells Saarth Bathra what to do. Nobody. My father got her for me. I can do whatever I want with her, and I will. And if she dares to say no to me one more time, I will—"

"You will fucking what?" I screamed.

"I WILL KILL YOU IF YOU TOUCH MY SISTER AGAIN!"

"Your sister?" Saarth growled. "Really? Your damn sister? You feel that bond with her in just a few days that you have spent here?" he looked at me. "I am your real brother, Savya, and don't you forget that. I am the one who shares the blood running in your veins, not her."

"Do you even know what it is like to love your siblings, Saarth? You despised Adah, Adar, and me since you were a little child. And now you suddenly want to bond with me?"

"I never despised you. I despised Adah and Adar," he said, turning his head away. "When it came to you, your unambitious choices merely disappointed me. The same way they disappointed Dad."

"Oh, fuck off," I hissed.

"Whatever, dead loss," he pulled a cigarette out of his pocket.

"Let bygones be bygones, Savya," Saarth slurred with the cigarette in his mouth, focussed on lighting it. "As it is, from now on, you need to be on my side. We need to stick together. I know how those two dead losers bullied you when you were a kid. Dad told me everything. We are his real sons, Savya. We are the real heirs of this golden legacy, the successors of this industry that Dad has flourished with his blood and sweat."

"Yes. With the blood of the powerless and sweat of the people he treated like slaves," I said. "And throw that cigarette out."

Sucking in his arrogance, Saarth puffed the smoke at my face with laughter. "I really thought you were different from those two. I thought you would join hands with your real family. Turns out one can't trust his own blood now," he said and laughed sarcastically.

I stopped the car near the sidewalk. "What do you mean?"

"We need to reach the police station at the earliest, Savya. Dad is waiting for us. Start driving, will you?"

"I am not driving till you tell me what you are hiding, Saarth."

He looked at me and sighed. "Our beloved mother had an affair before marrying Dad. An affair which was disapproved by her father because her lover was from another caste. A few days after her protests, she proposed to marry Mr Dev Bathra—the son of a rich industrialist and a man belonging to the same caste as theirs. Her father approached the elders of our family with the proposal, and it was accepted by them and Dad."

Saarth took a halt to take a puff at his cigarette. "Here," he said, passing one on to me.

"I don't smoke," I said. "And neither should you. Throw it out."

"Okay, doc," he sneered. "So, I was saying, the two happily got married and started planning their family. Mom gave birth to Adah and Adar a year after marriage. They planned for another child but couldn't conceive one for five long years until they had you. Ten years after which they had me. After Adah and Adar's birth, since mom couldn't get pregnant for a long period of time, Dad secretly got himself checked. The reports suggested that he had azoospermia. It wasn't possible for any lady to bear a child from him."

"But then," I gasped, "How did dad...? Did Mom know?"

"No." Saarth vehemently shook his head. "He discreetly underwent a surgical procedure in the States. He told everyone that he was going to be away on a long 'business trip'. And only after that, our mother was with child—you. But Adah and Adar's birth remained a mystery to him. He knew something wasn't right, but he really loved Mom, and he couldn't question her. Dad was in denial for years until one day after my birth, he finally decided to test the twins' DNA without letting our mother know. He lost it when he got to know the truth behind their birth. The truth he already knew somewhere deep within but had been denying the whole time. They were not his children. The twins were the result of his wife's unchaste desires, her infidelity! An extra-marital affair that she continued to have after their marriage with her old lover—"

"What!" I screeched in shock, cutting his words. "The... affair...twins...what?"

"I know," he said, taking another puff. "I was equally shocked...Poor Dad... man, I hated that fucking woman."

"Saarth, Mom would never—"

"She did, Savya. She did," said Saarth. "That bitch was a fucking *whor*...."

"Saarth!"

"Oh, come on," he snapped at me. "You don't know shit! She was pushing Dad to make Adar the head of the group's telecommunications business, and Adah, the leader of the retail business. What about me? What about you? She never fucking loved us, Savya! Never!"

"Please..." I sighed. "Just...please."

"After her death," he continued. "Dad decided to remove Adar and Adah as legal heirs from his will. He wanted them to have nothing that belonged to the *real* heirs of the Bathra industries. Adar got to know about this and decided to take advantage of the fact that Dad had kept the truth hidden. We knew he was up to something but couldn't figure out his next step. He even started acting to be threatened by us to show us in a bad light."

"Adar was planning to surrender all the evidence against Dad in the police station today. Do you think that was the reason Dad got him killed? Did he know about Adar's plan?" I asked, flabbergasted.

"What?" he yelled. "Even after getting to know the truth, Dad did so much for the two of them! That traitor sure deserved to die, but dad didn't tell me about any of this."

En route to the police station once again, I drove in a deep trance. Had dad really killed Adar? Was he behind mom and Adah's death too? Was he worse than I thought he was? In a few minutes, we reached the police station to find Ira and Ryan waiting outside the old building.

"What the hell are you doing here?" Saarth barked at Ira.

She ignored him and walked away with Ryan. When I asked her, she told me that there were some signatures

Ryan had to do on a few documents post his release, and she was there to pick him up. Asking her to drive home safely, I joined Saarth and went inside with the lawyer while the siblings left for Bathra Villa.

"You can meet him," said the constable guiding us to our father.

In a small dirty room, as far away as possible from the malodorous, damp spots with traces of defecation and urine, *The* Dev Bathra sat on the cold, mucky stone floor with his eyes closed and head leaning against the wall. Powerless. God has his own ways of dragging you to the ground, to humility, when the clouds need to be emptied for another arrogant soul, perhaps.

Saarth kneeled before the old man. "We are here, dad. We'll get you out in no time. I know you haven't killed Adar."

My father opened his eyes and looked at the both of us. "I have killed Adar," he declared rather calmly. "I take complete responsibility for his death."

"What? Dad! No!" cried Saarth. "I know you haven't killed him! You would've told me before taking such a drastic step. Why are you lying? Why are you doing this?"

Dad informed us that he had already distributed everything that he owned amongst Saarth and me. I knew my father was completely capable of killing Adar, but I was racked with indecision because of disbelief. Somehow, I was unsure of his confession. Had he really killed Adar? Or was he hiding something? *Someone*?

One arm clutched by the lawyer, another trying to hold on to dad's hands, Saarth was forcibly taken outside by the lawyer on dad's command since he wanted to talk to me in private. *"Dad! Dad no! You're all that I am left with, dad! You're all...,"* his screams faded with every step, the sight of his rebellion blurry. My father watched Saarth being dragged away with tears in his eyes. He then looked at me; for the first time without a dash of anger or disappointment on his face that generally took over at my sight. I went on my knees, curious to hear what he had to say. I was curious to learn how it felt like to have a peaceful, dispute-free conversation with your father.

"I know Saarth must've told you the truth by now, Savya," he said in a soft voice. A voice that was new to me. "After getting to know about Drishti's act of adultery, I had lost all hope. I couldn't accept Adah and Adar as my children. They were the result of her betrayal. They didn't let me forget what she had done to me. I could never look at them the same way, but I didn't want the kids to suffer because of their mother's wrong choices. I raised them like I would have if I hadn't known the truth of their birth. But my only hope was my real children—you and Saarth. I wanted you two to take over the family business. That is why I loathed your decision to disregard what you had inherited and choose something else. I wanted to see the drive in your eyes that I always, unfortunately, saw in Adar's," he said, his chin gathering the tears rolling down, holding my hand.

"Dad, I—"

"You don't have to give me an explanation, Savya," he softly firmed his grasp over my hands. "Your mother's death shook me. I was terrified by the thought of your and Saarth's future if something were to happen to me. I knew what I had raised. I was certain that if I died, Adar and Adah would dominate Saarth, and you wouldn't interfere due to your lack of interest in the business. Maybe you wouldn't even come back to India, ever. I knew those two wouldn't have hesitated or thought twice before throwing you both out of business—or even out of the picture if you created trouble for them. I had to protect you and Saarth, your futures, and your well-being after my death. So, I stealthily distributed everything among the two of you after Drishti's death without letting the evil twins know. I hid this even from Saarth, but Adar somehow got to know of it. He decided to expose me. I…I…had no other… choice…" he stuttered.

"I don't know what is making it so hard to believe you, dad," I said, sitting down, unbothered by the dirt.

My father laughed. Or maybe he had lost control over his senses.

"I have committed a lot of sins, son. It is time. It is my turn to pay for them—pay for each one of them…" he said.

"Dad, I know you haven't killed Adar," I said, shaking him. "Who are you trying to save? What are you hiding?"

He smiled at me and said,

'In the circle of life, he met me again, donning a new skin, a new name,

Tied in a different bond, but his hate for me remains the same.'

"Mr Savya, the allotted time is over," announced the constable. "I request you to come out with me."

"Please, sir!" I begged the man. "Just another minute!"

"I'm sorry, Mr Savya," he said, his fingers hesitantly touching my shoulder, signalling me to get up without him having to apply any force.

"I'm sorry, Savya, I couldn't be the father that you deserved." In a quaking voice, his words fighting with the lump on their way out, dad whispered as he watched me leave.

I ran to Nishika. "Did anyone meet dad before Saarth and me?"

"Why? What happened? Is he alright?" she asked me.

"The circle of life…he met me again…" I mumbled.

"What?" Nishika frowned. "Mishra, go check on Mr Dev Bathra."

"He's alright!" I said. "But please tell me, who met him before Saarth and me? Who was the last person he talked to?"

She looked at me, confused, *"Ira."*

* * *

Present Day

"Motherfu—" Ananya elbowed her younger sister before she could complete her raw reaction.

"Mother of father! Did you?" said Arya, trying to rectify her impulse.

"What?" screamed Eshan. "You did not...."

"No, of course, I didn't kill anyone," said Ira. "He had destroyed the life of my mother and me. I went to talk to him because...because I wanted to make him realise his mistakes. Nothing else," Ira defended her actions.

"Do you want to continue, Di?" asked Ryan adjusting his glasses.

"We could have easily skipped that part, Ryan," said Savya.

"No, they should know. I don't think what I did was wrong. I won't hide it," said Ira and continued.

26

Ira, 2010

After talking to Mr Bathra, cursing him for the wounds he had carved on my soul, cursing him for my mother's death, I left for Keshav Dham with Ryan. We were to leave Delhi the very day and fly back to Mumbai. I decided to file a divorce against Saarth. Ryan kept requesting me to file a complaint against him for the abuse and physical assault, but I refused. The man had already lost his entire family, and all I wanted was my freedom. On reaching the villa, we began packing our things. Hours went by in minutes, and I was extremely happy for myself. I was finally going to be freed from that horrendous cage. Leaving me alone for some time, Ryan went somewhere to meet up with a few people to arrange our stay in Mumbai.

"That smile on your face. That fucking smile after destroying my family!" screamed Saarth, who at the point was both mad and drunk. "**You are nothing but a curse of misfortune!**"

He entered my room, where I stood all alone.

He started cursing me and verbally abusing me. I tried to warn him of his actions, but he didn't stop. Incensed and out of control, he held me by my arm with all his strength and began mercilessly dragging me to his room. I screamed for help, but I was all alone in the entire villa. There was no one to rescue me from his grip.

I tried freeing myself but couldn't succeed. He lugged me out of my room, ruthlessly dragged me like a leashed dog for three storeys, then he threw me on the floor of his room and switched on the news that blazoned the truth about his family.

"My family has lost all the respect that we had earned. All because of you!" he thundered. "My father, my mother, our secrets, everything is out in the open! People are laughing at us, throwing muck at our name. All because of you!"

"Because of me?" I screamed at him, getting up. "All of this is because of their own sins. Their own deeds! Your own deeds, Saarth!"

He slapped me. I fell to the floor once again, my chin hitting the ground with a greater force this time, teeth dug into my lip, drawing out blood. My ears were ringing, my jaw hurt, and my cheek burnt like it was on fire. I lay on the floor, howling in excruciating pain. He then held my hair, jerking my face up and punched it hard. For several minutes, I lay on the ground, severely numb, almost lifeless. After a few moments of battling with and finally conquering the numbness, I tried getting up and running away, but he grabbed me again by my mane and banged my head on the table. The metallic taste of blood oozing from my lips and the gash on my forehead flooded my mouth. I pushed the brute away and ran out of his room towards the main door, but he chased me and caught hold of me on the stairway.

Saarth began dragging me back to his room, but with a strong prod in his eye, I escaped and ran towards the terrace. With an eye bleeding shut, he chased me there, screaming at me. I somehow managed to reach the terrace, my wounds and agony forgotten due to the drive to save myself. I was trying to lock the door, but he booted it open and entered the terrace. With all my vigour, lying on the floor crying for help, I started screaming for Ryan in the hope that if he came back, he would find me and save me, as Saarth vigorously kicked me. I tried to drag my bleeding skin, grated flesh, and broken bones away from that monster. His fist was armed with an empty beer bottle broken in half that he found lying in the corner of the terrace. He slowly walked towards me like I was his prey. His intentions were as transparent as they could get—he wanted to kill what he thought was the reason for the destruction of his family, of his life; me.

I knew no one would be able to help me. I knew only I could save myself from the beast. I had to do something. I had to save myself. It was time. It was time to finally fight for myself. It was time to unleash the fury I had been taming for what seemed like *ages*.

I stood up, my feet crawling towards the railing. His feet were inching towards me with the half-broken glass bottle clasped in his fingers till I reached the end of the terrace and couldn't move behind any further.

"Who's going to save you from me this time? Your brother? Or mine?" he sneered. "You deserve to die, Ira!"

As soon as Saarth attacked me with the glass, I moved aside and pushed him down the railing. His body fell to the ground with a loud bang. The security guard screamed in horror. I could hear the whispers and gasps of the people who had gathered near the gate. But I couldn't look down. I couldn't look at what I had just done. I stood there, shivering in shock. A lot of eyes had watched the entire visual from their house, their ears having heard my screams and yells of the brutal attacker. Some had informed the police about the man who was assaulting his wife, while others had informed Savya.

"*Ira! Ira, where are you!*" I could hear Savya call out my name, the intensity and pitch of the cries increasing as he neared the terrace.

* * *

Present Day

"Dadi..." Arya tightly hugged her grandmother, teary-eyed.

"The more you suffer, the more you're made to," sighed the fortunate young survivor's older self—saved but scarred for life—looking up at the ceiling, obstructing the flow of tears. "I can't do this...I think I'm going to go out in the fresh air for a while," said Ira and left the room.

Rohan sprang to his feet to follow his grandmother, tailed by Savya, but she motioned the two to stay back.

"Finish it," she told Savya on her way out. "Just finish it once and for all."

27

Savya, 2010

I kicked open the door of the terrace that Saarth had locked from within. As I dashed inside, I saw Ira standing against the railing, trembling, looking at me, weeping blood. Her crimson tears blended with the blood from the heavy bleeding, deep gash on her forehead. Another stream of blood dripped from her lips that were split apart. She had dark contusions all over her body. Saarth was a professional boxer, and his punch had given her a painful black eye which was beyond swollen. An arm of her pink *kurti* was almost ripped apart; the front splotched in her blood. The sight of her was enough to give me shivers. I ran towards her and tightly braced her as she broke down in my arms.

The neighbours who had been the witness to the heinous assault came ahead and supported Ira. They gave their statements to the police describing how she had been attacked. They narrated in detail everything that they had seen. What Ira had done was an act of self-defence. The trials acquitted her of all charges. Ira was innocent, *not guilty*.

18th March 2010: Seven days past Saarth's death, the nightmare finally ended. It was a bright morning. The case had been officially solved. I had decided to accompany Ira and Ryan to Mumbai, but before leaving the city, I had to fulfil my duties of being a human. A good one that I always hoped to be. Surrendering their bodies to nature, wishing prosperity, morality and wisdom for the three souls to choose better paths in their following lives, I ceremonially cremated my two brothers and a sister, burning with their mortal remains all the negative emotions nursing in my heart and mind for the dead. I donated everything that I had inherited to people in need and various charitable trusts.

The dark era of the Bathra industries had come to an end. It was finally our last day in Delhi. I stood at the stairs of her house, next to her—a place better at soothing me than my own house in front of it. The dusty stairs of her house felt more like a home than the luxurious villa ahead.

"So, that was it," I sighed, relieved, both our eyes on the villa.

"I guess so," said Nishika, tying her dark hair into a habitual top knot, her delicate lips gently parting into a tender smile, her warm beige skin catching the golden light and glowing.

"Is that a smile I see? So, we're finally friends now?" I teased her.

"Whatever," she said, trying to shoo me off as always.

"Nishika," I said. "I don't think I'll ever come back here."

Distracted by the pretty commotion for a moment, I watched the new residents of Keshav Dham before us. The new owners of the Bathra Villa had arrived. The family was busy shifting their things in the house. The house that had seen far more than it should have.

"I think this was my last case," she whispered. "I'm resigning."

"What? Why?" I shrieked, taken aback by her decision. "What do you mean resigning?"

"I think I've seen enough of this," she looked at me, and with a reflexive smile, back at the new family of four dancing in joviality in the front yard of the villa. "I want to live a peaceful life now."

"So...will you continue to live here or like shift to some other place?" I asked her indifferently, masking the eagerness racing from the hair to the tip of my toe by continuing to look at the family happily unpacking into the villa.

"I was thinking of Mumbai...."

"Really?" I yelled, nearly jumping out of exhilaration.

The officer softly chuckled at me.

"Yeah, right," I puffed. "At least my 'hideous' jokes don't break someone's heart," I said, narrowing my eyes at her.

"I haven't decided yet, but it would be someplace far from here, for sure," she said.

I looked at her, her eyes still on the family. "Do you think we should stay in touch?"

* * *

Present Day

Savya softly chuckled at himself, taking an abrupt pause.

"Savya Da, what did she say?" asked Eshan.

"Do you see her next to me?" Savya asked him with a smile.

"Were you in love with her? Is that why you never married anyone?" asked Ananya, dejected.

Everyone looked at the old man, impatiently waiting for a response.

"I didn't marry anyone because maybe I was better off alone," he said.

"But—"

"Read the last page, Ryan," Savya interrupted Arya with a hush, diverting everyone from the topic.

Ryan took his cue and flipped to the last page of the journal.

28

Nishika's Journal, 2010

I looked at the Bathra Villa, bathing in the morning sun, smiling at the streams of golden water, at the amber sun rays. Its time to live in bliss had come after the years of tragedy that it had seen. For the first time, the mammoth block of cement looked like a warm and beautiful home. No quarrels, violent fights, schemes, just a gentle silence delighted in getting interrupted by the gaiety of laughter and hoots of the family that had bought the villa, was unloading, and shifting their stuff. Two cheerful little girls being playfully chased by their puppy, parents lovingly looking at their kids, their new home, and then at each other—the mirth of the family seemed to have quenched the villa's thirst for happiness.

"Hello!" The lady saw me looking at them and approached with a friendly smile. "I'm Anusha Mehra, your new neighbour."

"Hey," I said, shaking the hand she gently thrust out. "Inspector Nishika Mehta."

The puppy followed its mother and entered my garden, sniffed the mango sapling, and wagged its little tail in excitement.

"He loves mangoes," she said, looking at the little baby.

I picked it up and watched it trying to lick my face. "It's adorable."

"I think he likes you," she said with an effusive laugh watching it wet my face with the soft unrestrained licks. "He's going to come here often now to meet you and his Mango tree."

I gently placed it back on the ground and watched it gallop back to the two little girls calling out his name. "*Bruno*!"

"Maybe he'll miss me then," I said, looking at the three little moppets. "I'm shifting in a few days…But don't worry, the new owners of this house are lovely. I'm sure they will let him meet his mango tree."

"Oh, are you?" she said. "Well, it was great meeting you, Nishika. I hope they're as warm and welcoming as you."

I waved the woman goodbye and watched her get attacked by the pounces and licks of the furball as soon as she entered the gate of her new home.

A golden Thursday, the eighteenth bright morning of March, coincidentally exactly eighteen days after it all started—eighteen days after Mrs Drishti Bathra's death, the file of the Bathras was officially shut forever. The case was no more than a war set in today's world. Blood turning against blood, conspiracies darker than moonless night skies, warriors (murderers and criminals as we have renamed them bearing in mind the yuga of Kali) all fighting for personal vendettas, revenge, greed, an immortal abhorrence. Heartfelt goodbyes, painful sacrifices of those innocent, unanticipated helpers—divine or not, who knows, and finally, liberation. It felt like the end of an era. The end of a ruthless war with one side victorious and the other defeated—to death. The war was caused by years of injustice, betrayals, vows of revenge, suffering, and of course, the infamous human emotions beyond their harbourer's control. A war that started way before it landed on the battlefield. A Mahabharata, indeed.

"How are you both?" I asked the two siblings walking towards me.

"We leave today…" said a watery-eyed Ryan, hugging me. "I'll miss you, Di. I always will."

Ira joined her brother without a moment's delay. "I don't know how to thank you," she said, pulling her head apart to seize a look at my face. "For the support, trust, and always being there. Thank you for everything."

"I'll miss you both, too," I said, trying to fit them in my tiny arms. The two of them had made a special place in my heart. They were family. My arms tightly wrapped around them, smile unabating and heart beating love, but eyes—unfocused, I looked around. Maybe I was expecting someone else to join us too.

Ryan ran towards the mango sapling and placed a daisy before it. "Bye Daisy…Until next time," he said, wiping his tears.

"Ryan, I think I have someone in mind for you," I winked, with hands tied behind, ambling to the boy and his two beautiful daisies peacefully lying on and in the earth. "You'll like her."

"Nishi Di, aren't you a bit late in introducing me to girls?" The boy laughed, his eyebrows united in question.

"*Coco!*" I called out loudly. "Come!"

A chocolate-coloured Labrador stormed out of my house on hearing her name and the command, pushing the door open, almost breaking it down, and sprinting towards us. Ryan crouched to the grass, catching the torpedo in his arms. The man and his best friend need no formal introduction, perhaps. The two bonded the very moment they saw each other. It was like witnessing love at first sight.

"She retired from the Force yesterday," I told him. "They were going to send her to a shelter. I thought I knew a better home for her."

He picked her up like a little child. “I love her,” he kissed her head. “I am the one who found shelter—a home, not her,” he sighed with recurred tears looking at the sapling and at the dog in his arms.

“It’s time to leave, Ryan,” said Ira.

She kissed Coco and gave me another hug before leaving. I saw the two of them walk away with Coco in their hands. They looked happy. All three of them. Alas, they found their home, maybe.

I looked at the mango sapling next to me. “Bye, Daisy, I’ll miss you.”

“So, I heard you are leaving,” said Krishna Da as he pushed open the gate, entering my front yard.

“Seriously,” I smiled. “How do you know everything?”

“That’s my job, you know,” he laughed.

“Yeah,” I said. “I’m leaving. I don’t think I’m made for this. I need to go somewhere far. Somewhere more peaceful.”

“Maybe you do,” he said, smiling, ruffling my hair like I was a child. “My warrior has seen enough wars now.”

“I’ll miss you, Krishna Da,” I said and gave the old man a tight hug. Like a toddler in her grandpa’s arms, I wept softly at the thought of his departure. “How can I meet you if I ever want to? Where do you live?”

“Hm, my abode…” he said, his hands on his waist, in deep thought. “Do you know how to swim?”

“What?” I asked, confused as always.

The old man burst out laughing. "Nothing," he said with that warm smile permanently glued to his face, his words forever cryptic. "Remember me. Call out my name, and I'll be there."

I laughed. I knew I was never going to see him again. I knew it was the last time I was seeing him.

The old private investigator I was once dithering to hire, a beat of my heart now, waved me goodbye and began walking towards the gate, away from me.

"Krishna…" I said with a crack in my voice. He turned around.

"देहिनोऽस्मिन्यथा देहे कौमारं यौवनं जरा |
तथा देहान्तरप्राप्तिर्धीरस्तत्र न मुह्यति ||

CHAPTER 2, VERSE 13

Just as the embodied soul continuously passes from childhood to youth to old age, similarly, at the time of death, the soul passes into another body. The wise are not deluded by this.

वासांसि जीर्णानि यथा विहाय
नवानि गृह्णाति नरोऽपराणि |
तथा शरीराणि विहाय जीर्णा
न्यन्यानि संयाति नवानि देही ||

CHAPTER 2, VERSE 22

As a person sheds worn-out garments and wears new ones, likewise, at the time of death, the soul casts off its worn-out body and enters a new one.

श्रीभगवानुवाच |
बहूनि मे व्यतीतानि जन्मानि तव चार्जुन |
तान्यहं वेद सर्वाणि न त्वं वत्थ परन्तप ||

Chapter 4, verse 5

The Supreme Lord said: Both you and I have had many births, O Arjun. You have forgotten them, while I remember them all, O Parantapa.

शरीरं यदवाप्नोति यच्चाप्युत्क्रामतीश्वरः |
गृहीत्वैतानि संयाति वायुर्गन्धानिवाशयात् ||

Chapter 15, verse 8.

As the air carries fragrance from place to place, so does the embodied soul carry the mind and senses with it, when it leaves an old body and enters a new one."

"Well done," he smiled. "So, maybe the Gita does have an answer to everything…."

"Or maybe you do," I said with tears in my eyes.

"Same thing," he shrugged.

"Don't go." The tears began flowing down. "Please…"

"There are a lot of people who need my help. This old man, this Krishna is in very much demand, you see," he laughed. "Don't worry. I'll always be with you. Always."

I watched the old man walk away. I watched my home walk away. And in the mystical haze, the magician disappeared once again.

I knew there was someone else I had to meet before going—the annoying Neurosurgeon with a heart bigger than any human I had met. The surgeon whose hideous jokes always made me laugh.

"Do you think we should stay in touch?" he asked me.

I wanted to, but I couldn't. I wanted no memory of that part of my life. I wanted to start my life from a fresh page with no traces of the crimson ink of so many people's sufferings dwelling in the past. I wanted to start over. I wanted a new life, one that involved peace and only peace. The peace that demands a clean slate. Demands solitariness.

"Do you think we should stay in touch?" the warmth of his gaze caressed my cheeks.

"Maybe I'm better off alone," I said, continuing to look ahead, avoiding his eyes. I was avoiding the gaze I knew I wasn't strong enough to hold. I wish I hadn't broken his heart. I wish I hadn't broken my heart. I wish I had told him…

He said nothing. He just smiled and bid me adieu. That was the last time I saw him. And once again, we parted ways like it was our thing. Only, forever this time. Neither did he look behind, nor did I call his name. We were always meant for goodbyes, maybe. Maybe, we only met again to part ways forever.

That was the last case of my career. In a few weeks, I quit my job, left the unrestful city and my past behind, and settled here in Dehradun to live a peaceful life—a life that I had always craved.

I wish the three of them the happiness and peace that they deserve.

Shakuni's Revenge (2010)
Case Closed

***

Present Day

Ryan shut the journal and held it close to his heart. "We came to Mumbai with a million hopes and dreams in our eyes. The three of us built all of this from scratch while Coco watched with her paws on top of the other, supervising us and awarding cuddles when needed," the old man softly laughed as he picked up the little Simba sleeping next to him and crushed him in his arms, peppering him with kisses.

"I began my practice as a Neurosurgeon here," said Savya. "Ryan recommenced his writing and direction, and

Ira gave her passion a chance to become one of the most celebrated artists in the country.

"We were each other's only family," chipped in the old woman who had re-entered the reading room.

"You're back," said Ryan, winking at his sister.

"Always will be," Savya added. "We all lived together until Ira and Ryan got married to their better halves."

Ryan looked at Rohan and Eshan. "I met your grandmother here in Mumbai, had a beautiful daughter and you two wonderful grandsons," he said. "I moved back in with Savya Da—the brother I was lucky enough to be blessed with—after her demise."

"And I met someone who loved me, and more importantly, respected me and was blessed with your father," said Ira as she kissed her granddaughters Ananya and Arya. "And your mother," she said, dishevelling Anuj's hair.

"Finally!" yelped Anuj and slung the two metal springs that he had untwined in the air. "No puzzle that I can't solve," he boasted with pride, his skills tested severely by the metal conundrum. Everyone laughed at the brainiac who had finally spoken in hours.

"Come on now. It is very late already. I want everyone down for dinner in five," ordered Ira and proceeded down.

Savya, Ryan, and Simba readily followed the woman down, but the audience stayed back.

29

"Something didn't add up," said Arya.

Eshan scratched the stubble on his chin. "Hmm…even I don't think Mr Dev Bathra killed Adar," he said. "Or Urvi killed Adah and Mrs Bathra."

The eight pairs of eyes sat silently, staring at each other. The same thought prisoned in their minds, unable to break free.

"I think it was Dadi," Ananya finally broke the silence.

Eshan looked at his sister, appalled. "Why do you think it was Dadi?"

"I don't know, it just…it adds up," she shrugged. "The young girl loathed the family—"

"As she should've," Arya interrupted.

"I agree, Arya, but that's not the point," said Ananya. "The point is—even then, could she not escape the family and go back to her own house because of her fiendish father? She was like a poor bird stuck in a net. And doesn't one flap its wings, try its best to get out of a trap until its last breath?"

"Hmm…technically, the only one around when all three of the Bathras—Mrs Bathra, Adah and Adar—died, was she," said Eshan, supplementing Ananya's theory. "While everyone thought Ryan Rana was the Shakuni, it might have been his sister they overlooked. The one giving refuge to delusions and false beliefs. The one suffering from the disorder…."

"She even had hallucinations—a symptom of the disorder!" said Rohan. "Compare the two characters; it was she who took care of her younger sibling, Ryan, like a parent since childhood, exactly like Shakuni. It was she who gave up her own life and happiness to ensure his well-being as he did for his sister. The doting elder sister lost it every time fingers were pointed at her little brother, every time conniving eyes were placed upon him."

"Yes!" said Ananya with a victorious clap of her hands. "The way Dadi attacked Urvi cannot be ignored. She's the calmest person I have ever seen. The hostility was unbelievable. Also, I'm still not convinced by the explanation that she gave about her last meeting with Mr Bathra."

"And she was also the sole witness to what actually happened the day Saarth died," added Rohan. "Maybe she provoked him…Maybe it was she who dragged him—the only remaining target—to the terrace and not vice-versa. She wanted him to attack her so that she could use it against him. Or else why would she go to the terrace instead of running outside the villa?"

"Saarth's room was on the fifth and the last floor. Maybe it was closer to her than the main door," debated Arya.

"It wasn't Dadi," said Eshan. "It can't be."

"Why not?" Ananya questioned him.

"Because, then that disrupts the whole pattern."

"What do you mean?"

"Why wasn't there a tape or some message after Saarth died?" he looked at everyone, confident about his theory. "So, clearly, the person who killed Saarth and the one who killed the rest of them isn't the same. It wasn't Dadi..."

"You know who I am unsure about?" said Arya. "Ryan Da."

"Even I was doubtful about him since the very beginning," Eshan pensively nodded. "He said that Mr and Mrs Bathra had been given a seat in the balcony exactly opposite them since the two had agreed on the plan at the last moment and there were no other seats available. But it is clearly mentioned in the journal that the entire balcony was reserved only for the Bathras and a few other VIPs."

"Did anyone else find it weird when Savya Da threatened his own brother, addressing the girl he had met just a few days ago as his sister?" Arya looked at everyone. "Or was it just me?"

"Actually, I did. It was pretty weird," said Rohan. "Also, the impatience with which he wanted to know Officer Nishika's views on Shakuni and if she thought the prince was the '*bad guy*' is equally questionable. Because I really think he liked her and her opinions mattered to him. What if he was the delusional mastermind?"

"And Savya Da was the last person who met Mr Bathra!" speculated Ananya, switching sides. "Maybe it was he who brainwashed the old man."

"Oh. My. God, hell no!" gasped Eshan.

"What?" the other three choired.

"In a way, all the three of them were at some point tormented by the Bathras," he said softly, his low voice edged with apprehension. "What if they did it together? Because they did successfully escape the 'hell hole' as Savya Da termed the Bathra Villa. Their only escape from that house was the death of the Bathras…."

"Look at you guys guessing which of your old, innocent grandparents is a murderer or a patient suffering from a severe mental disorder," said Anuj, dramatically shaking his head in disapproval.

"You didn't leave with them?" asked Rohan, oblivious of his presence.

"Do you even know what we're all talking about?" jeered Arya.

"Uh-huh," said Anuj. "I'm not deaf, Arya. I heard it all."

"No, you didn't," Arya frowned.

Anuj picked up the journal Ryan had left in his chair. "According to the killer's delusion, his arch enemies were also reincarnated, which in my view, are six."

"First, Mr Bathra: The mighty Bheeshma—the despotic commander-in-chief infamous for exploiting the weak. He who dragged Ira to the Bathra Villa and left her at the mercy of Saarth, his unworthy son."

"Saarth—the wicked, abusive husband, Dhritarashtra," added Ananya.

"Urvi, the insensitive Vidur who heartlessly targeted and made an innocent boy the murderer, a monster in everyone's eyes for the love and sake of her own brother," said Rohan.

"Adah, the one who killed an innocent dog exactly how Sahadev had killed Uluka, Shakuni's innocent son, who was not at fault for anything that happened," said Arya biting her nails.

"Stop doing that," said Rohan with a triggered pet peeve of nail biting.

"Don't look at me then!" protested Arya.

"Shush, you two!" rustled Eshan. "There are better things to talk about here."

With a riled finger on her lips, Ananya gestured for the two to shut up and continued. "The arrogant Adar would be—"

"Bheem," Eshan interceded.

"Right," she confirmed, "The way he bullied and abused that young student or thrashed the security guard on being asked an identity proof is evidence of his overpouring pride."

"Drishti Bathra, who everyone considered to be fair and righteous, unaware of her sins and fraudulent deeds, would be the one Shakuni had similar claims about—Yudhishtir," said Rohan, "The righteous prince who was not so righteous, according to him. The prince who was equally sinful as his nephew but was whitewashed by the same history that demonised his nephew."

"And we reach the dead-end!" groaned Arya.

"Not with me on your team," Anuj whispered to her. "*No puzzle that I can't solve....*"

Arya pulled a derisive face at her brother. "So, you know the killer?"

"Maybe," said Anuj and continued his theory. "The innocent boy, Ryan, who was targeted and hated by the Bathras for no good reason, would be Duryodhan, who had faced a similar situation as a child. Like Duryodhan, he was a hot headed-boy who picked up fights with everyone for his loved ones without any fear. He even broke Adar's nose—our Bheem—and fought with Saarth for torturing his sibling, exactly like the Kaurava who often fought with Bheem for bullying his younger brothers. The re-born hemophobic warrior who was terrified by the sight of blood that had drenched the soil of Kurukshetra due to his deeds in the past life."

"That does make sense...," said Eshan. "Continue. I want to hear the next ones."

With an uneven smirk on his face, Anuj looked at Eshan. "Ira Rana—our Gandhari. The woman hauled to hell on earth by Bheeshma, the woman abused by her husband, the woman everyone considers weak, timid, and helpless, but I think was one of the strongest characters of the epic. Sacrificing yourself for the welfare of your people and suffering in silence to ensure the security and well-being of your family isn't something everyone can do. Tying around your eyes a blindfold and resolutely embracing your words, decision and darkness till death driven by hatred and rage aren't the traits of a timid person."

"I never thought of her this way," said Ananya. "To me, she was just the...the poor blindfolded woman."

"The princess was a ferocious queen without a throne," said Arya. "A throne that she deserved owing to her own valour, patience, and integrity towards her words, unlike some of the deceitful men. The princess alone selflessly saved the lives of all her people. She saved her entire kingdom! She didn't need her husband or son to be crowned the king to become a queen. She already was one."

"I agree," said Rohan.

"So now remains our trickster," said Ananya after a musing silence.

"The evil trickster, the mastermind of the game who no one can defeat—*Shakuni* wh—"

"Savya Da!" Rohan interrupted Anuj. "The only one who remains. The whip-smart Neurosurgeon—the master of the game."

"Not really," laughed Anuj.

"What do you mean?" Rohan asked his brother, reduced to a state of unalloyed perplexity. "Then who?"

"Our Shakuni: the smartest of them all. The one who tricked everyone ages ago, the one who tricked everyone today. The mastermind who managed to entrap the entire world in a bubble of illusion," he smirked.

"Officer Nishika."

30

"One can only see what one observes, and one observes only things which are already in mind."

-Alphonse Bertillon

"What!" everyone shrieked altogether.

"How the fuck?" gasped Ananya, perplexed. "How can it be Officer Nishika?"

"Why not? Because she didn't write it in her journal like a fool for the world to read?" smiled Anuj. "Considering the angle from which Mrs Bathra was shot, the only people who were seated in the perfect spot and could have been the murderer were the Bathras and the one sitting right behind Ryan—Inspector Nishika."

'In front of me, in the first row of the balcony, sat Ryan, Ira, Saarth, Adah, Adar and his wife, Urvi.' Anuj read out.

"Oh my God. Yes!" exclaimed Ananya. "Being a police officer, even she was capable of that perfect shot!"

"No, wait...wait...but why would she?" asked Arya, befuddled.

"You remember how her parents died?" asked Anuj, tossing the journal at Arya, motioning her to check it.

'I lost my parents in an unfortunate accident when I was sixteen.' Arya read out loud.

"Now dig in the information Nishika's private investigator gave her about Adar Bathra," instructed Anuj.

Arya hastily flicked through the pages of the journal until she found the right one. On running her bewildered eyes through the inked page for about a minute, she gasped, "Wow…."

"What?" asked Rohan, impatiently snatching from her the journal.

'…Adar's father has also suppressed several cases of drinking and driving, including a major one that caused the death of three people while two were left severely injured.'

"But—"

"Nishika and her aunt were the two left severely injured," said Arya. "Amongst the dead must have been the widow aunt's late husband along with the officer's parents."

"She lost her entire family in an accident when she was just sixteen. The car accident that was caused by Adar Bathra. The young girl saw her parents die right in front of her eyes, saw the face of their murderer she could *never* forget…." Explained Anuj. "Exactly how she, as Shakuni, had lost all her beloved nephews to Bheem in her 'past life'. Exactly like the miserable uncle who saw his ninety-nine nephews die right in front of his eyes, saw the face of their slaughterer he could never forget."

"Six years after the accident, she shifted to Keshav Dham with the thirst for revenge ignited in her heart. The thirst that would only be quenched by killing the murderer, Adar, and Mr Bathra, who suppressed the case, denying justice to her dead parents."

"Di, do you think taking revenge is a sin?"

"Ryan, I–I don't know…I don't know if it's a sin, but with the crimes that I have seen, offenders, once upon a time victims, that I have met, it sure quenched the thirsts in their hearts they said…." Rohan read to all.

"And that she took," he added. "She killed Adar Bathra exactly the way he had killed her parents—crushed his body and his car."

"The Inspector lost her younger sister to cancer when she was just a child. The trauma caused by her sister's death must have worsened after the death of her family. She felt sad for Ira Rana after listening to the miseries her life was filled with from Ryan Da. Nishika found the sister she had lost in Ira. She found her lost family in the two siblings that were stranded on a path covered in thorns of agony by their own father after their mother's death. The siblings who also had no family."

"Wait," said Rohan reading out, *'I felt sad for the wretched girl. I wished I could do something to put a smile on her face.'*

"She finally got what she had always longed for," said Anuj.

"What?" asked Ananya.

"A family," answered Rohan. *"I always longed to have a family."* he showed Ananya.

"So, when she started to realize that she was drawn to the siblings to an abnormal extent and felt an unexplainable obsession for them growing at a dangerously rapid rate in her heart, she was unable to handle the overwhelming emotions. To counter these emotions, her distressed mind used Shakuni's story. She tried to convince herself that she felt so drawn to Ira and Ryan because she was related to them in her past life. She tried to convince herself that she was the brother of Gandhari—Ira, that she was the uncle of Duryodhan—Ryan, reincarnated," said Eshan, flipping the pages of the journal.

'What enraged me the most was the audacity of Mr Bathra, who walked with his head held high and chest pumped with pride after destroying the lives of innocent women.'

"Innocent women—Ira and her mother, Gandhari, and also the three abducted sisters of Kashi," he said.

"There is a saying by Sigmund Freud," Rohan took the diary from Eshan. "Unexpressed emotions will never die. They are buried alive and will come forth later, in uglier ways..." he said. "The evil disorder deep rooting delusions and beliefs in one was due to her traumatic past, unmanaged and suppressed emotions. She needed help...."

'I had always suppressed my emotions. That was the first time I was crying in years.' He showed everyone.

"Ryan and Ira's affection and trust towards her must've further strengthened her delusion," said Rohan. "It must've also strengthened every time she watched the recording of the play after Mrs Bathra's death under the name of investigation. Remember when she told Savya Da, *"Even I have watched the recording numerous times since the case started."*

"What about Dadi's hallucination?" he asked Anuj.

"It must have been due to the trauma that had been inflicted upon her since the past few days, or maybe the Ambien," answered Anuj. "She wasn't the one hallucinating because of the disorder. It was Officer Nishika."

"I don't get it..." said Ananya.

"Do you really think it is possible for someone to find an address in the city habituated by more than thirty million, with the help of just the first name written correctly? And how did the investigator even get to know it is the first name that is the correct detail which he has to trace to find her?" said Anuj, shrugging his shoulders.

"So Mr Krishna was..."

"Just a symptom of her disorder," said Anuj. "Unreal, imaginary, *a hallucination....*"

"Shakuni always wanted Lord Krishna by his side," Anuj explained. "The man was eternally fascinated by him. So, her mind gave birth to the Lord, who she had always longed for in her past life *to empower her delusion*. He looked exactly how she had imagined him to be in today's world. The information that Krishna gave her was everything she had already collected in the ten years that she spent in Keshav Dham to one day avenge the death of her parents. She just wanted to hear it from him to satisfy her age-old wish of being helped by Krishna like Arjun. She was hallucinating the whole time."

"And that is why he couldn't tell her about Adah's rage issues. An important detail that the Bathra family had managed to hide very well from everyone. A detail that she hadn't been able to find out," said Arya.

"That is also why he knew about the tape, which only Nishika and the Bathras knew," added Ananya.

"I thought it was like a…I don't know…a divine intervention," said Arya.

"Because she made it sound like one. Because she wanted the world to believe it was one. Because she herself believed it was one…" said Anuj. "Remember her conversation that night with Mr Krishna? Where he asked her the reasons behind Lord Krishna's actions."

"Yes!" said Eshan. "Wasn't it like how we solve our own queries? Find the answers to our questions?"

"Exactly. She answered her own questions that had risen in her mind during her past life as Shakuni in this life as Nishika after studying the epic in detail. It was a conversation that took place in the mind, which thought that it had seen two different eras as two different people," said Anuj, flipping to the page of the conversation.

"Does the epic interest you?" I asked him.

"It does. I always feel like I was a part of it, you know."

"Shakuni was always enthralled by Krishna but could never decrypt his actions, could never understand the reasons behind them…."

"Who was your favourite then?" he curiously asked me.

"Lord Krishna," I answered within a second.

"Ah. Never mind," he made a face on listening to my answer. "I don't like him that much."

"There are a few questions that arise in my mind every time I read the Mahabharata. Maybe if you could answer them, I would start liking him."

"Go ahead. I'll try to resolve your doubts with whatever information I have," I said, bracing myself for the questions.

"Remember her last dialogue with '*herself*?"

"The spontaneity with which you are answering my questions is impressive. It's like Krishna himself told you all of this."

"I wish…" I sighed.

"But Anuj, how did this thought even strike you?" asked Ananya.

"Only she was the one who had seen Krishna or had talked to him," Anuj answered.

"Really?" Savya frowned. "I mean, I didn't see anyone go out on my way in…."

"Huh? What?" I strode to the main gate and peeked outside. "Where'd he go?"

"Also, when Shalini Aunty came back from her Europe trip the evening of Daisy's death, didn't she see

Krishna? Wasn't he on the lawn with Nishika? Why was there no mention of him once she arrived? Did he just disappear?" Anuj laughed. "Her Krishna appeared every time she needed help or was disheartened. First, when she was frustrated by the warning of losing charge of the case. Next, when she wanted him to help her by telling her the details of the members of the Bathra family as her investigator. Then, it was the time when she wanted someone to share her grief with. Whenever she wanted her God to wipe her tears, he was there. Fourth, when she wanted to solve her doubts regarding the war, answer her questions—answer Shakuni's questions—and wanted a clue from him about the theory of reincarnation. Wanted Lord Krishna himself to prove to her that the theory of reincarnation is very much true. After that, when she was devastated by Daisy's death. He appeared next when she couldn't figure out why Ryan had absconded, when she was worried for the boy and wanted Krishna to help her save him by exposing Urvi. Next, to convince her when she was in doubt about her own beliefs. And for the last time, when she was disheartened to see her little sister and her nephew leave. When she knew that was the last time she was seeing them," Anuj further explained his theory.

"The mind has its own ways of dealing with situations and emotions once they go beyond its control. Those ways are sometimes sober, but most of the times ugly," said Rohan. “Hers came up with Krishna—the divine one who had come to guide her, stand by her side after years of loneliness and misery. The night of Adah’s death, when she was flabbergasted by Ryan’s escape and Urvi’s impromptu scheme, her first instinct was to call Mr Krishna; to talk to him. It was because that was the only thing that soothed her. The most beautiful ugly way her mind had come up with to deal with her emotions.”

“Here—” he said, showing everyone the page.

Supervising the subordinates with an eye, concurrently, I dialled up Mr Krishna, in dire need of his expertise and help.

“Hello!” he exclaimed, his soothing voice exuding abundant positivity any time of the day.

“I am extremely sorry to bother you so late—”

“Oh, it’s all good,” he said. “I don’t really sleep.”

“Uhm...okay...” I said, a little confused.

“Office hours: twenty-four hours a day, seven days a week—every moment at your service, child!”

His smiling words drew out of me a spontaneous chuckle of admiration, even in this grim situation. “Thank you, sir,” I said. “I need your help.”

“Is everything alright?” he asked from the other side.

“Ryan is absconding. He is accused of killing Miss Adah,” I told him. “Could you help me find him out?”

“Yes, sure,” he assured me. “I’ll inform you the moment I get any news related to him.”

"I understand why she killed Adar and Adah—to avenge the death of her parents and Daisy. But why Mrs Drishti Bathra?" Eshan asked Anuj.

"She initially arrived in Keshav Dham seeking revenge only against Adar and Dev Bathra, but after having remembered her past life as she believed, she began abhorring the entire family who were her enemies reborn. She took the chance and killed her Yudhishtir the night of the play," said Ananya clicking her fingers.

"But how did she get to know where Mrs Bathra would be seated?" questioned Arya.

"She didn't," said Rohan. "They were all on her hit list. The order wasn't important. She had shifted to Keshav Dham with nothing but vengeance on her mind. *She was always prepared.* She spared Mr Bathra then because she might have had better plans for him, something worse than death—suffering."

Arya looked at him, dazed. "Maybe that is why she kept insisting on checking the family that night. Maybe she was planning to frame one of them the night of the murder itself."

"Maybe," said Rohan. "The night of the murder when she said, *'I had a sleepless night for two reasons. A thought that kept arising in my mind, and the loud quarrels in the Bathra Villa.'* I'm sure she was hit by the thought that the young Ryan might end up as the prime suspect considering his feuds with the Bathra family."

"After Mrs Bathra, she marked Adah, who further pushed the roots of Nishika's delusions within her mind by trying to kill her '*once again*' in the police station during the interrogation, before '*recommitting*' the sin of killing an innocent who Nishika had developed a great bond with. She must've not been able to bear the death of Daisy," said Eshan.

'What I saw that day shattered my heart into a million pieces. A woman had killed an innocent animal to get her revenge against the people she abhorred, guided by her rage, guided by the honeyguides.' He read. "Remember what she said to Savya Da that night?"

"So Ira hadn't misunderstood the situation…Adah, really…" Nishika sighed. "Well, the girl was right…."

"About what?" I asked her, my head still lowered.

"She said that Adah shouldn't have dragged an innocent in this dirty war. That she should've kept Daisy away from it…." Nishika told me. "She really should have."

"9th March 2010—the night of the deliberate accident, she planned Adah's murder and decided to put the blame on Urvi, whose history, schemes, and ploys she had already figured out. She got an opportunity when Savya Da called her to the Villa to help him take care of Ira," continued Rohan. "The Officer told him that she was going to take her aunt to the hospital, but I'm sure she went to the Bathra Villa the very moment. Maybe her aunt was also a part of her plan but was unaware of Nishika's belief since the Inspector was cautious enough not to share it with anyone."

"You're right," said Ananya. "Nishika killed Adah and planted the murder weapon and the gun she had shot Mrs Bathra with in Urvi's surreptitious space."

"But her fingerprints? How did she not leave *any* evidence on the crime scene?" asked Arya.

"Nitrile gloves, disposable shoe covers, a surgical cap… She was a police officer, Arya."

"But—"

"The whole house was searched, but did anyone check *her* satchel that night?" Anuj shrugged. "Or did anyone check *her* in the auditorium?"

"Plus, Ryan Da contaminated the whole crime scene. And even if any little evidence like a strand of her hair or her DNA was found in the room, it would've obviously been assumed that it was because she was in that room investigating the crime scene being the officer in charge."

"So, after killing Adah, the officer hastily rushed to Savya Da's room. The swelling of her wrist had increased not because she had driven her aunt to the hospital but due to whatever resistance an unalarmed Adah must've put up."

"And the hair must've messed up due to the hasty removal of the surgical cap," suggested Eshan.

"Your hair," I gently fixed a few strands of her hair, escaping the bun messed up from all the relentless dashing around. "And how's your hand?" I asked her, removing it from

my shoulder, taking it into mine, and tightening the loosened Velcro of the compression wrap.

"It's okay now," she sighed.

"You drove your aunt to the hospital by yourself, didn't you?" I asked her. "You're supposed to give it rest, Nishika. It is clearly not yet okay. The swelling seems to have increased, in fact."

"Urvi, who must've seen Adah's dead body, decided to stick to her initial plan of trapping Ryan so that she could use Ira as a shield when she executed her plan of killing Adar," Anuj continued. "And so, she accused Ryan of murdering Adah and gave a drastic twist to Nishika's plan."

"It adds up," Arya thought to herself as she read, *'I knew Ryan was innocent and not the cold-blooded murderer that everyone thought he was. But why did he abscond like a criminal then? What about the horrifying sight that Urvi said she had witnessed? There was a war going on in my mind. A war that only Ryan could put an end to.'*

"Nishika had to disclose Urvi's secret as soon as possible to save Ryan, and so she did. The hints given to her by Krishna contributed in a way that her own mind was trying to help her out so that it could convince her that Krishna was on her side this time—on Shakuni's side this time and her delusion were not unreal. That she really was the trickster reborn," said Rohan pointing out Nishika's words;

"Actually, I'm not the only one who deserves the credit," I said. "It was my private investigator—'Elder siblings will die

for you. If needed, even kill for you,'—and that—'the heart is never void unless you are dead. There's always something that fills it. It could be anything. Love, sorrow or even revenge.' Yeah, it was all him."

"The intelligent police officer must've discovered Urvi's clandestine space when she first investigated her room after Mrs Bathra's death.

'I personally checked all the rooms that belonged to the members of the family...' Anuj reminded everyone.

"She was the only one who disregarded the Criminal Psychologist's theory the first time he proposed it like any other patient affected by the disorder," said Anuj—

"How can someone come up with such a belief out of nowhere?" I asked him incredulously, unconvinced by the entire theory.

Rohan sprinted his finger down to another instance—

"What the hell is all of this!" I thought to myself, my hands on my head, befuddled by his theory.

"But when Savya Da further explained the disorder to her the night of Ira's hallucination, she began doubting her belief," said Anuj.

'Savya's theory about the disorder and the related hallucinations kept me awake another night till three in the morning.'

"She hoped that her belief was not what she had begun to think it was—a delusion, *"I hope this is not what Savya and the Criminal Psychologist think it is," I thought, looking at the troubled girl shrinking every passing day, sleeping on the couch. "It can't be…. How can it be…? I am sure it is not," I tried to convince myself.*

"The doubt had put Officer Nishika in severe turmoil!" exclaimed Ananya as she read out the next part.

'I sat down on the couch with my head in my hands. The doubts that had been planted in my mind after listening to Savya's speculation last night continued to nurture. The case wasn't over—more people were yet to die. It made me question my efficiency as the protector of the law. It had taken a severe toll on my mental health. The suppressed powerlessness of not being able to have saved my sister or parents rose from depths I didn't even know existed. I couldn't witness any more deaths of people I was unable to save. The hungry beast just wasn't leaving me alone!'

"But her mind tricked her by giving birth to Lord Krishna one more time," read Anuj—

"Nishika, you cannot give up after coming so far," Krishna Da said in a calm yet firm voice. "You have worked diligently and determinedly on this case. You cannot give up after coming to the very end of it. It is shameful and craven to run away from the battlefield when you know war is inevitable."

"The police officer wanted to stop herself from killing any more people," said Arya, expressing pity.

"Krishna Da, I am terrified at the thought of not being able to save people when it is my duty to protect them! I wish I could've been able to save them all. Their blood is on my

hands. They appear in my dreams, asking for justice. The justice that I am unable to deliver," I cried, finally losing to the anguish. "I am not worthy of this uniform, these stars, this noble profession! I don't deserve any of this."

"Her mind persuaded her in the same way in which Krishna had convinced Arjun when he had dropped his weapons, terrified at the thought of killing his elders right before the great war. It strengthened her weakened belief once again. It convinced her that what she was doing was not at all wrong, and it was her duty to bring justice to her loved ones who were wronged in her past and present life," sighed Eshan.

"Death is predestined, Nishika," he chanted the verse, sitting next to me. "Neither you nor can anyone else stop the phenomenon, however hard you try. You are merely doing your duty—your Dharma. Stop blaming yourself for their death and do what is right. Finish what has been started instead of running away like a coward!"

I looked up at him with tears in my eyes. "I can't…."

"I know you can do this, child," he said and helped me up. "I shall stand by your side till the very end of it. Let justice prevail!"

"Who do you think was that man who killed Adar, wrongly claimed he was paid by Mr Bathra and then surrendered?" asked Arya.

"Anil Khatun," answered a voice entering the room.

"You knew?" asked Ananya. "How? And when did you get to know?"

Savya heaved a sigh of woe and sat down on the couch next to Ananya. "A few months after coming to Mumbai," he said. "I had treated my father's confession with scepticism since he first agreed to have killed Adar. I was sure he hadn't murdered his son and was lying. But why? This 'why' steered me back to Delhi after spending a few disconcerted months here. Using a few high-level contacts of my father, who showed a willingness to help me, I met the convicted driver who claimed he was paid by Mr Bathra to kill Adar. On begging him for the truth, the man told me the real name of the person who paid him to commit the accident. Told me everything."

"But who was he?" asked Arya.

"Just another victim of my family's brutality," said Savya. "Anil Khatun—the son of the airport security guard who died by suicide after being assaulted and insulted by Adar."

"Was he also the one…?"

"Yes," said Savya, reading Arya's mind. "He was also the one delivering the tapes for Nishika."

"The poor man was fuming over his father's death for years before he was found and approached by an unknown lady with a generous offer. An offer to fetch his revenge and get paid for it. He took the money his poverty-ridden family was in dire need of and the revenge his soul was ravenous for," Savya told everyone.

"Woah!" said Rohan, engrossed in what he was reading.

"What?" Eshan asked him.

'The entire society had gathered around the Bathra Villa to watch the once powerful businessman being helplessly dragged to the police station.'

"Officer Nishika accomplished her revenge against Dev Bathra by dragging him—her Bheeshma—to the police station to make him pay for his sins. She must have revealed her secret to Mr Bathra in the police van itself. It wasn't Dadi or Savya Da who brainwashed him. It was Inspector Nishika. It was Shakuni who brainwashed his Bheeshma and put him behind bars for his sins," said Rohan.

"We really overlooked a lot of things," said Ananya, slapping her forehead. "She made it look like any other case but couldn't hide the outcomes of her ingrained delusions—like when she unconsciously addressed Duryodhan as Suyodhan, something not commonly observed while people talk about him.

"So the ones Shakuni loved more than anything were Gandhari and—"

"Suyodhan," I promptly answered.

"Or her disbelief when the Criminal Psychologist was talking about the disorder," said Rohan. "She even asked him:

"Do you think it is possible for someone to remember his or her past life? Or is it impossible for something like that to happen?"

"What about the other religions and cultures?" I asked. "Are there any evidence, mentions or beliefs regarding the phenomenon endured by them?"

"What about you?" I asked him. "Do you believe in reincarnation?"

And let's not forget her unusual interest in the theory of reincarnation—the heap of books."

"The most important one?" I asked, perplexed. "I don't think so. I have all by Ian Stevenson, Walter Semkiw, Steven Rosen, William—"

"Technically, one would've been more inclined towards the theory of the disorder proposed by the Criminal Psychologist to find the murderer, but since the whole theory was absurd for her, she didn't take any of it much seriously in the beginning."

Arya raced her eyes through the journal. "Here!" the girl hooted. "Her inquisitiveness about Dadi's past that she had already been told about by Ryan during the time they spent together.

"Anyway, let's proceed with Ira. How was her childhood? What kind of a person was she before marrying Saarth? Tell me everything. Every little thing."

"She didn't want to lose the case to someone else—*All I know is that I have to solve this case before it is handed over to someone else*—not just because she was a competitive or dedicated officer but because that would ruin her plan of getting her vengeance. A plan that she had been waiting to execute for years," said Ananya.

"Give me Officer Nishika's note," said Anuj.

Rohan took out the note tucked in the journal and handed it to him.

Anuj laughed out loud, reading the piece of paper.

"What happened?" asked Savya.

"What a coincidence," said Anuj. "Savya Da, these names...."

Everyone looked at Anuj, confused.

"There's a Dev in Devavrata—Bheeshma's brith name, Drishti in Yudhishtira, Adar in Vrikodara Bheem, Urvi in Vidur, Adah in Sahadeva, Saarth in Dhritarashtra, Ryan in Duryodhana, Ira in Gandhari and Savya in Vyaas; the only one who understood the Mahabharata," he detailed.

"The surnames, too, then. Bathra in Bharat, the greatest ancestor of the Kuru Dynasty," added Ananya.

"And Rana in Gandhar..." added Eshan.

Anuj showed the note around, pointing at Nishika's name written on it.

"The hell!" shrieked Ananya on realising what Anuj was trying to show them. An anagram of the officer's name:

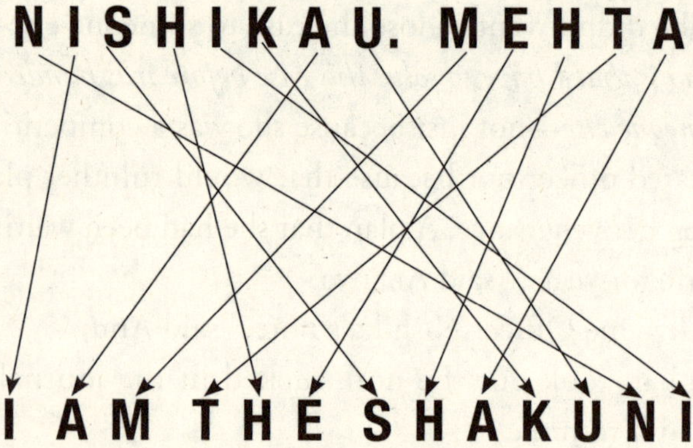

"I think she wanted to tell you the truth that day, Savya Da…" said Arya, flipping to the last page; '*I wish I had told him.*'

Savya grazed his hand over Nishika's name, her last words in the journal.

"Maybe I'm better off alone," I said, continuing to look ahead, avoiding his eyes. I was avoiding the gaze I knew I wasn't strong enough to hold. I wish I hadn't broken his heart. I wish I hadn't broken my heart. I wish I had told him…

"I wish she had told me…" the old man whispered in a frail, disconsolate voice, tearing up.

"Did you not try to find her, Savya Da?" asked Arya, settling next to the old man, her fingers of despair brushing his back.

"I did," he said. "But by the time I found out the truth, she was gone. Too far…Forever. She was exceptional at parting without leaving a trail behind. Never to be found out."

"Without leaving behind any evidence, too," said Ananya. "Rescued the two siblings, took her revenge, punished her culprits—everything without leaving behind any evidence against her."

"But why did she even write the journal?"

"Closure," Savya sighed. "Even after taking her revenge, Nishika didn't get the peace she thought she would. The peace she always craved. She *had to* make herself believe this is what happened to relieve her guilt."

"I don't know about the theory of her rebirth, but damn, she was just as smart, just as loving as Shakuni, for her loved ones, just as intelligent...," said Rohan. "Really managed to drape the whole world in her illusion, didn't she?"

"So, Shakuni did win this time...," said Eshan. "The Kauravas did win this time...."

"Maybe villains do win sometimes," said Ananya.

"Or maybe the heroes, too, deserve to lose sometimes," said Rohan.

"The villain did win. But it was never Shakuni. He wasn't the evil trickster she was fighting. He wasn't the evil trickster she lost to. It was the one stronger than us all, the most intelligent of us all, the real evil trickster; the mind. The mind that drives you on insane roads for revenge.

The mind that tricks you if you are unable to control it," said Savya.

'The evil trickster has always won,
And it shall always win, for it can be defeated by none.
For it is impossible to control it if time has gone,
If you are deep inside its cage, if you've become its pawn.
The evil trickster, the mind you must tame,
Before you become a puppet in its evil game.'

"I wish I could've helped her when she was at war with herself. When she needed my help. When she was all alone. When she was right in front of me, struggling for life, and I could do nothing. I'm sorry, Nishika. I'm sorry…." Tears streamed down the old man's eyes as he clutched the journal, his Nishika, to his heart with trembling fingers.

"Give me the strength, Lord, to live with myself."

'And in the mystical haze, the magician disappeared once again...'

-The Journal

उद्धरेदात्मनात्मानं नात्मानमवसादयेत् |
आत्मैव ह्यात्मनो बन्धुरात्मैव रिपुरात्मनः ||

Elevate yourself through the power of your mind, and not degrade yourself, for the mind can be the friend and the enemy of the self.
(The Bhagavad Gita; CHAPTER 6, VERSE 5)

ACKNOWLEDGEMENTS

And while I merely penned a story, all of them brought it to life.

Dear God, thank you for everything. I love you.

Thank you, Mom and Dad, for endlessly supporting my craziest dreams and always being there for me. This would've been impossible without your love, encouragement, merciless taunts for lazing around all day, and of course, the money. I love you guys. Special thanks to my lovely elder sister, the first reader of my very first draft, for her ruthless comments and suggestions that made this book a hundred times better than what it was and managed to humble my proud posterior (they said I couldn't put ass in here. Doesn't sound sophisticated!). And, of course, my dear little fur ball, Bruno, for (unwillingly) letting me sacrifice some of his play time so that I could tap some keys on a board and stare at some screen for hours. Your sacrifice shall be remembered, soldier.

Author S.M. Kashikar, my dearest grandpa, thank you for the writing gene and for always looking after me from up above. The only reason I dare to dream big is because I know by hook or by crook, you'll make sure God makes it come true. Keep troubling him until we succeed.

The Kevin Missal! Kevin, my main man, thank you for everything! For believing in me, in my book, and for trying your level best to teach my deadpan face how to smile (I'm getting there, by the way, don't worry). This would've been impossible without you, big man.

Thank you so much, Navya, my wonderful editor who deserves all the credit in the world for making this book what it is today.

Vini Bhati, Abhijeet Kataria, and Tanya Midha, my publishing partners, thanks a ton for helping my manuscript see the light of day.

Vitika Gupta, Tarun Negi, and Anusree Ghosh, thanks a ton for the wonderful book cover.

Tanishqa, my best friend, thank you for always being there for me. I love you, bro. Never leave me.

Theertha, my support system, I cannot express in words how thankful I am for everything. I hope you're always the first reader of all my manuscripts.

My inspirations — Shubha Aunty (Mrinmayee Bhave), my beloved principal, thank you for being the superwoman that you are and inspiring the little Harsha to dream big. Thank you for making school home, for igniting in me the fire to aim beyond the sky and teaching me the discipline to achieve it. Thank you for GURUKUL, Shubha Aunty.

My absolute favourite, Geeta Chandran Ma'am, thank you for all the love and support. For always pushing me to do better. Thank you for making me able enough to pen this book, ma'am. May God bless you with my share of joy.

Succhak Bhasskar, Anjali Mami, Vaidehi, Parth, CA Hanamanthrao Choudry, the readers of my manuscript, thank you so much for your time, words of encouragement, support and love.

Thank you, Saniya Khan Ma'am (Clinical Psychology Major), for your valuable insights on the topic, your time, and of course, your words full of love, care and motivation.

Special thanks to Dr Manish Kulkarni for all the valuable medical insights and your time, Doc.

Shreyas, Devendra, and the entire team, words shall *never* be enough to thank you guys, for your endless efforts, your time, and the mind-blowing book trailer! You truly breathed life into my story.

And most importantly, you, my dear reader. I know, generally, all of you skip this page, but if by chance you are reading this, I just want you to know you mean the world to me. Do get in touch with me via any of my social media handles in case you wish to talk about the book, me, how your day was, or absolutely anything under the sun. I'd love it.

Remember, you're not alone. If you *ever* need anyone to talk to, I'll always be there.

With love,
Harsha